Geoffrey Piper grew up in Bakewell, Derbyshire, studying at S. Anselm's and Repton School before gaining an honours degree in law at Cambridge. He enjoyed a long and successful career in accountancy and regional community development, working across much of the British Isles and Europe. A family man with four adult children and ten grandchildren, he has spent many happy holidays in Scotland and derived his inspiration for *The Seal of Promise* from family visits to Eilean Shona. *The Seal of Promise* is Geoffrey's first published novel.

For Sue

Geoffrey Piper

THE SEAL OF PROMISE

A Tale of Forbidden Love and Strange Discovery

AUSTIN MACAULEY PUBLISHERS™

LONDON • CAMBRIDGE • NEW YORK • SHARJAH

A CIP catalogue record for this title is available from the British Library.

ISBN 9781398400306 (Paperback)
ISBN 9781398400313 (ePub e-book)

www.austinmacauley.com

First Published (2021)
Austin Macauley Publishers Ltd
25 Canada Square
Canary Wharf
London
E14 5LQ

Author's Acknowledgements

I would like to acknowledge Charles Piper's original idea around which this story was built, and his initial research as well as very valuable technical support; to thank Hugh and Caroline Strickland and their family for their advice on numerous matters including many points of detail relating to Eilean Shona; and to express my gratitude also to Angela Golton and Jennifer Simms for their support for my work.

I am also greatly indebted to my long-suffering wife, Sue, my sister, Bridget Spurrier, and several members of our extended family who so kindly read my draft scripts and contributed helpful suggestions. Finally, I would like to record my sincere thanks to Vanessa Branson, the owner of Eilean Shona, not only for kindly contributing a most interesting foreword but also for so warmly welcoming my attempt to portray life on her island as it might have been two hundred years ago.

— Geoffrey Piper

Table of Contents

An historical, romantic adventure inspired by a curious discovery in a remote corner of the Scottish Highlands.

Historical Background

1688: The 'Glorious Revolution' results in the overthrow of the last catholic king to rule Great Britain. King James II of England (James VII of Scotland) flees the country and is succeeded by his daughter Mary and her protestant husband William of Orange, reigning jointly. Witnesses claimed that they saw the departing king throw the Great Seal of the Realm into the River Thames in the belief that its absence would hamper the future government of the nation.

1715: James II's son and heir, Prince James Francis Edward Stuart (The Old Pretender) lands in Scotland and attempts an uprising to reclaim the thrones of England and Scotland for the Stuarts. The uprising is soon put down by the British forces loyal to the new king of England (George I, Elector of Hanover).

1745-6: James II's grandson Prince Charles Edward Stuart (Bonnie Prince Charlie) leads a much bolder attempt to reclaim the throne for the Stuarts. He lands in Moidart and, with seven men, advances to Glenfinnan where he raises his standard and gathers the clans. He reaches Derby on his way to seize power in London before turning back owing to dwindling support. By the summer of 1746, after the annihilation of his army at Culloden Moor and several months on the run, he again passes through Moidart, miraculously evading Hanoverian search forces before being rescued by French ships in the Sound of Arisaig. The memory of his heroic effort on behalf of the Stuarts' claims to the throne would never be forgotten.

Author's Note

This story was inspired by a number of holidays enjoyed over the years by members of my family on Eilean Shona, a remote tidal island which forms part of the district of Moidart in Scotland's Western Highlands. Much of the action described takes place on or around this rugged but truly beautiful island. This is however a work of fiction – its depiction of the island's history is imaginary and any similarities between its characters and any actual person are entirely coincidental.

Foreword

Eilean Shona has long been an inspiration for writers, including J M Barrie, who is said to have written the screen play for Peter Pan whilst staying on the island in 1922. It is a joy to see this tradition thrive. *The Seal Trilogy* promises not only to grab our imagination but, by guiding us through the lives of one family and the inhabitants of this beautiful landscape, to immerse us in history itself.

When my family first stepped off the clinker-built rowing boat onto the ancient pier, we were immediately bewitched. This island with its craggy shores, its blue lagoon, wild hills and dark woodland must hold many a secret. And over the years its history has slowly unfolded as people who once lived there, or had elderly relatives who did so, have come forward with their wonderful stories.

In April 2012, two-thirds of the island was engulfed in flames after a prolonged drought. Thankfully no cottages were burned down and, to our surprise, nature restored the now blackened hills into a carpet of wild flowers in just a few weeks. A further surprise was the number of ruins the fire exposed – endless stone dwellings, monuments to all who once lived there.

I hope you enjoy following the MacDonell family's eventful journey as much as I have. They have certainly set my clan quite an example to follow!

– Vanessa Branson
Proprietor of Eilean Shona since 1995

Chapter One
An Island School

Eilean Shona is a small tidal island – wild, remote and often eerily beautiful – located just off the west coast of Scotland in the district of Moidart. It is far enough from the great cities of Glasgow and Edinburgh, and also from the larger Hebridean islands, to have developed over the years its own distinct character and identity, as well as its own customs and Gaelic traditions.

The history of Moidart is one which has seen both relative prosperity and abject poverty, but down the centuries its people have always shared a strong sense of pride in their local and national identity, being first and foremost men and women of Moidart but also fiercely Scottish. Importantly, the people of Eilean Shona and their neighbours across much of Moidart escaped the terrors of the notorious Highland clearances, whereby many land-owners had forced their impoverished and hungry tenant crofters off the land to enable them to put it to more profitable use for themselves.

At its peak in the early 1800s, the population of Eilean Shona numbered around one hundred and its community had for generations enjoyed a respectful and relatively friendly relationship with successive Lairds. This population comprised mainly crofters and their families, but it also included several loyal servants who worked personally for 'the Laird of Moidart', Alastair MacDonell, and his family to whom the whole island belonged along with much of mainland Moidart and some parts of Knoydart. A generous complement of house staff was always retained in the service of the Laird and his wife Lady Elspeth, who was herself the daughter of an eminent Scottish peer. These 'retainers' – men and women – provided a tried and trusted bridge between the crofting community and the Laird's own household.

By 1811, Alastair and Lady Elspeth had four small children (Euan, Archie, Margaret and Annie, ranging in age from eight years down to two). The family chose to spend most of their time at their island home, a relatively modest and very charming traditional Scottish 'Big House', known simply as 'Eilean Shona House', or sometimes simply 'The House'. Alastair had succeeded to the Moidart Estate on the death of his father in 1808, thus becoming the owner of lands comprising many thousands of acres and stretching across the wider district of Moidart to the shores of Loch Shiel and north to Knoydart, where a part of their estate had belonged to the MacDonells of Knoydart for generations.

Alastair and Elspeth were respected and much-liked by the majority of their tenants, unlike their counterparts in many other parts of the Scottish Highlands, and the relationship they personally enjoyed with the local population was key to maintaining the island's strong sense of community well-being.

Most of Eilean Shona's population at this time supported themselves through fishing or sheep farming, and by careful harvesting of their potato crops. Other than for a couple of years around the turn of the nineteenth century, the island had for many years been spared the worst extremes of weather, benefiting for much of the time from the gulf stream which helped to shield it through the worst of the winters.

In this respect the Moidart district as a whole was more fortunate than many other parts of Scotland. Indeed, it often seemed to the residents of Eilean Shona that nothing or nobody could ever disturb their relatively contented, routine existence. Only those with the longest of memories could recall much in the way of alarm or excitement on the island.

One notable exception – with a very long memory indeed – was the eighty-year-old Iain McGregor. Iain was the island's oldest inhabitant and reputed not to have set foot off the island for over forty years. By his own admission Iain now lived totally in the past, for he lived almost entirely on his memories. He had served Alastair MacDonell's father for many years, and his grandfather for a few years before that, officially as a footman, but in reality as a kind of odd job man, carrying out essential repairs to the House and generally maintaining most of the Laird's outhouses, his farm buildings, and occasionally his stables too.

Iain was also a prolific story-teller and in his advancing years loved nothing more than to tell stories of island life from days long gone, to anyone who cared to listen. The younger the listener, the more he enjoyed sharing his memories – and he was not averse to embellishing some of his favourite stories from the distant past, in the full knowledge that none of his listeners had any idea whether or not he was telling the truth.

"Och," Iain would say, "ha'e I ever told ye o' the day the Laird Angus married her Ladyship an' five o' Bonnie Charlie's men o' Moidart were there to form a guard outside the kirk? Now, let me see, tha' wid be in '75 – thirty years after Charlie's march – and them was all in their highland dress like tha' day they went wiv him ta Glenfinnan..."

Iain also prided himself on now being the only living islander to have met the 'Young Pretender' – otherwise known as 'Bonnie Prince Charlie'. According to him, he had as a young lad once met and spoken to the Prince face to face. This, he claimed, was on that memorable day back in 1745 when Prince Charlie had landed in Moidart, not very far from Eilean Shona, after sailing from France on his mission to reclaim the throne of Great Britain for its 'rightful heirs, the Stuarts'. And, as Iain never tired of telling anybody who came within earshot, the Prince had that day spoken to everybody he saw, including Iain himself, promising 'upon his life' that he would reclaim the kingdom of Great Britain for the Stuart dynasty 'to which it rightly belonged', and would honour all those good folk who were willing to support his claim and follow him along the length of Loch Shiel to Glenfinnan, and thence southwards to London and the throne of Great Britain. Glenfinnan was where he would be gathering the clans and raising his standard for the march south.

Over sixty years had now elapsed since that historic day when the young Prince had sailed into Loch Moidart with a mere handful of supporters. He had indeed then set about gathering the clans – the Clanranalds, the MacDonalds of Morar, the Gordons of Glenbucket, the MacDonells of Moidart and Knoydart and even some of the MacGregors of Rob Roy fame. Late one afternoon in August 1745 he had raised his standard at Glenfinnan, surrounded by several hundred fighting men willing to support the Prince and those original 'seven men of Moidart', and to do whatever it took to return the Stuarts to their rightful place as the rulers of all England, Wales, Scotland and Ireland.

Eilean Shona, as an integral part of the district of Moidart, had naturally remained closely associated with the story of this great uprising. Throughout the whole island community, the memory of Prince Charlie and his exploits had been marked every year on the anniversary of his arrival with toasts given to his 'Blessed Memory' at every wake or ceilidh or other local gathering. And tales of the whole 'Forty-Five' campaign, as this historic challenge to the Crown was later to become known, had immediately become a popular feature of the education received by all the island's children when, thanks to the initiative of Laird Alastair, Eilean Shona's own school opened for the first time in 1811.

The school was run by the local priest, Father Thomas McNaughton, and his cousin Miss Margaret McTavish, an energetic spinster who had been his companion and housekeeper for many years – long before they came to the island. Between them they now provided a stern and strict elementary education to any of the island's children whose parents wished them to receive it. Every morning other than Sundays and special feast days, the children walked from their homes in all corners of the island to receive their schooling in reading, writing and arithmetic, and to study the lessons of the Holy Bible.

There was the occasional respite for the youngsters when, instead of their normal lessons, they were treated to island tales and traditions, which generally meant stories from local history – and of these none appealed more to the young minds than those relating to 'the Forty-Five'. Those children who listened carefully could often detect differences between the school's supposedly accurate version of the Jacobite rising and some perhaps rather less authentic tales told to them by old Mr McGregor!

The establishment of the school had been a popular move with the island's population, although initially the Laird and Lady Elspeth had been concerned about the potential disturbance it could cause to other residents. In due course a suitably-located vacant cottage was identified and the school was formally opened by the Laird in the autumn of 1811.

By around 1814, what had initially been a mere handful of pupils had already reached sixteen and was continuing to grow steadily. Its pupils were mostly children from the island's impoverished crofting families, more and more of whom were attracted by the free bread and milk which Father Thomas arranged to have delivered to the school each morning with the generous support of the Laird. Some days, in addition to the health-giving, warming milk which came each morning straight from the MacDonell farm, there were slices of bacon too and occasionally, in season, there was fruit from the House's orchard or, provided the harvest was successful, an invitation to some of the children to come and help lift potatoes after the school day finished at noon.

The MacDonells were kindly, generous landlords who understood and respected their responsibility for the well-being of the island's whole community, and no child who so offered their services ever returned home without a bag of potatoes for them to give to their mother. It was through such gestures, and other such means of sharing the essentials of life, that the MacDonells ensured the survival and harmony of their island society. Year after year the community got by, contented in their own simple way, without for the most part the means, the knowledge or the desire to strike out and seek a better life elsewhere.

The MacDonells' own family – their sons Euan and Archie, and now their daughter Margaret – also attended the island school, like all the other Eilean Shona children, from the age of six. They mixed happily with the crofters' families, and would continue to do so until, in the case of the boys, the MacDonells considered it more appropriate for them to be sent away to board alongside other sons of the gentry. Euan had already learned that, once he reached his teenage years, he was destined to attend an English boarding establishment called Harrow School, near London, whose headmaster, the Reverend George Butler, was known and well-respected by the Laird. Happily for Euan, that time had not yet arrived.

For now, he and his siblings enjoyed an idyllic existence, playing daily amongst themselves every afternoon and making good friendships amongst the crofters' families. For the children there was never any sense that they were in any way superior or inferior to one another – this was something which the MacDonell children were only to learn about, and become personally influenced by, in years to come. When it came to lunch time, and the end of lessons for the day, they all shared equally hungrily in the meal on offer, before setting off, supposedly to walk home but, more often than not, to go exploring the island's crags, coves and crannies where they often indulged in impromptu games of hide-and-seek.

At playtime Euan and Archie usually joined a small group of a few crofters' children, including a lively lad called Billy and three athletic-looking young girls known as Kitty, Bernie and Ailsa. Kitty, or 'Kit' for short, was Billy's twin sister and Bernie was her best friend from a neighbouring cottage. Ailsa was Bernie's younger sister. Whenever they were so inclined (in other words when they wished to be treated as young ladies), the two older girls insisted that their names were really Katherine and Bernadette. But most of the time they were just Kit and Bernie. They would not have recognised the word 'tomboys' but that was surely what they were.

* * * *

Ever since they first heard the stories told by old Mr McGregor, the children had all taken an interest in the history and heritage of their island, so there was nothing they loved more than afternoons spent exploring different paths and caves, imagining where those adventurers of the past might have trod, and pretending to walk in their footsteps. Fuelled by a few drams of the locally distilled whisky, Mr McGregor had often convinced his young listeners that Bonnie Prince Charlie's arrival in Moidart in 1745 included a visit to Eilean Shona to recruit all those who honoured the memory of the Stuart kings. There might have been little or no truth in Mr McGregor's version of events but it was enough to excite young minds and fire their imagination.

One day Euan, in a mischievous mood, said that he had been told that when Prince Charlie visited Eilean Shona he had scaled Shona Craig, one of the steepest and most hazardous crags on the coast of the island, from where he had addressed a gathering of the islanders, calling them to join him on his march to 'glory and a prosperous future'. But Archie wasn't going to let his brother get away with that one.

"Nay, Euan, he couldn't have climbed up that rock," replied Archie, "nobody could get up on that rock and get down again."

To which young Bernie had responded, in her broad Scottish accent, "Och, Archie, it is nae sae hard, I'll do it ma'self a body ay these days – ye bide an' see – a body day when it's dry." It was always a point of honour amongst the children – both boys and girls – to show how they were game for anything, especially any challenge which showed them to have the courage and tenacity that was so essential on this remote island.

But unfortunately, Bernie wasn't allowed to forget this boast of hers, and every day for the next couple of weeks she was reminded of her promise by the boys, and especially by Euan and Archie. One sunny afternoon in late March, the six of them – Euan, Archie, Bernie, Ailsa, Billy and Kit – were making their way over towards Shona Craig, accompanied this time by a few other pupils from the school, both boys and girls. Tired of all the teasing and taunting, Bernie had finally relented. She had told all the children at school that she was going to show them what she was made of. This beautiful, breezy but sunny spring day seemed tailor-made for her assault on the crag. So by the time they had reached the start of her climb there was an air of excitement amongst them all.

Euan and Archie called the other children to keep quiet while Bernie set off on her climb. Several of them had wanted to go with her but Bernie turned them away, telling them this was her adventure, not theirs. She wanted to prove she could handle it on her own, she didn't want anyone else getting in her way.

The climb itself was not very high, perhaps fifty or sixty feet, and the first part of it, although steep, did not appear too daunting. For the first few minutes, Bernie slowly clambered up the slope and over rocks on which she and her friends had often played. There seemed no danger as she made her way over towards a steep grassy bank which took her twenty feet up to another ledge. But what none of them could see was the series of eroded, sloping rocks that lay beyond the next bank. Bernie was barefooted and wearing just her usual rather tattered outdoor clothes. The absence of footwear did nothing to help her achieve a safe and secure climb. Still, on she went, calling occasionally to the others below. They heard her cheerily shout that she was nearly there. But then she came to a ridge which took her round the headland altogether and out of sight of her friends.

For the next few minutes nothing further was heard from Bernie, then suddenly a distant call which both Euan and Archie thought sounded anxious. There was a sudden sense of fear amongst them, instinctively conveyed to the rest of the children as, one by one, they looked silently at one another, somehow all suddenly conscious that Bernie was in danger. Even Euan was now speechless as he began to realise how stupid they had all been to goad Bernie into taking on this perilous challenge.

Both he and Archie hurried around to the far side of the hill, followed by two of the other children. Along a footpath they ran, and up a steeply sloping potato field, desperate to obtain a view of Bernie's progress. For a moment she came into view, then they thought they heard a shrill scream, and then an eerie silence, save for the wind which had got up suddenly, hampering even their own progress on foot. Calling behind them to the other children to go back and call for help, Euan and Archie quickened their pace until, round the next corner, they could clearly see Bernie squatting on a tiny ledge, just a few feet from Shona Craig – the craggy platform from which Euan had mischievously suggested Bonnie Prince Charlie had addressed the islanders. Bernie had all but reached her destination, this tiny isolated promontory that had become the subject of a children's dare. And now she had lost her nerve. She could neither stand nor turn around. Again she screamed, not simply a call for help, more a cry of desperation and helplessness.

As the brothers both made to scramble over towards the terrified girl, Archie suggested that it might be more sensible to swim to the cove on the other side of the rock and then approach Bernie from there. The boys hesitated for a few moments before deciding they should try both routes. While Euan headed on over the hill, Archie retraced his steps and then, stripping down to his underclothes, took to the icy water. By this time a number of adults, including a horrified Father Thomas and a bewildered Miss McTavish, had arrived on the scene as word spread around the island that one of the children was attempting the climb.

Meanwhile, up on her ledge, the terrified, exhausted and embarrassed Bernie remained helpless, hearing cries from both boys for a while, then a reluctant call from Euan that he couldn't get any closer to her. The crowd below had grown in size, some too frightened to say – let alone do – anything to help. Father Thomas and Margaret McTavish had dithered, going first one way and then the other. Archie, meanwhile, was making good progress. He was a strong swimmer for his age and had reached a point immediately below the spot where Bernie was crouched, looking dazed and numb, her clothes even more tattered and torn than before. Shivering from his icy swim, Archie now tried to rock-climb up the steep precipice. It took him another fifteen agonising minutes, during which he slipped several times, accompanied on each occasion by screams, not only from Bernie who was following every inch of his progress, but also from those watching below.

They had all been racking their brains as to how they might help Archie and Bernie to descend from the ledge. By now a nearby crofter had brought pieces of rope but it was clear that they were too short to be of much help. And then there he was, Archie holding poor Bernie in his arms and calling for those below to make their way up to a lower ledge, bringing what ropes they had between them, as far as they could. The crofter did his best but was seemingly unable to reach close enough to Archie to throw him any of the ropes. It then occurred to him to take a stone, tie it tight with a knot to one end of the rope, and throw it up to Archie. Even this didn't reach him, but Archie was able to clamber down to where it had caught on the corner of a rock. Telling Bernie to stay where she was, he dropped down to a lower ledge, reached and secured the rope, and then clambered back up to where Bernie was squatting, now more hopeful but yet more terrified than ever.

And so, long before anybody had ever invented abseiling, Archie had used his common sense and his imagination to improvise, tying the rope around Bernie and letting her down the steep rocks, stage by stage. The process had taken almost an hour, as the two of them had struggled to work out how to use the ropes. But long before nightfall they were down at the foot of the cliff, now faced only with another icy cold swim across the bay to safety, where they were hugged, given blankets, and, much to the horror of Father Thomas, a small tot of whisky each. They were both still a few weeks short of their eleventh birthdays, but they had each had an early taste of the medicine which they would no doubt frequently require during the remainder of their adventurous lives. And neither of them would ever forget this traumatic afternoon.

The people of the island – and not just those who were present to witness the dramatic rescue of Bernadette – certainly took some time to come to terms with the whole episode. There were many questions to be answered. How had these young children (none of them more than twelve years old) been allowed to even consider such a hazardous climb, and without any adult supervision? Some wondered how long this kind of adventure had been happening. And why were there no barriers or warnings to stop people – either children or adults – from taking such a dangerous route?

These and numerous other questions occurred to the island population over the ensuing days and nobody had any satisfactory answers. Needless to say, it was the adults who worried the most. The children themselves soon shrugged it off, though Bernadette was chastised by her parents for days afterwards before gradually being forgiven by both, Mother and Father. They were more embarrassed that their daughter had to be rescued by the son of the Laird, of all people. And in the years to come the story would be told and retold, no doubt inaccurately and full of exaggeration, but always with the concluding comment, "Never again!"

* * * *

The main lasting outcome for the island, and for its school in particular, was the agreement by all concerned that there needed to be closer supervision of the children after school had finished each day at mid-day. But this was never going to be easy. Who was going to provide the extra supervision? At harvest time, and various other times of the year, all hands were needed to help on the land. But in winter and spring, the youngsters had boundless unexpended energy and somehow this needed to be channelled in a safe and sensible manner. More thought needed to be given to devising ways of keeping the youngsters occupied during the long afternoons after their school day was over.

Meanwhile the Laird and his wife Lady Elspeth had been as shocked as anyone to hear of the whole episode. They were surprised too to hear of the part played in Bernadette's rescue by their two sons, heroic though that may have been. As the owner of the land, it was of course for the Laird to ensure that proper barriers were erected, so as to warn and prevent any intruders from entering that area. Alastair MacDonell lost no time in getting his men to put these in place.

But they went further. Alastair had seen, at his old school, the benefits of children having an area set aside for them to play their own games – chasing one another, throwing or hitting a ball, or whatever else they wished to do, in a safe environment and in a way which provided a ready alternative to whatever mischief they might otherwise create. The topography of the island did not lend itself to the kind of spacious, level playing-fields which the Laird, with his privileged education, may have had in mind. But from now on he was determined that the children of Eilean Shona must at least have a dedicated area where – when they were not required to help on the land – they could play games, run around and generally work off their surplus energy.

Of course, this was not sufficient in itself. Father Thomas and Miss McTavish also set their minds to ways of encouraging some of the more adventurous children to use their time to better long-term effect in terms of enhancing their education. Their harshest, and most immediate, measure was to lengthen the school day. To some of the youngsters this seemed initially like punishing all of them for the sins of the few, but Miss McTavish – who would also be sacrificing some of her own leisure time – soon won most of them round when she suggested that some of the afternoon classes could be given over to stories and activities based around the traditions of their island and the district of Moidart as a whole, such as re-enacting various old Highland tales. She told them that, to help get this started, she and Father Thomas knew of one or two people who were knowledgeable about local history. She would see if they could persuade one of them to come and talk to the children from time to time.

This sounded to the older children like an invitation to old Mr McGregor to come and tell tall tales and they waited with interest to see who the school's visiting speaker would be.

Chapter Two
Tales and Theatricals

It did not take long for Eilean Shona School to arrange for a visiting speaker to come and talk to the children about the history and traditions of the island. Father Thomas was able to announce, within a few days of the Shona Craig episode, that a respected senior citizen by name Iain McGregor had kindly agreed to spend the following Thursday afternoon sharing his knowledge of the island's past. He had even offered to tell the children some of his own memories.

There were audible sighs from the boys in the class, accompanied by giggles from a couple of the girls, both of which Father Thomas chose to ignore. He finished by saying he was aware Mr McGregor was well-known to some of the children but he was a distinguished resident of the island who, he reminded the children, had 'forgotten more than any of you youngsters have ever learned'. He, Father Thomas, had an appointment with a parishioner that afternoon but Miss McTavish would be at school to welcome Mr McGregor and introduce him. It was most kind of Mr McGregor to agree to come and give a talk.

By the following Thursday, every one of the island's pupils had formed a clear idea of what they thought they could expect from Mr McGregor's talk. Most of them had heard the old man telling his tales of the old days, some of them several times. He would no doubt go straight into a long-winded description of the '45 rebellion, giving the names of all those involved – especially the famous 'seven men of Moidart' – and how Bonnie Prince Charlie had inspired them, and clansmen from all across the western Highlands, to assemble at Glenfinnan. Euan had even placed a bet with Archie that 'Old Iain', as they called him, would mention 'The 45' within forty-five seconds of starting his talk. Several of the other children had decided to draw pictures of him on their slates. But what none of them had expected was that he would arrive at the school dressed as Flora MacDonald's maid, a character called Betty Burke into whom Prince Charlie had been disguised while on the run after his defeat. And Miss McTavish was herself dressed as Flora MacDonald, the lady from the Isle of Skye who had harboured the Prince and helped keep him hidden at the time when he was in the greatest danger of being discovered and arrested. She, Miss McTavish explained, was a real heroine and one whom all true Jacobites rightly honoured and celebrated.

But all this time there was the sound of giggling from amongst the children. They had never seen anything quite so funny in the whole of their young lives. As Mr McGregor pranced across the room calling out, "I'm Betty Burke, I'm only a humble maid, Miss MacDonald's maid," in a squeaky falsetto, the children all fell about laughing. It was several minutes before order could be restored, and when Iain McGregor started speaking again, they were all still laughing so much they didn't listen to a word he was saying.

Eventually both he and Miss McTavish sat down in front of the children and started a conversation with one another about why Bonnie Prince Charlie was having to be disguised, why it was essential for him to escape, and why he had come to Moidart in the first place. Half an hour had elapsed before they paused and Miss McTavish asked the children if they wanted to ask Mr McGregor any questions. At this the class fell silent, but only for a moment, before Euan, and then Bernie and Kit, and then a boy called Robbie, all put up their hands at almost the same time. They all wanted to ask Mr McGregor questions.

They wanted to ask him why he was dressed as he was, and who Betty Burke was. Was there really such a person, asked Bernadette? No there wasn't, Mr McGregor was able to explain, but the Prince had to be disguised to avoid being caught. Young Kitty asked whether the Prince would have been able to run in those clothes, at which they all started laughing. And then one of the boys asked why Prince Charlie thought he should have been King, and why he came to Moidart and not Edinburgh, or straight to London. One of them asked whether he was ever caught, and one boy even asked what would have happened to him if he had been caught.

By now Margaret McTavish had come to the conclusion that this was the best day she had ever known at the school. The children were all, in their different ways, captivated by the topic and the way Iain McGregor was talking to them. The questions kept coming and most, but not all, of them received answers from Mr McGregor. After a while he went quiet and asked for a drink. The class went quiet too. Miss McTavish noticed how white Iain McGregor had become. He was clutching his chest. She felt his pulse. And then he gasped and fell sideways. Euan, Archie and Bernie all got up from their seats to ask the old man if he needed help. But Margaret McTavish said nothing. It was clear to her that Iain McGregor had had a heart attack. She had seen her own father suffer in the same way. By this time, she had torn off some of Iain's 'Betty Burke' clothing to try and help him breathe. But he didn't breathe. He wouldn't breathe. Mr Iain McGregor had died.

* * * *

There was nothing they could have done. There was no doctor on the island, nor could much in the way of medical help have been found anywhere in Moidart. Miss McTavish asked all the children to make their way home, as quickly and quietly as possible. She did not expect there would be any school for a few days. Euan and Archie offered to run back to the Big House to tell their father – the Laird – and their mother. Inside the hour Alastair MacDonell had arranged for Iain's body to be collected and one of the outbuildings at Eilean Shona House became a temporary morgue. Father Tom was fetched from his afternoon appointment and came over to administer the last rites and offer prayers for Iain's soul. As far as anybody knew, Iain had no living relatives. He had never married and had lived alone in a tiny cottage alongside the Big House. But the whole island population were his family. Everybody on the island was devastated. Iain had been one of those characters you could never forget.

Iain McGregor's funeral took place at Eilean Shona's little kirk later that week. Father Tom conducted the service and Alastair MacDonell spoke movingly about how fond of 'McGregor' everybody had been and how much he would be missed. Alastair's father and grandfather had both depended upon him for all the odd jobs that needed to be done and he had never let anybody down. He was also the island's unofficial historian and had managed to keep alive many of the old stories about Eilean Shona and preserve its unique folklore. Above all he had done his best to pass on his knowledge and his many memories to younger generations. It was perhaps rather appropriate that he had spent his final afternoon doing what he loved best, telling the island's children his stories about the Jacobites and the '15 and '45 uprisings.

And then the Laird offered drinks outside the House, beside the kirk, for all the mourners. It was a sunny afternoon and there was a generous supply of the local whisky to be shared. Many of the islanders stayed on, exchanging stories and memories of Iain. They would never see his like again. Father Tom told the Laird that the children had learned a great deal from Mr McGregor, and Miss McTavish added that the children had been greatly enjoying that fascinating afternoon listening to Iain. They were sadder than anyone to have lost him. She mentioned that it might be nice if the children could be encouraged to put on a little play about Bonnie Prince Charlie in Iain's memory, and invite anyone who wanted to come and watch. Alastair and Elspeth MacDonell both agreed that was a lovely idea – Lady Elspeth thought that they might be able to find a room in Eilean Shona House which the school could use as a small theatre.

It did not take Margaret McTavish long to interest the children in the idea of making up, and producing, such a play. She suggested that the story of Bonnie Prince Charlie was an obvious theme. They all felt so inspired by having listened to Mr McGregor at the end of his long life – some still felt a sense of shame about the fun they had previously made of his tales, but they now all readily agreed that, in addition to doing something in honour of the old man, there was an important story to be told about the whole Bonnie Prince Charlie adventure.

* * * *

Iain McGregor had died in April 1815 and a decision had to be made soon about the timing of the play. Given that this year marked not only the centenary of the Old Pretender's uprising (the Fifteen) but also the 70th anniversary of the 'Forty-five', Margaret McTavish thought 1815 would be an appropriate year to perform a commemorative play about the Jacobites. But could it be written, cast, rehearsed and produced before the turn of the year? It was clear that, if that was to be achieved, the children would need a great deal of help.

"Och, I nay think we ha' the time to do such a thing thi' year," Father Tom told Margaret. "There's all the harvesting and if we ha'e a year like these last twa' ha'e been, 'tis all the youngsters tha'll be needed on the land."

"Nay, Tom," replied Miss McTavish, "we cuid do a' the writing ourselves i' the summer, then gi' th' bairns their parts and put on the show afair Christmas."

"Aside from that," she added, "ha' we no' bin looking for things to keep them oot o' trouble after lessons?" That was a point, Father Tom conceded, and so Margaret had won the argument.

"Besides," she added, "I cuid name five or six of the youngsters who canna' wait to guit started. Ah shall hae it aw written thes summer, gie all the kids a part ta lairn an' perform it i' guid time afair Christmas."

And to help keep Father Tom happy, Margaret offered to write, and produce, the play herself.

* * * *

Sad though everyone was at Iain McGregor's sudden death, his passing had brought the whole island together and, as word spread that the school was going to produce a play, there was mounting interest across the whole community. By mid-summer the Laird and Lady Elspeth were able to confirm that they could allocate a suitable room – their ballroom in fact – and that this could be reserved for the event, provided it was held by early December. Lady Elspeth explained to Margaret McTavish that the Laird did sometimes decide to entertain over Christmas, or more likely over Hogmanay, so it would be convenient if the play could take place well before then.

Miss McTavish was delighted when she was shown the spacious room later that week – it was clear that there would be ample space for a small stage to be erected and for an audience of up to fifty or sixty to be accommodated, some of the men standing if necessary. If there were to be so great a level of interest amongst the local community that even more people wished to attend, she felt sure the children would be delighted to give two performances.

There was great excitement at the school when Miss McTavish, accompanied by Father Thomas, gave the news to the children on the last morning of the summer term. Bernie, Ailsa and Kitty immediately asked Euan and Archie what this 'bull room' was like but the MacDonell boys had been forbidden to reveal anything about the geography of the House. Several of the children also wanted to know straightaway exactly who would be playing which part. Happily for Margaret McTavish, it appeared that every child in the school, apart from one very shy seven-year-old called Donald, was keen to appear in the play. Several asked if they could be given a leading role, or at least a speaking part. Miss McTavish promised that they would all have speaking roles.

She explained to the children that the play had not even been written yet, she would be doing that during her summer holiday, but they would all hear about the roles they were to be offered in good time to learn their lines.

Miss McTavish then made the children all laugh when she warned them that they couldn't have more than one Bonnie Prince Charlie – nor, she added, more than one Duke of Cumberland! Some of the children already knew that Cumberland was the Jacobites' arch-enemy for it was he who commanded the British (or 'Hanoverian') forces who were so intent on destroying all remaining support for the Stuart dynasty. One of the boys, Billy, replied that he would quite enjoy being the Duke of Cumberland. "I think he'll win the battle. I'd like that. Shall I be carrying a rifle or a musket, Miss?" he asked excitedly. He had evidently heard about the campaign the British forces had been waging against Napoleon. Miss McTavish, who was loving the enthusiasm shown by the children, then pretended to write a note – *'Billy to play Cumberland'*. The school broke up that afternoon for the children to make themselves useful on the farms and in the fields and Billy skipped home cheerfully, confident that next term he was to be the Duke of Cumberland.

* * * *

The weather was kind to Moidart that summer, so it was helpful to have the extra pairs of hands which the children provided on the land. As always, the main harvest of potatoes was the priority for everybody from the Laird to the humble crofter. A good year meant survival for crofters and their families and every hand, and every extra hour spent on the land, could help make the difference in terms of the success of the harvest. Billy worked long and hard through his summer holidays, alongside his two elder brothers and three sisters, to ensure that he made his contribution to the family's potato and turnip crop. And as he worked, he longed for the next term at school and the chance to play the part of the Duke of Cumberland.

Across Eilean Shona, as in Moidart and throughout the western isles, the dedication of children to the survival of their family, and their clan, was of paramount importance. Young and old laboured alongside one another until the crop was ready and the potatoes had all been lifted or re-planted for the next season. Potato formed the staple diet for the people of the Scottish isles, as it did for much of the Highlands, and all of Ireland, where weather conditions were normally ideal for the crop and generally provided bountiful harvests. The success of the potato was somewhat more uncertain in Eilean Shona but, so long as a strict regime of planting, lifting and storing was followed, the results were generally satisfactory. The children's contribution could be useful in many different ways – if they were not assisting with the potatoes themselves, they could be milking the cow or helping with the herring catch. Whatever their involvement, they were expected to be playing their part each hour of every day towards their family's survival.

This work did have another benefit as far as Billy was concerned. It helped to pass the time until autumn, when the school was to be re-opened. And when the time came for that, Billy was the first to go and speak to Miss McTavish. "Please miss, can I be the Duke of Cum-whatever it was, please?" Billy was desperate for the role and Miss McTavish fully understood his anxiety. But there were other children who might want that part in the play.

"Yes Billy, I'll let you know who is to take which part, as soon as that is all decided. I hope you've been helpful to your ma and pa in the summer?"

"Yes of course, miss. I've worked every day for me ma and me pa and we've had a guid harvest this year I think," was Billy's reply.

"That's guid, Billy," replied Margaret McTavish, now firmly making up her mind to give Billy the part he so wanted and deserved. She had already given a great deal of thought to which child would suit which character, while she wrote the script of the play, and she had more or less made up her mind about all the main roles. But she would keep the children waiting just a wee while longer, as she saw how they settled back into the school routine. She also needed to speak to Father Thomas in case he had any reservations about the way the play should be produced and how much time could be set aside for the rehearsals. She was already conscious that some parts in the play would require considerable dedication by the children who were chosen to play them, and did not wish Father Thomas to feel any child was being unduly burdened by the commitment they were making to the production.

Miss McTavish had decided to call the play 'The '15 and the '45'. Over the summer, as she scripted the lines, she had toyed with other potential titles such as 'The Uprisings' or 'The Jacobite cause'. But she preferred 'The '15 and the '45' as it marked more clearly the anniversaries they were seeking to celebrate. Father Thomas readily agreed, and, more important than that, so did the Laird and Lady Elspeth. "Miss McTavish, that is an excellent title," Lady Elspeth said to her one morning, whilst showing her the ballroom in which the play was to be produced. "Even if they eventually forget every word of your play, they will always remember those dates. And, if nothing else, that will keep the cause of the Stuarts alive for another generation or two."

And so it was decided. 'The '15 and the '45' was to be staged at Eilean Shona House in early December 1815. The Laird had suggested Saturday 2nd December, at two o'clock in the afternoon, with a dress rehearsal the previous day, open to islanders who could not attend on the Saturday. Margaret offered to show Lady Elspeth and the Laird her script, but Lady Elspeth declined this suggestion.

"It will spoil the show for us if we know what happens," she said with a smile, adding after a moment's thought, "Do you know, I don't think Alastair and I have been to the theatre since 'Macbeth' was on in Edinburgh the year we wed. That was back in '02. I shall have to get a new gown." This made Margaret McTavish decidedly nervous, she had not intended anyone to attach such importance to her little play. There was only one thing for it – she and all the children were going to have to work especially hard to ensure that the occasion merited Lady Elspeth's investment.

* * * *

The first day back at school was exciting for all the children. Most of them had seen a little of one another from time to time during the summer, but the work that occupied them during the harvesting had prevented much in the way of discourse. So as they assembled back in the classroom there was plenty of chatter. At nine o'clock sharp, Father Thomas called for silence so that the day could begin with the customary prayers. "Our father, which art in Heaven," he chanted, and the children's attention was focused upon the lines that they too were expected to recite. It occurred to some that they could soon expect to be given some more lines to memorise – and what those lines were would depend on the parts they were to be allocated.

I do hope I'm to be Charlie, thought both Euan and Archie. During the holidays they had frequently argued with one another as to which of them was best suited to playing the Prince. Meanwhile Bernie was praying to be given the part of Flora MacDonald and Billy, of course, was hoping to be Cumberland.

At mid-day there was the customary break, which, prior to Bernie's hairy adventure on Shona Craig, would have marked the end of school for the day. But now the new regime, that of keeping the children occupied in the afternoons, was swinging into action. After the children had been given their food rations for the day, Father Thomas called for attention and announced that for the new term the main afternoon activity would be to prepare for the school play. He then handed over to Miss McTavish to announce what role each child was expected to perform.

"Now then, boys and girls, I know you will all have your preferences, and I hope that most of you will be pleased with the parts you have been allocated. But some of you may be a little disappointed – you cannot all be Bonnie Prince Charlie, nor can you all be Flora MacDonald – or the Duke of Cumberland for that matter, Billy. So please no tears and no squabbling when you hear which parts you are to play."

"First of all, can I explain that I have received a special request from the Laird that, as you, Euan, have important examinations in the near future for your entrance to your next school, you should not be involved in any stage role which might distract you from your studies. Instead, you are to be allocated the role of theatre host, so you will be asked to welcome the audience to the Big House on the day and show them through to their seats. You won't therefore need to spend any time doing rehearsals." Euan and Archie smiled at one another; they were both happy with this decision.

"I will leave the role of Prince Charles Edward Stuart for the time being," Margaret McTavish continued. "Now the next important role will be the King of England. The boy who is chosen for this role won't actually have to do anything – or even say anything. He will just sit on a throne wearing a rather handsome crown. I wonder if, Donald, you might like to be our king?" Donald, the shy boy who had not wanted to take part, nodded his head and gave a little smile – he rather liked the idea of this play now.

"Next, boys and girls, I'd like to suggest that Archie would make a very suitable prince." This was very popular, everybody seemed to agree that he would be ideal for this. Archie grinned, and blushed a little. Bernie looked pleased too, and began to wonder whether she might get the part of Flora MacDonald. She had become very keen on Archie ever since he helped her down from Shona Craig. She tried to look at Archie without looking as though she was looking.

Miss McTavish continued. "Now, next there's the nasty cruel man who was head of the British forces, The Duke of Cumberland. Somebody is going to have to play him. Fortunately, I think we have a kind offer from Billy for this role, isn't that right Billy?"

Billy looked thrilled – he nodded furiously and said, "Yes miss," with a huge grin. His whole summer had been spent hoping he would get to play this role. Miss McTavish went on: "Now the Duke can't fight on his own, he will need to have some other soldiers to help him, and so you, Robbie; and you, Andy; and you too, Fergus, you will all be soldiers under the Duke of Cumberland's command." The boys all glanced and grinned at one another.

"So now," Miss McTavish continued, "that just leaves us with the famous 'seven men of Moidart', who were the prince's initial supporters when he first began the uprising. Oh, and also Miss Flora MacDonald – I'll come to her in a moment. Some of the girls looked round the room – several had not yet been given a part. Which of them would be Flora? And where were the seven men of Moidart to be found? I would like to ask the following to be the seven men of Moidart," Miss McTavish was saying. "They were very important, as the prince could not have set off on his own. Now we don't have any more boys, so, Margaret and Annie MacDonell, Kitty, Ailsa, Lorna, Rhona and Biddy, I'd like you all to pretend you are men – it's all right, you can wear your kilts, you'll look just like they did," Miss McTavish added with a smile, "and I'm sure you'll make a fine body of men." At this the boys all laughed, while the girls all glanced at one another and nodded in agreement. This was going to be fun.

There was a slight pause and then, just as Bernie was about to put up her hand and ask what part she could have, Miss McTavish added that there was still one part to be allocated – a very important part, without which the prince would never have survived. "This just leaves the part of Flora MacDonald," she went on, "and I cannot think of anyone better suited to this role than the brave and daring Bernadette. It's quite a major role, Bernadette, now do you think you can manage that for us?"

And Bernie, privately thrilled to be given the role, calmly responded, "Yes of course, miss, if you think I'm suitable."

"Of course, you're suitable, Bernadette," came Miss McTavish's response, "but like all the others you'll have to do plenty of rehearsing." And something stirred then inside

Bernie as she wondered if she might get a kiss from the prince while she was hiding him from the enemy.

* * * *

Thanks to the hard work of all the children, and the skill and dedication of Margaret McTavish, the play was a huge success when it was duly staged in the ballroom at the Big House in December. All through October and November, 'Tavvy' – as the children had started calling her when she couldn't hear them – had kept them hard at rehearsal, going over every scene until they could all play their parts without having to stop and think. It had been hard work at the beginning, but everybody agreed it had been well worthwhile. Enthusiastic applause greeted every child as they appeared on stage, and there was a special cheer from the fifty or so islanders who had packed into the ballroom when 'Prince Charlie' attempted to thank 'Flora Macdonald' with a hasty attempt at a kiss.

As the final curtain came down, the Laird stepped forward and reminded everybody that the play could never have taken place without two people in particular – the late Iain McGregor, of course, in whose honour it was staged – he would never be forgotten; and Miss McTavish, whose idea the play had been, and who had dedicated so much of her time to making it such a success and a really happy learning experience for all the children. And then Euan MacDonell appeared with a basket of fruit and delicacies as a Christmas present for 'Tavvy'. As Miss McTavish accepted the gift, she congratulated Euan on the news that he had passed his entrance examination to Harrow School, saying how much he would be missed at Eilean Shona School. She was sure he would be back for his holidays from time to time, and hopefully one day would return to live here.

Euan received a respectful round of applause as he returned to his seat. Nobody quite said it but there was a feeling that, after the events of the last few months, the island would never be quite the same again. There had developed such a happy relationship between the people of the island and the whole MacDonell family. It had come together, in a spirit of friendship between young and old, and, with such an excellent bunch of children growing up on the island, the future was in good hands.

Chapter Three
Departures and Discoveries

In the years that followed these memorable few months, the island slipped gradually back into its old routines. The school reverted to its traditional curriculum, further stretching the hours devoted to its reading, writing, arithmetic and bible studies in order to meet the higher standards of literacy and numeracy which their teachers considered were now essential, not only for the children's own future well-being but also for that of the Eilean Shona community as a whole. This meant that except on Wednesdays and Saturdays, school lessons now continued into the afternoons as a matter of course.

Other changes took place over time. Mostly it was just a very gradual process, although from time to time there were particular moments which brought home to the island community that it was moving into a new era. First of all, and only a little more than a month after the island's school play had so thrilled the whole Eilean Shona community, there came the day of departure for Euan. This was an event in itself. Into the depths of the January snow, the Laird's coach was driven out of the stables at Eilean Shona House, with Euan and his father both on board and a fully laden trunk carrying all Euan's requirements for his first term at boarding school.

Despite the weather, the farewell gathering included several of the other children – Archie, Bernie, Ailsa, Kitty, Billy and Margaret and Annie were all there. They and their parents, and a few of their neighbours and friends, had gathered outside to wave Euan good-bye. He would not be returning until April, and from now on, Eilean Shona would be his home for only a small part of each year. Suddenly the thought hit the younger children that time did not stand still. They would miss Master Euan more than they had ever realised.

And two years later the same procedure would be followed for Archie's departure. Of course, by then Archie would have his big brother to travel with him and, hopefully, to show him the ropes when he arrived at the big school. Not that Archie had ever lived in Euan's shadow – ever since the episode on Shona Craig, Archie had carved out his own place in the island's history and hierarchy. He was the one who had come to the rescue. Certainly for Bernie, and probably for several of the other children, they would miss his reassuring presence while he was away. But somehow, while they had started to refer to Euan as 'Master Euan' – and this had soon become quite natural for them all – nobody yet thought of Archie as 'Master Archie'. Perhaps they never would.

Those two years passed quite quickly for both Euan and Archie. Euan responded very positively to the demanding regime of his famous boarding school. The school expected high standards of study, of personal conduct and discipline, and of social interaction. As he found pleasure in many of the activities, including the playing of team sports and the military training, Euan grew in confidence and the weeks and months sped by. It was noticeable, whenever he returned to Eilean Shona for his school holidays, how fast he was maturing. Some of the islanders remarked privately that they could see Euan becoming an inspiring and very popular Laird when his time came.

Archie had of course stayed at Eilean Shona School during his brother's first two years away. He had inevitably become closer to the other, older children who were still at the school – particularly Bernadette. But then, after those two years had passed, Archie too was heading off to Harrow. He had satisfied the examiners with distinction and he followed his brother there in January 1818. Archie soon thrived on the boarding environment and, in his case, he benefited from the school's academic focus upon the classics and an all-round syllabus which was designed, as the headmaster put it, to provide the 'leaders of tomorrow' with the skills and confidence necessary to take on responsible roles in the years ahead. In addition to Latin, ancient Greek and classical mythology, Archie also studied English and European history and he enjoyed the expert tuition that was available to him and his fellow students. These were the years immediately following the Napoleonic wars and Arthur Wellesley's great victory at Waterloo. Like others up and down the country, Archie took pride in the great victory which had by now earned Wellesley the honour of being created the first Duke of Wellington.

* * * *

Meanwhile, in terms of the MacDonell family itself, only the two young sisters now remained at Eilean Shona School. Margaret and Annie were both very bright girls, intelligent and confident, and they too would no doubt have been capable of passing the Harrow entrance exams, had they had the opportunity. However, as girls, and particularly as daughters of the gentry, there was at this time no expectation that they would pursue their academic studies to a higher level. Instead they were encouraged to become accomplished in the more feminine pursuits, such as playing the violin or singing, or dancing or drama or other such pastimes. One day they could expect to be introduced to Edinburgh's social scene, or perhaps even London's, in the expectation that they would find themselves suitably well-to-do husbands.

They had therefore stayed at Eilean Shona School after Euan and Archie had both moved on; and the Laird and Lady Elspeth arranged with Father Thomas and Miss McTavish that they would be allowed to remain there beyond their fourteenth birthdays, and study subjects such as languages and the arts, until they had both reached their sixteenth birthdays. Despite their superior background, all the MacDonell family had remained popular with the other children. Margaret and Annie continued for the most part to enjoy the company of their fellow students, particularly Kitty, Ailsa and Lorna, who all belonged somewhere between the MacDonell girls in age. Margaret had also tried to remain close to Bernadette, despite the two years between them. She sensed that Bernadette was missing Archie, who she knew would forever have a place in Bernadette's heart as her saviour on Shona Craig. And now she reasoned that, in Archie's absence, Bernie would welcome some other close contact with his family.

But, as she soon discovered, Bernie seemed to be behaving differently these days. She no longer answered to the name 'Bernie', now that she was in her teens. This was because, she told Margaret and her friend Kitty, 'Bernie' was not a very dignified name for a young lady. From now on, she wished to be known as Bernadette. Besides, she was now the oldest pupil at the school and needed to maintain her dignity in the eyes of the younger children.

Kitty responded by announcing that she now wished to be known as Katherine: she also wanted to maintain her 'dingety', or whatever that was. But, in her case, the pretence lasted only a couple of days before she reverted to being Kitty. Kitty had never been one to put on appearances. She considered it absurd to do so, given the humble conditions in which she and all her friends existed. But Bernadette was adamant – she was now Bernadette, and that was that.

For some while, neither Bernadette nor Kitty had taken much interest in the junior children, but Kitty suggested after school one day that they should at least befriend Margaret as a means of renewing contact with Archie when he came home. But Bernadette was adamant. "Where do we stop, Kitty?" she asked. "In no time at all we'd have that baby Annie tagging along." And anyway, Bernadette pointed out, Margaret was a poor substitute for Archie when it came to making friends. Quite apart from being two years younger than him, she lacked the obvious attraction of belonging to the opposite sex. She wasn't even particularly adventurous. Margaret and Annie's idea of exercise, she said, was simply to skip or play the occasional game of hide and seek. Bernadette had long since grown tired of these childish amusements and wanted to spread her wings and take interesting walks and explore the surrounding countryside. She thought it would be stimulating to study the various plants, grasses and mosses for which the area was renowned.

* * * *

Beneath this façade, and although she kept her feelings to herself, Bernadette spent most of every school term yearning for Euan and Archie to return home to Eilean Shona for their holidays. She hoped they would then be available to take her with them on some of their boat trips and hikes around the Moidart district. She knew they were keen on exploring local history and places of interest and she dreamed of going out with them, perhaps discovering old remains of treasure from shipwrecks off the nearby coastline or the ruins of castles long deserted by ancient clansmen.

On his first holiday back on the island, Archie did not disappoint Bernadette. It was April and he and Euan were home for three weeks, including Easter week. Of these Bernadette soon found that the first week, 'Holy Week', was of no use to her. Archie's parents were devout Catholics and expected him, and Euan and the family as a whole, all to observe Holy Week strictly. This meant periods of total silence and contemplation at certain times of the day. Going out climbing or on boat trips, both of which would occupy most of the day, were quite out of the question. There would be plenty of time for trips out, and whatever escapades they had in mind, once Easter had been properly observed. Meanwhile there was still Good Friday to be respected. The regime on Good Friday was even stricter, for on that day Father Thomas presided over a traditional 'Crucifixion' observance, which lasted three hours.

These traditions were all part of the routine of the Eilean Shona community – they had all grown up with such established customs. But to Bernadette they were now becoming a nuisance. Easter Day itself was also closely observed, but in a much more joyous mood. Christ had risen, so it was now permissible to run and dance and have fun. At least they might be able to meet for some games of chase on the playing field area, but as far as Bernadette was concerned, time was running out for getting out and about with Archie – and of course with Euan. She told herself she mustn't have eyes only for Archie.

It was not until they all came out of church after the Easter morning service that Bernadette had any chance to speak with Archie. Discreetly biding her time, she stood with her mother and smiled politely at the other worshippers who were busy exchanging Easter greetings. Meanwhile the Laird and his family were slowly making their way around, enquiring of their tenants' health and wishing everybody a fruitful harvest this year. Euan and Archie followed close behind, with Margaret and Annie, making similarly polite conversation but mostly aimed at the young people of the island in their case. As they approached Bernadette and her mother, Euan asked Mrs Neish about her husband's health, leaving Archie free to speak briefly with Bernadette. "And how is my friend Bernie?" Archie politely enquired, smiling broadly at the young lady he had helped to rescue a couple of years or so earlier, "you must be top of the class at school by now." And Bernadette, ignoring the reference to her academic progress, simply answered in her own cheeky manner.

"Yes, but I'm missing my knight in shining armour. I canna go exploring now." By now Euan and Mrs Neish had fallen silent and they heard Archie continue.

"Oh, that's a shame. Where would you have liked to explore? Euan and I have been thinking we might arrange a hike while we're home, if you and Kitty would be game?"

"Och, Master Archie," Mrs Neish replied, "I trust ye won't be leadin' Bairnie into any danger this time."

As the Laird's family walked across from the kirk back to the house, Euan teased Archie about the interest he'd shown in Bernie. "You still have a liking for peasant girls eh?" he teased. "Wait till I tell our friends at Harrow about the kind of young lady you fancy!" And Archie was quite unable to hide his embarrassment.

"Oh Euan, we're only being decent to the young kids, they don't get a lot of fun here." Euan decided to leave it at that, it would make a good day out for them all and he didn't wish to embarrass his younger brother any further.

Meanwhile their parents had picked up on the plans the boys were making for an expedition. "I gather you have plans for one of your days out," the Laird had said that evening to them both. "May I ask where you're planning to go, and who might be going with you?" He looked from one boy to the other, and for a moment Archie feared that his father might be about to impose restrictions on where they went to amuse themselves on their holidays, and with whom they intended to pass the time. Feeling somewhat guilty that they hadn't already thought to discuss the arrangements with their parents, Archie was on the point of breaking into a profuse apology.

But his brother beat him to it. "Yes, Papa," Euan intervened, "I'm keen to be able to talk a little more knowledgably about this part of the country when we return to Harrow next term. I know they are planning to cover geography in our syllabus from now on, and I'm sure Archie and I will need to be able to show we've seen something of the district in which we live. We thought a hike over towards Glenuig and back would be a good start."

"Oh, what an excellent idea, my boys," came their father's response. "You'll need to pick a day when the tide is low, or be willing to wade or row across the water, and you'll find Glenuig and back is a good day's walking but if you stick to the tracks you should be all right. Is anybody going with you?"

Archie sensibly left Euan to handle this question as well. "Oh yes, Father, Mrs Neish has given permission for her daughters Bernadette and Ailsa to accompany us, if you and Mama are happy for us to do so." And the Laird now remembered Bernie from the school play a couple of years earlier.

"Ah yes, I remember her – wasn't she the one who played Miss Flora MacDonald? Pretty girl, I seem to remember. Make sure you look after her. Young lads like you should be able to cover that distance within a good day's walking but if you have lasses with you be sure to look after them."

By this time Lady Elspeth had entered the room and was looking quizzically at her husband. But Euan simply thanked his father, and Archie nodded his agreement. Lady Elspeth kept her thoughts to herself, for the time being.

* * * *

Having successfully handled the negotiations with his father, Euan decided to leave Archie to walk across to the Neishes that afternoon and confirm the invitation to Bernie and Ailsa to join their proposed day's walking. He told them they were thinking in terms of the following Thursday, when he had noticed the tide would be right down in the early morning and evening so should allow them to walk across the sands to the Moidart mainland. Billy and Kitty's mother happened to be there with 'Ma Neish', as she was known locally, so Archie decided to assure both women that he and Euan had discussed the proposal with their parents and received their approval, which both women were relieved to learn. It was kind of the Laird's family to maintain friendship with the likes of themselves, they thought, and Ma Neish immediately offered to put together a wee bag of potatoes and a slice of her home-made cheese for them all to take with them on the trip. "Ye'll a' be hungry afore ye are half way roond," she said to the children.

Archie nodded his gratitude and hurried home to tell Euan they were to be a party of six. They could now start planning their day out, and they looked forward to sharing it with Bernie and Ailsa, and Billy and Kitty. Having heard their father's reaction, the boys decided this was an ideal opportunity to spend a day going across to the Moidart mainland. The days were drawing out now that spring had arrived, so if they made an early start on Thursday, they should be able to enjoy a really good hike, hopefully at least as far as Glenuig, and maybe even further. The boys checked on the tides again and then got out an old map of their father's, from which they deduced that they should be able to walk across from Shona Beag towards Kylesbeg and then join the track towards Glenuig. The Laird suggested to Euan that they take the map with them, mentioning that he remembered once climbing a small hill near there, which provided great views over to the Sound of Arisaig.

At this Euan recalled old McGregor saying that the Sound of Arisaig was where the Bonnie Prince had finally been rescued by French ships after his lucky escape with Flora MacDonald, and Archie suggested they try and reach there. Euan wasn't so sure. "It looks a good distance, might be a bit far for any of the bairns from school," he said.

"Oh, I dunno, I'll wager Bernie an' Ailsa cuid manage that alright," was Archie's response. They were starting to slip back into the Scottish accent they had picked up as children, but which they had begun to lose after months of mixing with well-to-do English boys at Harrow. Meanwhile something had stirred inside him at the reference to the Prince and Flora MacDonald.

By the Tuesday morning they had worked out their precise route which they estimated would be around ten miles there and back. Archie volunteered to go across to Bernie's and Kitty's cottages, to explain to them what they would be letting themselves in for and to check whether the girls and Billy still wanted to come with them. Bernie's response was definite – they were all used to long days on their feet and quite accustomed to walking long distances. "Tis no worry Archie, we's all used to walking, this woan be beyond any of us – aye, only worry now is Ma – she's wondering, if the sun isn't shining, how will we keep track o' time and beat the tide for coming back in the evening?"

"That's no problem Bernadette," Archie replied with a smile, pulling a pocket watch out from inside his jacket. "My present for passing my Harrow exams," he added. "I'm told,

Bernadette, that it once belonged to an uncle of my father's. It might come in handy on Thursday."

"Och, what presents you have, me and ma sis jus git an extra tattie if we do well. Och, and what's all this wi calling me Bernadette. I'm still Bernie you know." Bernie she certainly was, now that Euan and Archie were back to keep her in her place...

* * * *

Thursday dawned bright and sunny and they were all wide awake and raring to go by daybreak. Ma Neish was also up and about at dawn. They had agreed to meet up at her cottage, partly on account of its location on the east side of the island, close to the path leading straight over to Shona Beag and the ford across to the mainland, but also to take advantage of her kind offer of potatoes and cheese to help sustain them through the day. Euan and Archie did not want to appear ungrateful and sure enough, Ma Neish had the rations all ready, sorted into six little piles. She now took the trouble to check that they each took their share, stuffing them into the pockets of their shirts or coats or, in the case of Euan and Archie, into the knapsacks that only they were fortunate to possess.

Euan noticed that poor Billy didn't have pockets to the rough shirt he wore, so he generously offered to look after his share. As he opened his own knapsack to slip Billy's potatoes and cheese inside, he noticed a small parcel of food hiding at the bottom, wrapped in the familiar-looking grease paper which his family's cook was forever using whenever they went anywhere. Not wishing to embarrass Ma Neish, who had shown such warmth and generosity towards him and Archie over the whole idea of the outing, he closed up the knapsack without a word. Perhaps he would 'miraculously' discover these extra rations if they were still hungry later in the day.

An early morning haze hovered over them as they all set off, promising them a warm sunny day, and the birds were already up and about, providing them with a cheerful chorus to see them on their way. These were mostly seabirds –

redshank, oyster catcher, herring gull – but there was also an early cuckoo to be heard that morning, sounding its warning to the doomed pipits already settling into their nests.

Carefully following the map which the Laird had agreed to lend them, the gang walked briskly along, Euan and Archie both grateful to have shared their plans with their parents. Their father's advice now gave them the confidence to know which tracks were the safest to follow. Little did they know at this time that their parents, particularly their mother, had been harbouring fears that they would suffer socially themselves if their boys continued to fraternise with humble, crofters' children. It was more for this reason that their parents had initially had reservations about this expedition. Only after lengthy discussion had they decided that for the time being it would be good for future relationships on the island for their boys to 'muck in' occasionally with the 'local kids'. After all, as Lady Elspeth had eventually acknowledged, these same children had been their school friends only a year or two earlier. So they had settled on lending their support for the expedition; the Laird had fished out his old map for Euan to borrow; and Lady Elspeth had instructed Cook to wrap some sandwiches and slip them into the boys' knapsacks.

* * * *

The path was less hilly than they had feared and, despite the occasional pause to take a drink from a stream, they reached Glenuig well before mid-day. From here a track to the left offered what promised to be a scenic coastal walk, with delightful views over Glenuig Bay and a tiny outcrop called Samalaman Island. Consulting the map, Archie and Bernie estimated that they could take this track around the coast, past Samalaman Island and Rubha na Faing Moire, and eventually back across the sands to Eilean Shona, all in much the same time that it would take to retrace their steps on the track they had taken this morning. Bernie mentioned that she would like to see Samalaman Island, it sounded romantic and she adored islands, especially really small ones. She would definitely like to take this path. Billy, too, thought this would be fun and wanted to take that route.

Kitty and Ailsa, meanwhile, were already beginning to feel quite weary – Kitty said she didn't want to spoil the day for anyone but she would prefer to turn back. She thought she and Ailsa wouldn't have too much trouble finding their way back if they just followed the route they had been on all morning. Euan was torn, he still felt quite fresh, he was enjoying the day but he didn't want to spoil it for any of them. He looked in Archie's direction, nodded at Bernie standing close by him, and thought for a moment. Perhaps he ought to keep an eye on Kitty and Ailsa, and see them safely home. So they all sat and consumed their potato and cheese, before embarking upon their two separate routes back to Eilean Shona. There was a brief discussion as to which trio should take the map but Archie soon pointed out that he agreed with Kitty and Ailsa. Even with Euan to distract them, they certainly shouldn't need it unless they had had their eyes shut all morning. So the map went with Archie, Bernie and Billy. To even things up, Euan insisted on his team having the watch.

And so they set off, around one o'clock, to take their separate routes home. Then, after no more than two minutes, Billy changed his mind – he'd seen his sister Kitty skipping along with Euan and Ailsa and he decided he'd prefer to join them. Archie and Bernie said it was up to him, but to take care and make sure he caught up with the others before they went out of view. They watched him run off and soon they saw him joining up with Euan, Kitty and Ailsa.

Euan made the return journey good fun for his younger companions, telling them stories he had heard from his parents about the things that happened in Eilean Shona, and then – at Kitty's request – about the funny or strange things that happened at his school. These made them gasp, for he told them how the 'beaks' (the teachers) used sticks to beat any boys who didn't do as they were told, or simply didn't do well enough in class. They thought he was very brave to attend such a school but he said that mostly it was good fun, and he'd made some 'topping' friends who did 'stunning' things like diving off the top of one of the school buildings into a lake. He kept them talking and asking questions most of the way back, and it was only when they were three-quarters of the way home that he realised he still had all Cook's food packs sitting at the bottom of his knapsack. They stopped, sat on a rock, and guzzled away for more than half an hour. But they still arrived back in Eilean Shona soon after seven o'clock in the evening.

Meanwhile Archie and Bernie had made their way along the coastal path towards Samalaman. The views were inspiring and Bernie had never felt happier in all her young life. She had dreamed of spending some time alone with Archie ever since that unforgettable afternoon when he had come to her rescue almost three years ago. Archie teased her now that, if she became stranded on any of the rocks that they passed, he wouldn't bother to save her this time. But she knew he cared for her and, even though she detected differences in his attitude since he had been away at boarding school, she felt a deeper friendship than she had ever known before.

After a while they stopped and sat down for a rest, fairly close to a large, solitary stone – a stone that looked almost like a monument, but with no writing on it. They wondered whether it had once formed part of a ring, like the kind of dolmens which Archie said he believed were worshipped by the ancient Celts many hundreds of years ago. Bernie went over to it and made to bend over the stone in mock prayer, but she slipped and fell over on a grassy bank. Archie hurried over to her to check she wasn't hurt and, as he pulled her up onto her feet, they both noticed the pointed corner of some kind of box protruding from the ground where she had fallen.

"Do I always have to come to your rescue, fair maiden," Archie teased, but Bernie's attention was on the strange object that appeared almost completely buried beside them.

"What is it?" she asked.

"I don't know, how do you expect me to know?" came Archie's response. "But, young lady, if you now consider yourself rescued, I will try and deal with your other demand

and find out what on earth it is." So they started digging with their hands and gradually they uncovered more and more of the box. After several minutes they were able to examine the whole of its exterior. It was clearly very old, Archie decided, but had been made of sufficiently strong material – a leather of some kind on top of some very hard wood, he guessed. It needed to be, to protect it against not only the elements but also all the worms and insects that had inhabited that spot, presumably over a very long period of time. Archie and Bernie looked at one another, both sensing that they had made a really interesting discovery. Then, as they heaved and pulled the box out of the ground altogether, Bernie noticed the remains of an old glove. "Ah Bernie, a nice glove for you to keep your hands warm in winter," he joked. But, as they lifted and examined first the box and then the glove, they both felt mesmerised by their intriguing find.

* * * *

They sat for a while, pondering and discussing the possible significance of this double discovery. How and why had somebody decided to bury and leave these mysterious items? Maybe the glove could have been dropped by mistake, but to leave a sturdy, possibly quite valuable, box seemed strange. What was in it? Archie decided to see if he could open the box. He wrenched and pulled, using first one piece of stone and then another, and suddenly it flew open – or rather about half-open. He couldn't open it any further. They held the box under the full glare of the afternoon sun, peered inside it and saw a tiny part of its contents glinting in the sun. Could it contain something valuable, they wondered? Archie wiped away as much of the dirt inside the box as he could reach. And then, bit by bit, they were able to see what it was, this object that had sat in its box, in this wild and remote spot, and for who knows how many years, and yet was still glinting in today's spring sunshine. It was circular in shape but with some intricate engraving like a Seal with a Coat of Arms or the insignia of some special organisation. As they continued to clean as much of the Seal as they could, and to study it, they became more certain in their minds that it was, or had been, somebody's personal seal – the kind whose use on documents would signify its owner's personal approval or authority.

They stared at one another for ages, asking themselves over and over again what they should do. Should they pick it up and take it back with them to Eilean Shona? How important might it turn out to be? If it was potentially very valuable, should they move it at all? Perhaps it was best to leave it alone for the time being, they thought. And, in the meantime, who should they tell about their find? Would anyone believe them anyway?

They sat still, considering all the options and, as they talked it all over, they looked out to the sea before them. "So this is what they call the Sound of Arisaig," said Archie. Wasn't this the place where old Iain McGregor had told them Bonnie Prince Charlie's great adventure had ended? Where he had finally escaped Cumberland's massive search to bring him to justice? And where he had been picked up by two French ships in this remote bay, despite it being closely guarded by the Hanoverian forces?

Bernie's mind was also racing ahead. Was it just a coincidence that this important-looking Seal, and somebody's old glove, had finished up buried together, so close to the site of that historic rescue? Bernie's imagination told her that there were no limits as to the potential significance of their find. If this was the case, she suggested, they should keep the secret to themselves, at least until they could work out what was the best thing to do. In the meantime, it was their find, and nobody else's, and they should take care not to tell a soul. Archie agreed – they must tread carefully, very carefully, in case its significance really did know no bounds. They could always come back and claim it once they knew how important, and how valuable, it might be.

They decided to re-bury both objects exactly where they found them, but also to make a mental note as to precisely where they were in relation to the solitary stone. Archie suggested that, as soon as he had an opportunity, he would try and learn more about seals, such as what kind of people had them and what they were used for. What were they worth? He felt sure some of the masters at Harrow would know about these things. In the meantime, they should be very careful who they spoke to about their discovery. Their secret find would no longer be theirs if they started telling other people.

As they completed the re-burial, Archie looked Bernie in the eye and said they must faithfully promise one another on this. And Bernie replied, "Of course, dear Archie, I share with you my Seal of Promise on that." And they agreed that the 'Seal of Promise' would be their watchword, their own private code and guarantee of secrecy. At this, Archie put his arms around Bernie and, as they looked out over the Sound of Arisaig, they kissed – not for long, but they kissed, for the first time since their stage 'hug' at their little school play over two years ago.

As they broke away from one another, Archie repeated to Bernie, "I share my Seal of Promise with you too, my dear Bernie." And they again solemnly pronounced their 'Seal of Promise' to be "their watchword, their own private code, their guarantee of secrecy." And neither would ever forget that precious moment that they had spent in each other's arms. *This was a real kiss,* Bernie thought to herself, *not a pretend one this time.*

Then suddenly, sensing that they had spent much longer on this part of their walk than they had ever expected, they picked up their pace and began to hurry back towards the nearest crossing point to Eilean Shona. It wouldn't do for their families to notice how long they had been out together, unaccompanied and now dishevelled and dirty from Bernie's fall and the digging they had both been doing with their hands. It was all going to take some explaining.

Chapter Four
Island Games

It was certainly going to be difficult for Archie and Bernadette to keep completely silent about their remarkable discovery. Not only this, but they were also going to have to explain what the two of them had been up to all afternoon on a remote coastal path. For a start, they returned to Eilean Shona almost two hours after the other four children, wading back across the water as the tide started to turn and with Bernie in particular looking very flushed and shaken after her fall on the grassy bank and the ensuing excitement over their remarkable find. They had talked through the situation over and over again as they made their way back, but who was ever going to believe whatever reasons they gave as to why they were so late and so unkempt?

For a while their two families had coped reasonably well with the children's delayed arrival home, the Laird and Lady Elspeth managing somehow to hide their anxiety. They had been looking forward to welcoming all the six youngsters back together from their adventure, having decided that if they made it feel like a special occasion, they could perhaps arrange it so that such excursions occurred less regularly in the future. They had wanted to show their support but at the same time were concerned that, if this kind of activity became a regular occurrence, inappropriate friendships might begin to develop. In such a small island they did not wish to place unbearable restrictions upon the company which their sons kept during their holiday and leisure time. However, taking into account their social standing, they were now becoming distinctly uncomfortable about their sons becoming unduly friendly with the crofters or labourers' families.

Lady Elspeth in particular became very agitated as the clock ticked past eight in the evening and there was still no sign of either Archie or Bernadette. She was aware that her son was thought to be quite an admirer of the spirited crofters' daughter, and this friendship had been reciprocated ever since he helped to save her from a fall on the rocks a few years ago. They were both healthy, bright children, but from such very different backgrounds. She could not bring herself to contemplate the worst – that her son should have compromised himself in some dreadful way with this girl. How could he have even considered separating off from their companions, taking with him just this one young lass – a lively girl but somewhat flighty too, she had heard – the two of them walking off together on an unknown path open to any passer-by who might happen to walk that way? Oh, the shame of it all, if such a thing had happened. But then again, something else, more terrible still, could have occurred. Euan had mentioned on his return that they had chosen to walk the coastal path. Could one of them have slipped and fallen into the sea? Could they both have perished, the one attempting to rescue the other? They had a history of daring exploits, as they all well knew...

And the Laird himself, sitting all this time attempting to calm his wife, had his own fears. If Archie had disgraced himself, how would he explain his son's behaviour to his headmaster – just one term after he had passed his entrance with flying colours? And if the outcome of it all was expulsion from Harrow, or even just suspension, how would the family ever live this down? Never had there been such disgrace in the MacDonell family. But then the Laird checked himself – why were they fearing the worst of their beloved son? He had always conducted himself sensibly and honourably in the past. Why did they think he should suddenly have fallen from grace? No doubt there was a perfectly good reason for Archie to have stopped to look after this girl – or perhaps it was just that they had accidentally taken a wrong turn on the way home. He suggested to Lady Elspeth that they should wait until the two youngsters were home before jumping to any conclusions.

* * * *

As they finally came in sight of Eilean Shona, with the sun now low over towards Baramore and Rubha Aird an Fheidh, Archie and Bernie repeated their solemn promise to one another not to give away even a hint of their exciting discovery, their 'Seal of Promise'. This was their discovery, their find, and, to their minds, 'finders were keepers'. Even their own parents, even the Laird, should be kept in the dark. If necessary, they should invent some other plausible explanation as to why it had taken them so much longer to return home than the others. Bernie suggested that she should pretend she had tripped and sprained her ankle, and that Archie had kindly carried her part of the way home. But Archie pointed out, neither of her ankles looked at all swollen or bruised – so no, they needed a better explanation than that. They then considered telling a part of what had happened – that they had reached a point on the headland which provided a stunning view over the Sound of Arisaig, and had stopped to imagine the scene when the French ships, according to Iain McGregor, had come to rescue Prince Charlie. This too was rejected as being a bit too close to the truth – it might encourage others to make their own way to the same spot and then they might notice that something appeared to have been buried there... So instead they decided just to say that they had misjudged how far out of the way their return route was taking them. They had probably walked twice as far as Euan and the others.

When they finally made it back to Eilean Shona, in the twilight and around half-past eight in the evening, they were greeted by what seemed like half the island's population, with a great cheer and a relieved welcome all round. Warming refreshments were hurriedly brought out – by Ma Neish, and by Euan and his mother as well – and no-one spent much time investigating what had taken the two of them so long. Like the prodigal son, two of the island's favourite young people had returned after all, and this was a cause for celebration.

It might, however, be a while before either family encouraged any further such expeditions.

* * * *

Little more than a week now remained before Euan and Archie were due to return to Harrow. Their parents reminded them both to be sure that they had completed all their holiday reading, so that they could give a good account of themselves when they got back to the school for the summer term. So there was little time for Archie to worry about the discovery he had made with Bernie. In fact, there was not much time for him even to say hello to Bernie before she and the other island children were themselves being called back to the school house to resume their own studies.

It was only during their long coach journey back down south that Euan mischievously challenged his young brother as to exactly what had happened that eventful afternoon.

"So, brother, you must have enjoyed your few hours with young Bernie the other day? Jolly clever of you to send poor Billy running back to our group, I'd say! Gave you plenty of time alone with the love of your life eh?"

And Archie had blushed and stammered that they didn't do anything like that, they simply enjoyed the scenery and it just took them a lot longer going that way. "You try walking all round that coast, Euan, it's a long way I assure you."

"Aye, I think I should, dear brother, that's a really bonny idea of yours. Next holidays, in the summer, how about we all take that road and you and Bernie can show us where you went, and all the interesting places where you stopped to enjoy… one another. You can't fool me, you know, I saw how dirty you both were when you got back that night!"

Archie decided not to prolong the conversation. He wasn't keen to be pressed any further, nor did he fancy the three of them paying a visit to the site of their discovery, if that could be avoided. It would be difficult not to end up sharing their secret with Euan, and he had given Bernie his faithful assurance that only the two of them should ever know about it – their 'Seal of Promise'.

Soon afterwards their coach reached Glasgow where two other Harrow boys, and one who was destined for Eton College, joined them for the remainder of the journey. So Archie felt his secret was safe now, at least until they returned to Eilean Shona in July. He only hoped that Bernie would be able to avoid giving anything away between now and then.

* * * *

The matter was completely forgotten for many months afterwards. Mid-way through their summer term Euan and Archie received a letter from their father to tell them he had arranged for the boys to spend three weeks of their summer holidays with a Perthshire family that he and their mother knew well. The grouse season would, as ever, be starting on 12th August – the 'Glorious Twelfth' – and they would have an excellent opportunity to experience the shoots that had been arranged. Prior to this, he hoped they would both join the school's cricket society, which would afford them the chance to stay the first few days of the holidays in London attending the annual Eton and Harrow, and Gentlemen v Players, matches at Lord's. Their aunt Hermione, their mother's sister, would be delighted to have them to stay at her home in Dorset Square.

So there would not be very much time between these commitments for them to spend at home on Eilean Shona. Their father had however made sure that his latest innovation – the island's own Highland Games (to be called the 'Island Games' but, as he put it, who would know the difference?) – were being held during the time they were there. Both boys were now well-built and athletic and should be strong contenders for some of the races, and possibly the caber tossing. It was clear to Euan and Archie that a great effort was being made by their parents to minimise the time that they were able to spend with their former school friends on the island, now that they were all in their teens. "I think we're being grounded, to make sure there's no repetition of your scandalous behaviour with Bernie," teased Euan. And Archie, still sensitive about the whole affair, rose to the bait and snapped back,

"Oh, give over, Euan, we never did much that day." But even that response, Archie mused afterwards, might have given Euan the wrong impression. He was secretly glad that there would be little opportunity to follow up the 'Seal of Promise' discovery, at least for the foreseeable future.

* * * *

Their week in London, with their cricketing friends from school, was to prove a fascinating experience for the boys. Euan and Archie both appreciated the opportunity to pass time with their Harrow school friends without the demands of any school work or the chores they were required to undertake on behalf of the older boys in the name of 'fagging'. A dozen or more from each of their age groups had chosen to attend the day at Lord's cricket ground to watch a match between Harrow and their great rivals Eton, and there were also quite a few sisters and cousins, and their fathers and uncles, all dressed very smartly as though they were attending a friend's wedding. Some of the gentlemen were evidently members of a Marylebone cricket club which, Euan gathered, not only owned this delightful cricket field beside St John's Wood, but was planning to purchase an adjoining field so that a thousand spectators might be accommodated in comfort, under a roof and in fixed seats. Not only here, but everywhere they went in London, they noticed how many houses were being built and how many carriages were making their way along the busy streets.

After the cricket was over, the boys were invited to a soiree at one of their school friends' houses in Dorset Square, close to where their Aunt Hermione had invited them to stay. This was a relaxed occasion, their aunt had informed them, so there was no need for them to bring their dinner suits. She had checked with their hosts and they would be fine in the suits they had worn to the cricket. There were several other young people there whom the MacDonell boys were being given the opportunity to meet. One girl, who was introduced as Lady Caroline Ponsonby, was almost exactly Archie's age – her parents were the Earl and Countess of Hardenby. Aunt Hermione made a point of introducing Lady Caroline to both Euan and Archie, repeating her full name and title to make sure the boys heard. Caroline turned out to be delightful company and later in the evening Archie heard her discussing with Euan the possibility of coming to visit them in Eilean Shona next summer. Their parents should be very pleased to receive Lady Caroline, Archie mused. He wondered how Caroline would get on with Bernadette, if they had the opportunity to meet.

All through their week in the capital, Euan and Archie found themselves chaperoned and carefully observed, their every move watched so that they could be steered in the most advantageous direction for meeting suitable friends. They never complained, it was all most enjoyable and entertaining, and it was certainly giving them a useful introduction to some potentially influential acquaintances. But it was tiring too, and towards the end of the week they found themselves looking forward to the prospect of a few days at home in Eilean Shona before it was time to set off for their next arranged activity – their grouse shooting on the Camerons' estate in Perthshire.

* * * *

When they did get back to Eilean Shona, in the first week of August, it still felt to Euan and Archie that they were purposely being kept fully occupied so that neither of them wandered off to mingle with the islanders. After their week in London it was clearer to them than ever that, as young members of the social elite like their other friends at Harrow, they were expected to mix only with sons or daughters of the upper classes. The British class system had developed systematically over many years and neither Alastair MacDonell nor Lady Elspeth wanted to risk their sons being ridiculed for straying outside the appropriate circles. The occasional afternoon with local children for a sports day or a village cricket match was acceptable, but anything that smacked of building close personal friendships with young people of inferior breeding was most definitely out of the question.

So Euan and Archie were soon well aware that they were expected to toe the line. On the day they arrived home, their mother informed them that there were activities arranged for almost every weekday between then and their departure to Perthshire for the grouse season. Most of these were simply days out fishing with their father, or helping with specific tasks on the farm, neither of which, Archie noted, held out much prospect of meeting up with Bernie.

The one exception would be the Island Games afternoon, which the Laird had decided should now take place on the small playing field he had created a few years ago, with a view to becoming an annual event if it proved popular. He had made it clear that this traditional Scottish event would be one to which every local inhabitant of the island was welcome, together with any visitors if they wished, and he had expressed the hope that as many people as possible would take part. Euan and Archie decided to try and enter their names for as many of the contests as they could, noting that the event was scheduled for the following Saturday, the sixth of August.

Before then, Archie made one unsuccessful attempt to contact Bernie. He decided to write her a letter telling her that he was now home for a week or so and offering to come over and help her mother with her livestock and crops. In the letter he said how much he and Euan had appreciated the trouble Mrs Neish had taken to provide food for their day out in April and they wanted to repay her generosity. But Bernie never received the letter, which Archie had dropped through the open front door of their tiny cottage. "That's strange," Archie said when they did eventually manage to meet at the Games. And Bernie's response was frank and to the point.

"Och, Archie, Ma tol' me tha'd bin some paper but she used it to help light t' fire, anyway Ma canna read so tha's no point in writin' letters." Archie was left wondering whether he had done something to upset the Neish family.

So Archie's, and Euan's, time for conversing with the young people of the island was strictly limited. And with all the events in which they were expected to compete at Saturday's Games, they envisaged that there would be very little opportunity then either. Euan, it appeared, had been entered in the caber-tossing, and also a ploughing match, and Archie found that he had been put down for both the sixty yards dash and the round-the-island race. Archie had explained to his mother, who had already entered their names to make sure they were included, that he would have preferred to go for the long jump and, anyway, he couldn't be both a 'sprinter' and a 'stayer', but she didn't understand that. "If I'd waited till you came home from London, it would have been too late to enter you, so I just put you in for both. Anyhow, you're a good runner, aren't you?" she had added. To Lady Elspeth all running was the same, however long the race.

Euan's caber-tossing seemed to occupy him most of the afternoon, leaving him little time for the ploughing which was the kind of thing he particularly enjoyed. The upshot was that he did not have as successful a day as he had hoped for. Nor did it seem would Archie, at least not in the sixty-yard dash in which he was narrowly beaten by Billy. He saw Bernie run over to Billy and give him her congratulations, while he was left cursing a small mound which had hampered his own progress twenty yards from the finish. It was not at all like the sports day at Harrow, he thought to himself, taking care not to complain that the Eilean Shona games field, hurriedly created as a result of his own father's initiative a few years earlier, was not as well prepared as the one on which he competed at school.

But Archie had little time to worry about his sprinting disappointment, before he heard his name being called to line up for the round-the-island race. This, it emerged, was not simply one circuit of the island. Instead it was a true test of endurance amounting to five laps, each of approximately two miles, up and down hills and glens. Archie took a drink of water as he contemplated this ordeal, for which he noted there were five other competitors. Before long they were off. Initially Archie found the pace frighteningly quick, he could not believe that the other competitors would maintain this speed for five long laps. Next he came to a ditch, and then a small hedge over which they all had to jump. This was like a hurdles race, combined with a steeplechase. He had heard that such races took place these days in other places but had not expected it back home on Eilean Shona.

Gradually the pace settled down and Archie began to feel quite comfortable. They turned a corner and found themselves re-entering the games field for the first time. Four more laps. He noticed Bernie standing there with Ailsa and Billy, and his own mother and father nearby. They all called, "Come on Archie," as he ran by them. One of the other competitors tripped up on the next lap and lay nursing what looked like a twisted ankle. They were certainly racing over some rough terrain. The next lap seemed slower, as the runners all braced themselves for the final two laps.

As they passed the winning line for the third time, Archie noticed that his mother was standing alongside Bernie. He thought he saw them exchange smiles and this gave him a lift. Could Lady Elspeth have been having a friendly word with Bernie? On and on he ran, careful to keep a little in reserve for a finishing sprint on the last lap. And then they entered the last lap. The crowd around the finishing line had grown now, all of them cheering for their favourite. Archie redoubled his effort and overtook the young man in front of him. There were now just two competitors ahead of him, both slightly older runners, neither of whom he recognised as islanders. He had heard there were professional runners who came from all over Scotland to win prizes at these events, could that be what these men were doing? This made Archie more determined than ever and he sped down one of the slopes on the far side, still out of sight of the finish but only a miie from the line. He passed one of the older runners, then moved alongside the other.

Five hundred yards now, certainly no more. Archie thought of his mother and Bernie, they would be at the line, wouldn't they? He must make sure he won. Then, all of a sudden, they were into the final straight, running over the same area they had used for the sixty-yard dash earlier. Archie looked out for the mound that had cost him that race. He moved over slightly so he wouldn't be impeded by it this time. This left the other man running straight at the mound. They both accelerated, one last effort, even if it killed them. And then, there was the other runner, flat on his face, cursing that little mound. And ahead of him there was Archie, the winner – and the hero of Eilean Shona, for the islanders all knew he was one of theirs and he had beaten two of the professionals.

His mother, Lady Elspeth, was the first to congratulate him, followed by his father, the Laird, and of course Euan, who was smiling happily despite his own lack of success in the ploughing match over the next-door field. And then there was Bernie, with her mother and Ailsa, and Billy and Kit and all their friends. After a few minutes Father Tom was asked to present the prize, which for this special occasion was a small silver cup generously awarded by the Laird. True to form, Alastair MacDonell had decided to present a trophy each year for the most demanding and gruelling event of the Games. It had never occurred to him that it would be won by one of his own family, but, as Father Tom put it, there could be no more deserving winner.

And with that the party started, with ale and the local whisky flowing and two pipers playing a reel. Archie grabbed hold of Bernie's hand, and Euan took hold of Ailsa, and they and the other islanders all took to the grassy dance floor. All of a sudden there was an open-air ceilidh taking place, and that's the way it would stay for a few hours yet. But the two professional runners had taken their leave – they were last seen heading over towards Glenuig.

* * * *

The Laird and his wife stayed for a short while but then slipped away quietly. The experiment of staging Eilean Shona's own 'Highland Games' had clearly been a success and it was good to see almost all of the island's population taking part or watching. Meanwhile everybody seemed to want to congratulate Archie on his magnificent run; and Bernie, who had earlier been rather shy about being seen with him, started to relax. Nobody seemed particularly surprised at their friendship now. There had been a small amount of gossip after their late return from the walk in April but many islanders were now only too pleased to see the crofter's daughter enjoying her evening with such a gentleman.

But there still would not be much opportunity to discuss what to do about the 'Seal of Promise'. As they took a break after an energetic reel, which Archie now found almost as tiring as the race that he had won earlier, Bernie discreetly enquired of Archie how long he and Euan would be staying on the island this summer. She was amazed to learn that they were spending most of their holiday either on grouse moors or socialising in London. Was this normal for Lairds' families? For a moment she was glad she didn't belong to such a rich and privileged class of society. But then another half of her thought of the dreadful struggle that she, Ailsa and their ma and pa faced whenever the harvests were poor and the winters were long and bleak. As her thoughts wandered, Archie continued to be constantly congratulated, almost worshipped by other islanders who all treated him as a hero, the brightest star in the firmament, a symbol of success and prosperity. This was no time for her to ask him if he'd had any further thoughts about what they should do with the Seal of Promise.

She watched as Archie calmly accepted all the plaudits, modestly praising other competitors and saying how lucky he had been to avoid any of the humps and bumps. And then Euan strolled up and jovially called out to Archie that he must have cheated. "I'll wager you only went round four times, brother, you couldn't have won it any other way," and then, winking at Bernie, he told her that Archie would be too exhausted to dance any more.

With that, Euan took Bernie's hand and whisked her off for the next dance, leaving Archie with his sisters Margaret and Annie, who had rushed across to watch him receive his trophy after hearing that he had won. For several minutes they all danced their reels and then, as Archie continued to be besieged by other spectators, Euan took Bernie over to the hut where the Laird's seemingly endless supply of whisky was still being poured by the MacDonells' butler, a genial soul called Ritchie.

"Will ye tak' a wee dram, fair maid?" Ritchie enquired of Bernie. And after she and Euan had both been poured generous tipples, they went and sat by a small tree away from the others. There was silence between them for a moment, before Bernie cheekily asked Euan whether he and Archie really wanted to pass their summer holidays at cricket and shooting, when there was so much fun to be had here on Shona. Euan tried to explain why it was important for them to do these things, but could see that to the young island lass they made no sense. He paused for a moment and then, glancing over at Archie, who was still surrounded by admirers young and old, he decided to tease Bernie a bit. "So you'd like us to stay longer on the island would you, or should I say, you'd like Archie to stay a while longer?" he enquired with a wide grin on his face.

Bernie blushed, then straightened her kilt, and then looked Euan in the eye. "Master Euan," she began. "What do you know about Bonnie Prince Charlie and the Forty-five?"

Euan began to wonder where this was going. Why on earth was young Bernie suddenly thinking of Prince Charlie? So he simply replied, "Well, not much, I'm afraid, Bernadette." He had heard that Bernie had been putting on airs and graces since he and Archie had left the island school, and he decided that if she was going to address him as 'Master Euan' he would certainly give Bernie her full title. And then he added, "But why, young lady, do you ask about the prince? Come to think of it, I did watch a very good play a year or two ago, in which Prince Charlie was rescued by a charming lady called Flora." And looking sideways at her over his glass, he teased her by adding that the very same Prince Charlie had done the rescuing himself on a couple of other occasions. "In fact, just this last Easter, I believe, he had to help Flora out on the coastal path out Samalaman way. A very interesting afternoon that must have been, don't you think?"

Bernie was suddenly panic stricken. What did Euan know? Had Archie inadvertently revealed to Euan something of their 'Seal of Promise' adventure? Could it all have been discussed by the brothers when they were together on their own, perhaps on their long coach ride back to school? Taking another sip of the whisky, which she was beginning to find stimulating, she asked Euan what was so interesting about that coastal path. Had someone found something there? And then she went quiet, as she realised she might have said too much.

* * * *

Euan kindly escorted Bernie back to her cottage that evening. As they made their way along the path across the bleak moorland, Euan casually enquired whether she and Archie had actually seen something interesting on that path at Easter? He had picked up on her earlier remark and guessed that their late return that evening might have been caused by them coming across something unusual.

For poor Bernie, the realisation that she had betrayed Archie was now too much to handle, all the more so with more than a dram or two of whisky inside her. "Marshter Euan," she said, now slurring her words more than she herself realised, "Can ye keep a sheecret? A vairy important sheecret?"

"Of course, Bernie, of course I can keep a secret. Is it something between you and my brother?" came Euan's reply. And then there was a moment's silence and Bernie realised she couldn't hold back any longer. So she poured out her account of the discovery she and Archie had made, and Euan listened, amazed but utterly fascinated, to every word. She may have been intoxicated but Bernie was certainly giving an interesting, if somewhat disjointed, description of what she and Archie had come across on the headland that glorious sunny afternoon in April.

As she finished, Bernie burst into tears, sobbing as they now sat together on the deserted moorland a few hundred yards from her home. "I shud na hae told ye," she kept saying. "I gave ma promise to Archie, I shud nah ae told ye." But Euan understood. He understood her grief at having betrayed a confidence. He understood how difficult it must also have been to have kept the secret for all these months, not telling a soul at home, or at school or anywhere. But above all, he sensed the possible significance of the mysterious discovery that she and Archie had evidently made last spring.

* * * *

For days, and nights, after sharing her secret with Euan, poor Bernie cursed herself for letting Archie down over their 'Seal of Promise'. They had promised one another faithfully to keep the existence of the mysterious Seal entirely between themselves. And now she had allowed the whisky to get to her, and she had lost all sense of responsibility. How could she ever forgive herself? And to have told Euan, of all people – he was sure to take it out on Archie, probably while they were on their way to their shooting holiday, which was now only days away. Archie would never forgive her when he discovered that Euan was now in on the secret, and just as she had started to so enjoy his company. Oh, how stupid she had been.

But Bernie need not have worried. Euan had listened politely, and with some amusement, at what the inebriated Bernie had said that Saturday evening, but when she came to describing a dirty old box, he had totally lost track of what on earth she was talking about. But she was too sweet a girl to be going home in distress, so he had decided to comfort and console her at the end of that exciting day, to ignore all the nonsense she had talked, and above all to get her back home to the Neishes' cottage safely.

Chapter Five
Peace Offering

As It happened there was very little opportunity for Bernie to speak with either Euan or Archie for a long time afterwards. Soon after all the excitement of the Island Games the boys were off to Perthshire for the next three weeks, although not before their father had sat them both down for a chat in his study at Eilean Shona House. Their mother had tactfully left 'the men', as she now referred to them, to talk in private and Alastair decided to strike while the iron was hot and use the success of the Games as his starting-point.

"Great success boys, don't you think?" he began, without waiting for any response. "Your mother and I were so proud of you both. My goodness, Archie, I don't know where you get all your energy from these days, and as for you Euan, I gather you took to the ploughing as though you'd been doing it all your life. Well, that's what Laing was saying and what he doesn't know about these things isn't worth knowing." Laing was a stable lad who had been talked into preparing two of the cart-horses and organising the ploughing match. Archie was flattered that he thought he had done well.

"Thoroughly good day all round, I'd say," continued the Laird, "and the island folk all seemed to enjoy themselves, don't you think? Very good for relationships with them, I find it. They need to know we appreciate who they are and what they each do for the estate. Take that young Neish girl, for example – you know the one, I believe you were both talking with her."

"Yes Papa," came the reply, from Archie first. "Yes, we've known Bernadette for years, we were at the school here

73

with her and her sister before we started at Harrow. She's very intelligent and works really hard too."

And Euan added, "She'll go places I'm sure, a very bright spark."

"Well, Father Thomas and I have decided to give her a role in helping the teachers at the school. We think that's the best way to keep her out of mischief," their father said, looking straight from one boy to the other but mainly at Archie. "There's almost twenty children at the school these days, not like it was for you chaps when you started there. No, Bernadette Neish does seem quite intelligent, and she helps her poor parents a great deal. But your mother and I don't think you should see so much of her from now on. So she's having a few days helping out at the school now, before they break up to help with the harvest, and then she'll be busy helping with the teaching every day in the future. But not to worry yourselves, she's not one of us, anyway, and she never will be."

Archie had guessed where this conversation was going, and, if Euan had not also been present, he might have broken into an argument with his father about class divisions and so on. He and some of the other boys at Harrow had already had some interesting conversations at school on this topic. But he had no wish to provide Euan with any more ammunition with which to tease him while they were away this summer. So Archie bit his lip and resolved to set his mind to finding other ways of communicating with Bernie, without his parents knowing. They simply had to keep in touch with one another about that discovery of theirs, if they did nothing else.

* * * *

It was easier said than done, Archie found. He had already tried writing a note to her and that had simply ended up being used to light Bernie's mother's fire. He had noticed there was always a fire burning at their cottage and any further letters would presumably receive the same treatment. So the day before he and Euan were due to set off for their shooting in

Perthshire, he decided to go over to the school, on his own, and see if he could catch Bernie for a word there when lessons finished that afternoon. He had heard it was the last day of term before they broke up for the harvest break. As Archie approached the school, a place he knew so well from all those happy days he used to spend there, he could hear from outside that Bernie was talking to the class. It sounded as though she had now taken over Miss McTavish's role. So he waited, and he waited.

It was almost an hour before the class came to an end and he heard Bernie telling the children to leave the tables tidy and take care going home. She sounded like a really experienced teacher, he thought. They were going to start a new project next term, she was saying, so they were all to make a note of the starting date of 20th September, when it was hoped they would no longer be needed in the fields. A few minutes later, she emerged from the school and was taken aback to find Archie waiting for her. "You canna wait here, Archie, we canna carry on." And then, furtively looking around her, she added, "We've had warnings, Ma was told after church on Sunday, by Lady Elspeth, that we've to stop seeing one another, we're not right for people of their standing, she said."

"But what about our 'Seal of Promise'?" responded Archie, and then continued, "Bernie, I've been told the same by my papa, but I still hope we can keep in touch. We must, for the sake of our..." And then Bernie saw Father Tom approaching.

"Go Archie," she whispered, as she hurriedly disappeared back into the school.

* * * *

Bernie was genuinely sorry that their relationship could not continue as before. Over the past few years she had become increasingly fond of Archie and now had strong feelings for him, to which she had been unable to give full expression. She and Archie were both fourteen, and physically maturing, and it was difficult to accept that they could take things no further, simply because of their different family backgrounds. Meanwhile she realised that they still had the problem of what to do about the Seal – neither of them would ever forget their find, she was sure. She only hoped that Euan wouldn't ever tell a soul about what she had told him on the night of the Island Games – least of all tell Archie himself, for then he would really feel that she couldn't be trusted.

* * * *

While they were preparing themselves for their visit to Perthshire, and then on the journey over there, Euan and Archie had plenty of time together to chat about everything that had been going on. Much of this time they found themselves chatting generally about island life, and how things had really livened up in the past few years. Euan said he thought their mama should take much of the credit for this, she had really entered into the spirit of the island and was always making suggestions to Papa, like having the school play in their ballroom and arranging for a ceilidh to take place after the Games – and Archie agreed, he didn't think Papa would have changed anything without Mama pressing him, other than possibly having the games area built, and even that would not have happened if they hadn't had their crisis with Bernie getting into trouble on Shona Craig! But he didn't regret that at all, Archie added – he had quite enjoyed the challenge of teaching himself to rock-climb!

"You've always enjoyed anything involving Bernie, dear brother," Euan said in response, and then added, "especially quiet country walks on coastal paths, eh?"

"Oh, give over, Euan you never will believe it was just that it was a rather long and difficult path to follow. I've told you that before but you never believe me, do you?"

Euan paused for a moment, just a brief moment. "No, Archie, I never do." And he left it at that.

* * * *

The shooting was in the north of Perthshire, quite near Dalwhinnie on the Glenshera estate, and proved to be great fun for the boys. They arrived at the Lodge on the eve of the Glorious Twelfth and found that their parents' friends, the Camerons, had also invited a few others of a similar age to join them. They included a couple of Eton boys, Jeremy and Alexander Colquhoun, and their sister Felicity and a friend of hers from Northumberland, Daphne Talbot-Clarke.

They all got on famously. Of course, they all turned out for the main shoot itself on the 12th and Euan, despite hardly ever having held a gun before, had great success bringing down several birds within his first hour on the moor. 'Beginner's Luck', Archie called it, having had no luck at all himself. And Euan, ever the gentleman, had agreed totally. "Don't expect me to do that again," he replied modestly.

They didn't all shoot every day. After their first few days at Glenshera, they were taken over to stay in a new lodge which the Camerons had borrowed from friends for the week, so they could try their hands at salmon fishing on a stretch of the River Tay, near Aberfeldy. This was more to the girls' liking and both Felicity and Daphne perked up when they saw the opportunity for a catch.

The evenings were fun too: there was a piano at the lodge where they were staying, and they all sang their favourite songs, while Daphne, who showed herself to be a talented musician, accompanied them on the piano. Night after night they sang and danced, or played cards or charades, and by the end of their three weeks, Euan and Archie were both very taken with Felicity and Daphne. As they waved them farewell, Archie had somehow quite forgotten about Bernie and the 'Seal of Promise'. He hoped there would be further opportunities to meet up with Felicity and Daphne.

* * * *

But their lives at Eilean Shona had certainly not been forgotten. It did not take long, upon their return home, for Euan to start suggesting to Archie that they do another day's walking over to Glenuig – just the two of them. He suggested that this time they could take the coastal path from there round towards Samalaman island, so that Archie could show him what an interesting path it was. He realised that it would not be possible to invite Bernie now but he would very much enjoy the walk anyway. He eyed his brother carefully as he made this suggestion.

This created something of a problem for Archie. If he agreed to go there with Euan, he would face the dilemma of whether to secretly share the 'Seal of Promise' discovery with his brother; or to solemnly walk past the spot where he and Bernie had re-buried their extraordinary find. He had faithfully promised Bernie he would never divulge their secret discovery to anyone else, at least until they could establish whether it carried potential significance or value. They had both taken very seriously their responsibility to one another on this matter. Was he to renege on this promise, only a matter of a few short weeks since they had made their pact? Despite all the excitements and interesting young people they had met in London and away in Perthshire, Bernie still mattered a great deal to him. He thought for a moment, pretending he hadn't been listening to Euan.

"Sorry brother, did you say something?" he responded.

"Of course, I did, Archie. You know perfectly well what I'm suggesting. A nice day out to Glenuig and back home via Samalaman Point. Just like you and Bernie did in April. What's the problem?"

And Archie had to admit, there was no problem – except, he thought, that he would have to deceive either his good friend or his brother. He decided to accept Euan's cheeky proposal but suggested they leave it till the last day or two before going back to school. There was always the chance that something might intervene between now and then.

Euan and Archie looked one another in the eye. Both knew that the other knew, or strongly suspected, more than he was letting on.

* * * *

The date for their departure to Harrow for the new school term had been set for September 12 and, after studying the tidal movements which showed high tides for most of that week, they finally agreed on the previous Saturday as a suitable day for their walk. They shared their proposal with their parents but with no-one else. Certainly, neither of them had any reason to let Bernie know what they were doing.

The Saturday dawned with a typical early mist, a regular feature for the west of Scotland at that time of year, and Archie suggested they should think again before risking getting trapped in a really thick fog. He was rather hoping for low visibility, which he thought would prompt their parents – and particularly their mother – to insist on them abandoning the walk. But just as he was hoping that the mist would co-operate and deteriorate, it suddenly lifted to reveal the kind of bright sun that promised one of those glorious early autumn days. It was now eight o'clock and there was no alternative for Archie than to agree they should set off without further delay. They needed to bear in mind the earlier sunset now that they were into September – certainly they could not afford to take as long over the walk as he and Bernie had in April.

They happily followed the route they had all taken then and, with none of the younger children to keep an eye on, they managed to reach Glenuig by mid-day, which Euan pointed out was exactly the time they had arrived there in April having set off at five o'clock. This time they had each taken one of Cook's neatly wrapped food packs, which took only a few minutes to consume.

"Now, brother, you're the expert on the remainder of this walk," said Euan. "So I'll leave it to you to be our guide."

"Aye, aye, skipper," came Archie's cheerful response, "happy to oblige." And they continued their gentle banter as they made their way along the coastal path, westwards towards Samalaman island and the glorious views across the sound of Arisaig. He couldn't resist reminding Euan at this point that it was not far from this part of the coast that Prince Charlie had finally been rescued by French ships and been able to escape the clutches of Cumberland's frustrated search parties. Since listening to poor old Iain McGregor, Archie told Euan, he had been reading some more detail about the Prince's escape. Apparently two French ships, each flying British colours at their mast in case the Royal Navy spotted them, had been piloted into Loch nan Uamh and dropped anchor there.

"That all happened, I read the other day, on September 6th, 1746 – almost exactly seventy-two years ago today, Euan," added Archie. "And look over there, below those hills opposite – that is Loch nan Uamh. Just imagine, brother, that is precisely where they dropped anchor and Bonnie Prince Charlie was finally picked up and taken back to safety with his supporters in France."

"You're joking, Archie," replied Euan, "are you really telling me this is where it all ended – and not far from where he first landed and began his great campaign?"

"Yes, it seems this was the very spot, Euan. And not only that, but all along this coast, his supporters from all around Moidart and the isles were here to see him safely out to sea. He had so many loyal friends who would do anything to help. It wasn't just people like Flora Macdonald, though she's the one we're always told about."

At this point Archie realised that they were just about to reach the dolmen-like stone, where he and Bernie had stopped, and where, after Bernie had slipped and fallen on the ground, they had accidentally uncovered what they now knew as the 'Seal of Promise'. Archie went quiet for a moment. This was the moment of reckoning. Was he going to be honest with his brother Euan, or stay loyal to Bernie – still, he hoped, his good friend and the one who had helped him make the discovery in the first place? That was what it all boiled down to now. But there could be only one answer.

"Euan," he heard himself saying. "Can you keep a secret, a really important secret?" Euan thought for a moment. Had not somebody else asked him that very same question, and with the same concern in their voice? He soon realised that person had been Bernie. Was this just a coincidence? It all seemed very strange.

"Yes Archie, of course I can keep a secret. Can you?" he replied.

A good question, thought Archie, knowing that despite everything he was now about to betray Bernie and defy their solemn pact, their 'Seal of Promise'.

"Well, normally I think I can," Archie replied. "But you see that stone over there, that solitary stone? Come over there and let me show you something."

* * * *

For what seemed only a matter of minutes but was actually well over an hour, the boys proceeded to locate, then exhume, then carefully study the remarkable object to which Archie and Bernie had accorded the title 'Seal of Promise' a few months earlier. The leather box required further cleaning after spending another summer underground, but Archie had now found it a little easier to open and he showed Euan the old Seal with its magnificent engraving. "My goodness Archie," gasped Euan, "no wonder you and Bernie have been so protective of this. It's unbelievable. It's probably worth a fortune."

"That's exactly what Bernie and I both thought, Euan," was Archie's response, "There's something very special and important-looking about it, don't you think?" He was relieved to now be sharing their find with his elder brother, his sensible elder brother. If Euan was equally excited about the discovery, that was certainly reassuring. Archie felt a weight had dropped from his mind, and from his conscience. He felt sure that Bernie would now understand him, and forgive him, for sharing their secret with Euan. He then picked up the muddy old glove and offered it to his brother.

"A glove, Archie? What has that got to do with the Seal of Promise? Looks to me like somebody just happened to lose one of their gloves, perhaps while they were taking a look at the stone. I don't think that dirty old glove has anything to do with our Seal," replied Euan, rejecting the grubby object out of hand. "But I do think the Seal is interesting. We really

81

ought to do something about it, at least get it somewhere safer, and where it won't get damaged any more by the elements."

"Yes, I agree with that, Euan," said Archie, "but where? And do we really want to go telling people we think we might have found a really valuable treasure, and risk making fools of ourselves when they say it's some sort of a fake? I certainly don't know enough about these things to judge whether it's the real thing. And what happens if it is valuable but we're told we had no right to move it, because the law says it must belong to the Crown or something. I've been living with these questions, and so has Bernie, for the past four or five months, and anyway, I've actually felt all along that part of its value lies in where it was found and the fact that it might – it just might – have something to do with either the arrival or the departure of Prince Charlie."

"Give over Archie," replied Euan. "You're letting yourself get carried away. But I have to say, it is a fascinating discovery, and it does look like it could be a really beautiful and valuable jewel, once it's been cleaned up and restored to its original state. And whoever left it there, or presumably hid it there, must have either been a thief, or on the run from somebody, and perhaps planning to return at a later date to retrieve it. It's all most mysterious."

The boys looked at one another, and then at the silent Sound of Arisaig – all quiet now, but presumably a hive of activity seventy odd years ago when Bonnie Prince Charlie, so close to being hunted down by the search parties that had been after his blood for months, had finally been picked up by those French ships. And then they glanced at the sun, still shining bright but now itself heading out west, over towards Eigg. "It's time we made our way back," said Archie as they returned the box, Seal and glove to their earthy grave. With a final glance at the spot where their treasure had now been buried for a third time, they set off home.

* * * *

On their return home, their mother greeted them with the news that their father had been taken ill quite suddenly that afternoon. She had asked Ritchie to arrange for a doctor to visit as soon as one could be fetched and, in the meantime the Laird was resting and had taken a dose of some medication they had purchased when they were last in Edinburgh. Lady Elspeth felt her husband had had too much excitement in the last few weeks and they just needed to ensure he could enjoy peace and quiet, and a complete rest for the next few weeks. The boys were due to return to school in a few days' time, so it should be possible for him to recover gradually and be well enough to enjoy the Christmas and New Year's holiday with the family.

Euan and Archie saw this as a signal to stay out of his way, and so they made a point of getting out of the house as much as possible. They decided to go fishing next day and very soon had landed a few herring, which they would take back to the House and offer to Cook. Their mother was well pleased and when they said they could have caught plenty more, she suggested they keep at it. The tides were clearly conducive to some sizeable shoals circulating around the island.

Sure enough, their catch the next day was even greater. This was their last day at home before they were due to set off to school for the Michaelmas term, so Archie suggested that they take a few of the herring to the Neishes' cottage and offer these to Ma Neish. "Some sort of peace offering, eh brother?" enquired Euan, and Archie blushed and simply responded that it was the least they could do to provide these poor people with some assistance before he and his brother had to go back to Harrow. He thought it would be best to visit the Neishes alone, so there was no need for Euan to come with him. Euan secretly wondered whether Archie was feeling guilty about sharing the 'Seal of Promise' with him and was looking for an opportunity to square things off with Bernie. But he was content to leave his young brother to pay the visit alone and went off to catch a few more of the herring himself while there were so many to be had.

* * * *

When Archie arrived at the cottage, he was pleased to find Bernie and Ailsa playing hoops outside the front door. School had not yet re-started on the island and they were both enjoying a rare opportunity for some relaxation.

"Och, Bernie, look who's here," called out Ailsa, and Archie quickly apologised for disturbing their game. The girls both picked up their skirts and ran over to meet him, but Bernie's greeting was sour. "Ah thought ye was not to see the likes of us any more, Master Archibald," she said, somewhat sarcastically. "Ye'd better no' let your mama and papa see ye here."

But Archie looked sorrowful and responded that his father wasn't well and his mother wished him and Euan to stay out of his way. They were off down south tomorrow anyway for the new school term.

"Och, well that is a shame. Shall ye have a slice o' tattie pie wi' us then, while you're here?" replied Bernie, and Ailsa hurried off to fetch the pie and set a stool out for Archie to sit.

"So wha's the matter wi' the Laird?" asked Bernie, and Archie explained that his mother thought it was just a case of exhaustion after all the excitements of the summer. The Laird wasn't used to such activity as there had been this past year, even though a lot of it had been of his own making with ideas such as the Island Games.

"Och, they were wonderful," said the sisters in unison, as Ailsa returned with the pie. And Bernie added, "I hope they're going to be ev'ry year like he said, I want to see ye win the round-the-island again. Me and my ma loved that." Bernie's resentment at the enforced separation from the Laird's family was starting to soften. Archie took his chance to respond in a similarly friendly manner, assuring her that he would certainly be aiming to defend his trophy but would need all the support he could muster from the likes of Bernie and Ailsa.

They had a little meal together, the three of them, with the potato pie, some of the herring that Archie had caught, and some home-made ale, and then, while Ailsa went off to wash the pots, Archie raised his glass of ale and quietly proposed a toast to Bernie 'to the Seal of Promise'. And Bernie responded "to the Seal of Promise" with a gentle smile.

As he made his way back to the House, first to see how his father was, then to check whether his mother needed any help, and finally to ascertain whether Euan had returned home with any more herring, Archie congratulated himself on restoring some sign of affection in Bernie. For all the fun he and his brother had enjoyed with Felicity and Daphne, it was still Bernie whose flame flickered strongest in his heart. He was glad he had re-established contact, perhaps by next year they could start to see one another again. Little did he realise that it would take much, much longer than that.

Chapter Six
Serious Business

Alastair MacDonell's sudden illness threw a shadow over life on the island for quite some while. He appeared to have been in perfectly good health that summer, much enjoying the success of his Island Games and the news that his two sons had created a very favourable impression during their holidays, both with his sister-in-law Hermione in London and with the Camerons in Perthshire. And then he had suffered what the doctor, when he eventually arrived on the island two days later, pronounced was a mild heart attack. The doctor prescribed complete rest for the Laird for the foreseeable future and left several weeks' supply of some tablets that were now recommended by the medical profession.

Lady Elspeth found herself constantly attending to her husband's needs, which seemed to grow pettier and more frequent by the day. She was glad she had the support of several maids and an excellent housekeeper, Dalgleish, a Glaswegian woman who had originally joined them on what was supposed to be a temporary arrangement when Elspeth was expecting Euan, back in 1803. Dalgleish was a strong, well-built woman who seemed to be able to cope with anything, and there were also the men such as Ritchie and Brown who could be relied upon outside.

After the fun and joys of summer, and in particular the delightful day they had all enjoyed watching the Island Games, it was a difficult autumn and an even more difficult winter, with the weather being worse than any of them could remember. The Laird croaked one morning, when they were despairing at the damage caused by the storms, that he remembered '94 being similar to this. "You always end up paying for the good days," he grunted. The thought of the winter weather was not improving his demeanour, nor his appetite for recovery.

Meanwhile, Euan and Archie were way down south and Alastair and Elspeth now heard from them ever more rarely. In November a letter from Euan arrived, saying that they had both been invited to spend Christmas with the Earl and Countess of Hardenby, whose daughter Caroline they had met when they were staying with Aunt Hermione. This meant that it was going to be hardly worth their while undertaking the long and, in winter, generally very slow and hazardous journey north. He and Archie hoped Mama and Papa wouldn't mind. They both sent their love to the parents and to Margaret and Annie and would be sure to get home for Easter.

The Laird and Lady Elspeth had mixed feelings on receiving the letter. On the one hand they were bitterly disappointed that, for the first time in their young lives, the boys were not going to be home to celebrate Christmas and Hogmanay. It just wouldn't feel right without them. On the other hand, as Lady Elspeth pointed out to her husband, it was good to see that they had evidently created a favourable impression with Lady Caroline Ponsonby, whom they had met at the soiree after the Eton and Harrow cricket match. It appeared that Caroline's parents had offered to have the boys to stay for the duration of the Christmas holidays and, sure enough, a separate letter arrived at Eilean Shona House two days later, from Viola, Countess of Hardenby, writing from her Edenborough Hall address, confirming this invitation.

With little hesitation Lady Elspeth responded to say that her sons would be honoured to join the Countess's family for the Christmas holidays and that she was sure they would both greatly enjoy their stay. It was most kind of the Earl and Countess to extend this generous invitation. If there was anything they wished the boys to bring with them for their stay, please let her know. Secretly she was delighted to know that they had both begun to mix with well-connected young people such as Caroline Ponsonby, as she had started to become seriously concerned that Archie in particular had become too comfortable associating with the lower classes.

So Euan and Archie MacDonell spent their Christmas holidays of 1818-19 at Edenborough Hall in Kent, where they not only renewed their friendship with Lady Caroline Ponsonby but also met her younger sister and her three brothers. It was a very different experience for them from any of the Christmases they had spent at home on Eilean Shona, or indeed elsewhere in Scotland, such as in Edinburgh where they had occasionally been taken for the Hogmanay celebrations. With Lady Caroline's family there seemed to be parties to attend almost every other day, either with other well-to-do neighbouring families or up in London where Viola Hardenby was preparing Lady Caroline for the following year's Queen Charlotte's Ball. It was altogether a different world for Euan and Archie – a far cry from a ceilidh at the Island Games on Eilean Shona.

* * * *

By the time Euan and Archie visited Eilean Shona again, at Easter 1819, they were noticeably more grown up. They were confident, well-mannered young gentlemen now, looking ahead to their future careers. For Euan, he hoped this would be military service and he had set his sights on earning himself a commission with the 72nd Highlanders regiment, in which his father had served during the Napoleonic Wars. Archie meanwhile was contemplating a career in the legal profession, perhaps as a Writer to the Signet, the traditional legal qualification in Scotland. For them both, time spent as young men on the London social scene had been advantageous. It was always going to be helpful to meet as many of the most influential people in the land as they could.

They found their father greatly improved when they saw him at Easter, after his winter's rest. Lady Elspeth was also more cheerful, having nursed her husband through the worst of his illness with Dalgleish's help and that of an increasing compliment of maids which now included two more local girls. It made all the difference to the Laird's recovery to see bonny young girls smiling at him as they brought him his food and his daily doses of medication.

He also overheard snippets of their gossip from time to time and was amused to hear them refer to a very strict teacher at the local school by name Bernadette Neish. Wasn't that the name of the lass who his son Archie had become friendly with last summer? He was sure that was the name. Strict, eh? Well done her!

* * * *

It was good for the Laird and Lady Elspeth to see their sons again, but sadly Euan and Archie now found life on Eilean Shona very limited after all the exciting experiences they had been enjoying for the remainder of their time. Not surprisingly, neither of them spent much time back on the island from now on.

Nor were they regular letter writers, so over the next few years their mother and father learned only spasmodically about their respective officer training and academic studies. It was however a particular delight for Euan when the time came for him to write and inform his parents that he had passed out with distinction and was now 2nd Lieutenant MacDonell. This was something he was only too happy to write home about. He expected to see action in faraway India in the near future, but he told them not to worry, he would be sure to look after himself.

Meanwhile Archie, who had left Harrow a year early after winning a scholarship to St Andrews University, had duly completed his law degree at the ancient university on the Fife coast and was now being granted articles by a firm of Edinburgh lawyers. It took years of hard work to get there but he hoped to qualify as a Writer to the Signet in a few years' time. Visits by either of them to see their parents on Eilean Shona were becoming fewer and farther between, but both Alastair and Elspeth were enormously proud of them both, whenever they saw them.

Together they paid a visit to St Andrews to watch Archie receive his degree. Euan happened to be home on leave at this time, and both Margaret and Anne, who were now living in Glasgow, were free to attend too. So they were all able to celebrate Archie's graduation as a family – it was the first time they had all six been together for several years and they marked the occasion by eating in a fine St Andrews hostelry from which they watched the playing of a game called golf which none of them had seen before.

The one thing that seemed to be missing from both Euan and Archie's lives was any sign of romantic attachment. For two such handsome young men (Lady Elspeth assured her husband that they were definitely very handsome, against his better judgement), it was surprising that they seemed so set on remaining single. Maybe it was too soon for them to form serious relationships? Alastair and Elspeth persuaded themselves that their sons were wise to make sure they had good careers under way first, if they wished to make successful marriages.

However, as Alastair ordered an extra bottle of the hotelier's finest claret wine, Euan and Archie began to be teased a little by their sisters. Archie in particular had earned himself quite a reputation as a teenager – what had happened since, they asked him, to deprive all those young ladies of his irresistible charms?

Their parents listened with amusement to the banter, privately hoping that such teasing might stimulate Archie into thinking about settling down, now that he had achieved his degree. But life was serious business for Archie, as it was for Euan too, and although their respective careers offered very different opportunities for romantic attachment, they both knew only too well that when it came to the serious business of marriage, that would be the most important decision of their lives.

* * * *

When Alastair and Elspeth returned to Eilean Shona after this family reunion at St Andrews, they were able to offer first-hand news of their family to their staff, their tenants and all the island inhabitants in a way they had not been able for some years. Although neither Euan nor Archie, nor Margaret nor Anne, were there to participate in this summer's Island Games, the Games had now become a firm date in the island's calendar in exactly the way Alastair had originally envisaged. And this was an excellent opportunity for the Laird and Lady Elspeth to update many of the older island residents who had seen the family grow up.

Father Thomas, now completely retired, and Miss McTavish (Tavvy), who was working only two days each week, were among the first to enquire how the Laird's family were, as was Mary Neish and of course her daughters Bernadette and Ailsa.

Lady Elspeth was pleased to pass on news of her own family but also saw the opportunity to thank both the Neish girls for what they were contributing to island life. Bernadette, now in her twenties, was in the process of taking over from Miss McTavish as the principal teacher at the school. She was not in any way professionally qualified but had a depth of understanding of children that all who knew her readily acknowledged. Ailsa was assisting her as and when required, but she was also heavily committed to nursing her sick father and helping her ma with their livestock and crops. Their family, like others on the island, needed to work hard just to stay alive.

The little bit of money that the Laird and a few others contributed to the costs of the school provided Bernie with a modest remuneration, and Ailsa's occasional teaching was also rewarded if the school could afford it. They never complained, but as she spoke with the Neish family Lady Elspeth made a mental note to discuss with her husband the possibility of increasing their salaries.

As the Laird and Lady Elspeth spoke to other such families, exchanging news of their respective loved ones, they were able somehow to connect their own faraway family with the community of their childhood. It was apparent that their sons and daughters were much loved and admired by the island people, perhaps more so than the Laird had ever realised. He loved his island, as he loved the whole of his estate, but sometimes found it difficult to communicate that love and relate it to the everyday challenges that the community faced. However, these conversations with island families were breaking down some of those barriers and in the process encouraging Alastair and Elspeth to feel more optimistic about the future well-being of the island than they had for some time.

Several of the younger islanders suggested, to either the Laird or Lady Elspeth, that in addition to the excellent Island Games, which had now become a delightful annual tradition, they would also welcome an annual expedition, enabling islanders to explore other parts of the Moidart estate and surrounding countryside with their friends. Some of them were aware that there had been an expedition of a kind some years ago, involving members of the Laird's own family they seemed to remember, and they thought this could perhaps be a good way of bringing the young people of the island together in a way which they would enjoy. Some of them had hardly ever had a chance to step off Eilean Shona, they added.

The Laird and his wife listened with interest, readily recalling the worry which had been caused by their own son Archie being late home on that previous occasion. But they promised to look at the idea and, much to the islanders' surprise, they announced a few days later that they would favour an annual trek – in late April or May each year – provided it took place entirely within their Moidart estate. They went further and said they would offer a small prize to all participants who completed the trek, but only if all those who set off had returned by 6 pm. They did not wish the event to be spoiled by anyone losing their way, so it was important that they all stayed fairly close to one another in case of any mishap.

* * * *

The first such trek was to be held on May Day the following year, 1829. A small, informal committee was asked to organise the event and this included three of the young people who had taken part in the previous trek led by Euan and Archie MacDonell back in April 1818. When they were told it was now more than ten years since that expedition the Laird could not believe it was that long ago. "How time flies!" he exclaimed to Lady Elspeth. Comparatively few people even remembered that one taking place and even fewer were involved themselves.

Bernadette and Ailsa Neish, and their friends Katherine and Bill Taggart were the exceptions, so it was decided to ask them to join the committee, so that any necessary lessons could be learned from that experience. Bernadette hesitated briefly, before deciding it would be more sensible to be involved and to keep in touch with the event, rather than risk something unfortunate happening which she could have helped to avoid.

It was agreed that, as in 1818, it would be appropriate to follow the direct route across the sands at low tide, joining the track up the glen towards Glenuig. Sensibly, it was decided to do a trial walk over the proposed course later that autumn, before winter set in, to make sure that there were no insuperable obstacles which might now create difficulties for the participants in the expedition itself the following spring.

Before they undertook this 'trial run', Bernadette was asked by the committee whether she felt there were any particular risks which she might recall from the previous event. Bernadette was ready for this and, amongst other comments, she expressed the opinion that they should not attempt to make any detours, which she admitted was a mistake that she and Master Archie had made on the earlier expedition. Privately she had been thinking that it might be wise for her to visit the site of the 'Seal of Promise' alone some time, just to check that if anybody did take the route she and Archie had followed ten years ago, they wouldn't notice anything untoward which might alert them to the discovery they had made. Bernie had not been near the site since that memorable afternoon with Archie and started to worry that if, in their haste, they had failed to re-bury the box with sufficient care, it might by now have become visible to passers-by. She couldn't imagine that anybody would have spotted it if it were buried properly, but she wanted to make sure.

Over the course of the next few days Bernie gave some thought as to when would be the best time to go and check the state of the 'Seal of Promise' burial. She came to the conclusion that it needed to be done sooner rather than later, and certainly before the members of next year's organising committee went on their trial run. The problem was that she was fully committed every weekday with her school duties, and that just left Sundays.

Would people notice if she failed to attend church one Sunday, she wondered? She could always say she was recovering from a cold. But then that would require her sister Ailsa and her mother to back her up. No, she would simply tell them that she had some private preparation to do in readiness for the following week's school lessons. What lengths she was having to go to for the sake of the secrecy of the Seal of Promise, she thought! But she would be so worried that somebody would discover it, if she didn't take precautions...

Bernie soon decided that it would be as well to make this surreptitious inspection before there was the likelihood of severe winter weather. By now it was already October and she decided she should carry out her secret mission whilst it was still relatively mild. The tides were low the following Sunday so she casually announced to her mother that she was having to miss church that morning in order to collect some specimens for a botany class at school.

She was on her way by eight, clutching a knapsack that she normally used for carrying school books, before Ailsa could offer to come with her. Bernie still did not want anybody to see the Seal of Promise other than her and Archie, and certainly not her sister. That would have been like Archie showing it to Euan and she couldn't imagine that ever happening. No, that was completely out of the question...

* * * *

So Bernie set off alone, repeating the trek that she and Archie, and Euan and Billy and Kitty and Ailsa had undertaken ten years or so ago. It all seemed so different now. They were mere kids then, and she recalled thinking they were very brave to undertake such an ambitious expedition. Archie had been such a gentleman to her, very responsible for his fourteen years and encouraging her every step of the way.

Thinking about her time-table for today, she remembered that for the previous expedition they had set off really early in the morning and still didn't reach Glenuig until mid-day. Ailsa and Billy were only ten or eleven years old then, so hopefully she would make more rapid progress now. But she needed to press on, as she would need to allow time for the detour to the Seal of Promise burial site as well as the return journey. Fortunately, it was a cool day, dry and slightly misty – ideal, she decided, for this solitary trek. She wondered also what Archie would be saying if he had been with her today – with his legal training, she thought he might have refused to waste time visiting the site, instead he would probably have advised that they should take out an injunction, or some such legal protection, to prevent anybody interfering with the find that they had made together in April 1818. Bernie would not have favoured that approach for their secret would no longer be theirs, and this was all part of what it was that she treasured.

She made good progress, benefiting from her distant memories of having previously followed this route, as well as the lack of any distractions, and reached Glenuig before mid-day. She turned straight off towards the Seal of Promise burial site, taking care to remember this part of the route as well. And then she spotted the single dolmen stone, standing as though it was looking out to sea and the Sound of Arisaig. She stopped and looked, and for a while she couldn't see any disturbed ground, or any sign of anything having been buried or re-buried.

For a moment she wondered whether she had stopped at the right dolmen stone. And then she noticed a small piece of turf which seemed to be lying at an ever-so-slightly different angle from the rest of that grassy bank. She lifted this piece of turf, and then noticed another piece which looked as if it might have been disturbed, and then, after lifting that too, she could see a tiny corner of the box that contained the… Seal of Promise.

Excited beyond words, she now felt she was only fourteen years old again. And then she pulled at more of the turf, and then some more, and some more, and eventually she pulled the whole box out of the ground, and with it that grubby old glove. It was all still there, looking much the same as it had looked ten years ago.

But what should she do now? Was she to re-bury it, like they did then? If she did that, she would need to ensure that the turf was replaced much more carefully than they did last time. She wasn't sure she could manage that, and anyway it would take time, and she was conscious that she would need to get back to Eilean Shona by four o'clock, with the evenings drawing in now that it was October.

Should she take it home with her? Perhaps that was the answer, after all she was one of the people who had discovered it. Surely, she could not be blamed for taking it away for safe keeping. It was not what she had agreed with Archie, but then would Archie have advised against taking it away? Again, she imagined him weighing up the legal arguments for and against, smiled to herself at this thought, and decided she should take it away – the box could just fit inside her school knapsack, so it wouldn't be too difficult to carry it home. Hiding it in the Neishes' tiny cottage might be a problem, but maybe she could find somewhere else to put it – maybe somewhere at the school, where she was the keyholder these days.

Bernie squeezed the glove inside the box and set off back to Glenuig. She felt sure she would get home faster by retracing her steps, rather than taking the rough cross-country route she and Archie had taken. And she was right – she reached the ford over to Shona Beag shortly after four o'clock and was easily able to cross over to her home. Only when she reached the cottage and found her mother and sister waiting anxiously did she realise she had completely forgotten to bring back any botanic specimens...

* * * *

Bernie's immediate concern was more for the privacy of the 'Seal of Promise' box than for explaining the absence of any botanic specimens to her sister Ailsa. She really had to conceal the box, but where? She certainly couldn't hide it anywhere in the cottage and the only alternative was the school. It was growing darker by the minute now, and the school building was a further ten minutes' walk away. Thinking quickly, Bernie simply said, "Sorry, ma sis. I'll need to get all these samples into school before dark," and set off along the well-worn track that she trod daily on her way to Eilean Shona School.

By the time she reached the school building it was almost totally dark but, reaching for her keys, she was able to open the door and feel her way to a small corner cupboard which she knew contained only some French and Latin text books that were rarely used. She fumbled with her keys, not sure which, if any of them, would open the cupboard door. For a few moments she thought she must have the wrong set of keys, but then at last one of them fit the lock. With a sigh of relief, Bernie squeezed the box into the back of the cupboard and hid it behind the books, re-locking the cupboard with care. As she locked the building and set off home, she began to ask herself how and why she had become quite so secretive about the 'Seal of Promise'. She had felt like a burglar disposing of stolen property, but why?

Was it the power of love and respect she had had for Archie when the two of them had come across this extraordinary find? The two of them had reasoned that they had to maintain secrecy about the discovery. But why, exactly why? She had a premonition that somehow the Seal held some special significance, but what could that be? She vaguely remembered Archie saying he would try and find out more about seals, who had them and what they were used for, that sort of thing. Wasn't he going to ask his teachers at school? But, as far as Bernie could remember, he never did discover anything or, if he did, he certainly hadn't told her about it.

By the time Bernie finally reached home for the evening, she had begun to think she really ought to try and contact Archie and ask him if he ever did discover more about seals. But then, she thought, what would his family think if she started meeting up with him again, or even just writing to him? Anyhow, they rarely saw either him or Euan on the island these days and she certainly didn't know how she would contact him. Bernie decided she would just have to bide her time still further. Maybe one day there would be an opportunity to speak with Archie again.

"Urr ye day dreaming again Bernadette?" she heard her mother say. "Ah dunnae ken what you've been up tae today, sounds like all them bairns are in for plenty of lairning tae do this week. But ye, yoong lady, swatch loch ye havnae eaten all day. Come haur lassie and help yersel tae some of this tattie pie afore ye fall fast asleep."

* * * *

The expedition duly took place next spring, by which time twenty-six islanders had registered their interest in taking part. Bernadette took part herself, of course, without any of the concerns she might have had if she had not undertaken her private mission to remove the 'Seal of Promise'. As it happened, none of the party ventured along the coastal path where she and Archie had made their discovery ten years before. But the event was pronounced a great success by all who took part and it was agreed that, from now on, an expedition along these lines should be organised every spring. One fairly elderly islander suggested that one year they should take the route over by Samalaman which was where, somebody had told him when he was young, Jacobite supporters had kept a lookout for Bonnie Prince Charlie, expecting him to sail into Glenuig before he went on into Loch nan Uamh.

Chapter Seven
Chance Meetings

For the next three years the 'Seal of Promise' remained well hidden in the French and Latin book cupboard at the school. Bernadette occasionally opened the cupboard to clean inside, or rather to check that her 'treasure' was still safely hidden. She was in her late twenties now and had become very set in her ways as the island schoolmistress, known to all the children as Miss Bernadette or, behind her back, as 'Bernie'. She didn't mind her nickname now – she remembered fondly how she and her childhood friends had always referred to Miss McTavish as 'Tavvy'.

But she did sometimes worry how much longer she would have to remain teaching on Eilean Shona before something happened that might offer her something a bit more exciting. She had had a pleasant enough childhood, just playing with friends around the island, but there must be more to life than that.

One afternoon that summer, she was walking away from the school with two of the younger pupils, Maggie and Tommy McClean, seeing them safely home in the way she did every day for that particular family. Their mother was of a somewhat nervous disposition and preferred her children to be escorted home in the afternoons. Mrs McClean always walked them to school in the morning herself but she had a part-time job at the Big House, working in the kitchen, which prevented her collecting her children at the end of the school day. Bernie never minded being Maggie and Tommy's escort in the afternoons and usually sang songs with them as they went.

On this occasion a lady and gentleman suddenly emerged from around a small hill and enquired of her which was the easiest route back to the pier. They were taking a holiday from their home in Glasgow and had been brought over to Eilean Shona by a boatman from a point near Castle Tioram.

Bernadette took the trouble to point the way to the correct path but warned them to take care round the next corner where she had noticed there were rather a lot of sheep droppings. At this, the lady asked whether these lovely children were hers and, when Bernadette answered, she didn't merely tell them that they weren't hers, but explained that they were a couple of the pupils at the school where she taught. She added that she had been in charge of the island school these past few years and hoped one day to get work in one of the big cities, perhaps in Edinburgh.

"Of course, I am sure you would find that interesting," retorted the lady, "sorry, I'm afraid we're from Glasgow, not Edinburgh, but you seem to me like a natural schoolteacher. I'm sure if you were ever to come to our city, it would not be long before you were offered a position in one of our schools. We have many new schools opening in our city these days and I can't imagine it would be long before you found something suitable." And then she added, by way of an afterthought, "And if you didn't find a school to suit you, I know our daughter is looking for a tutor for her three children."

Bernadette just couldn't believe her luck. She explained that she felt committed to Eilean Shona for the rest of this summer but would be interested in going to Glasgow in September, if they thought she would be suitable for their daughter's family. The couple, who then mentioned that their names were Donald and Anne Henderson, promptly gave Bernadette a card showing their address and suggested she travel down some time in August if she were still interested in the position. As they went on their way, Bernie noticed that the card gave their names as Sir Donald and Lady Henderson. *Sir and Lady, indeed,* thought Bernie.

* * * *

Ma Neish knew something was up the minute she saw Bernie arrive home that afternoon. "Ha'e ye foond a pot o' gold, young lady?" she said as her elder daughter skipped into the cottage.

And "yes, Ma" was the reply she received.

"Wha' do ye mean by that?" asked Mrs Neish, as younger daughter Ailsa joined them.

"Well, this pot of gold – by name Sir Donald Henders, or something like that, and his wife," replied Bernie, looking at the card, "appeared to me and Maggie and Tommy McClean as I was walking them home and asked the way to the pier. They were really nice and we chatted for a bit and they said I might be able to teach at a school in Glasgow next term. Glasgow, Ma!!! I canna believe it!"

"Steady on, young lady, what's our school here going to do wi'out ye? And what's ya pa an' ya ma gonna do wi'out ye? We need ye here, don't ye care aboot us now?"

"Oh Ma," chipped in Ailsa, "ye've got me, remember. I can look after ye and Pa an' I can do teaching in school too, h've been doin' that these three years anyway."

"I still don't like it," said Ma Neish, weeping now. "Are we no' gonna see ye?"

And Bernie reassured her ma that it was only Glasgow she was going to. It wasn't London, or even Edinburgh. She could get back to the island in a few hours whenever she was needed. She added that she would need to take Ailsa through a few things about school but neither girl thought it would be any problem for her to take over school duties. It might create an opportunity for their friend Kitty to take over some of the teaching duties now.

Ma Neish finally relented. She had sensed for some time that Bernadette was ready for more responsibility and, in the absence of any sign of her marrying, this might be just what her elder daughter needed to bring the best out of her. She knew she was a talented and an attractive girl, and the time had come for her to spread her wings.

* * * *

102

After exchanging letters with the Hendersons, Bernie duly made her way to Glasgow in August, as Sir Donald Henderson and his wife Anne had suggested, and at their invitation – and their expense, she was relieved to find, for the coach fare was paid entirely by Sir Donald. The coachman had been instructed to deliver Miss Neish to the Hendersons' home, which was located in one of the smartest areas of the city.

Bernadette could not help noticing that their carriage passed near some other areas of Glasgow which looked dreadfully poor, and if she was required to go and work in these parts, she felt she would prefer to return home. But this was not to be the case, for that same afternoon the Hendersons' daughter, Fiona, appeared with her three children – Donald, aged 9; Isobel, aged 7; and Hannah, aged 6. They lived close to the Hendersons and Bernadette took an instant liking to these three charming young children, just as they did to her. It turned out that Fiona was married to a Mr Galbraith, the son of one of Glasgow's most successful tobacco merchants. Later, Bernie was to discover that Sir Donald had himself been highly successful in the same industry.

Bernie was immediately granted a temporary position as the children's 'tutor'. This was the title she was given by Mr and Mrs Galbraith, although Sir Donald and Lady Henderson referred to her as their 'governess'. It was agreed that if all parties were content, the arrangement would be confirmed after a month. Bernie could not believe her good luck. She hit it off straightaway with all the family and, long before the trial month was over, there was no doubt that Bernie would be staying on with the Galbraiths. She wrote a letter home informing her parents that she had the perfect job with a wonderful family, and she intended to stay as long as she could. She was being paid much, much more than she had ever thought possible, and she would be able to save almost all of it, as her board and lodging was all provided for. She had also been promised two weeks' holiday at Christmas and a further three weeks in the summer, so she would be able to return home twice each year.

Ailsa read her sister's letter to her parents, as neither their mother nor father had ever been taught to read or write. The girls often counted their blessings that a school had been opened on Eilean Shona just in time for them to be taught such life-enhancing skills. Ailsa then replied to her sister's letter on behalf of their parents as well as herself, congratulating Bernie on finding herself such excellent employment and assuring her that Ma and Pa were both well, or in their father's case, as well as could be expected. Ken Neish had been suffering from what he called his 'aches and pains' for the past six years, ever since he had fallen while re-thatching the roof of their cottage late one winter's afternoon. Since then he had never left the cottage and was only rarely off his bed. He depended upon his wife and daughters – now just the one daughter who was at home – for his survival.

Ailsa finished her letter by asking whether Bernie could remember where they might find the key to the corner cupboard in the school room. Somebody had said they thought there were some French text books in there but nobody could find the key...

* * * *

Bernie was glad to learn that everything was carrying on as normal at home. She admired the way her mother coped with her bedridden father, while making sure all the family were fed, in one way or another, through good times and bad. Ma Neish had always ensured that nothing stood in the way of her daughters' healthy development, and Bernie was grateful that she and her sister had been brought up in the way they were. Theirs had always been a frugal existence, but that was what it had to be. Neither girl had ever had the luxury of smart clothes, and often they had no shoes on their feet. Nevertheless, it had been a happy childhood and Bernie felt now that it should serve as a platform for her to seek something better, not just for herself but for both her parents and her sister. She must make the most of the opportunity that Sir Donald and Lady Henderson, and their daughter and son-in-law, now offered her.

However, she was irritated by the query raised by Ailsa at the end of her letter. This, she now realised, was entirely her fault. She should have found somewhere much less prominent for hiding the Seal of Promise, or else she should have simply left it buried where it was. She had foolishly fretted about the possibility of somebody happening to do exactly what she and Archie had done, at an extremely remote spot miles from where people ever went, and that that person might have gone on to make a fortune from it. How likely was it, she now reflected, that somebody else would not only choose to go that way but that they would then also decide to dig up the ground? Of course, it was much, much less likely than a teacher wanting to look inside a locker in their classroom. It was elementary, and Bernie cursed herself for having worried so much about this infernal Seal. It was probably of little value anyway, she now thought.

As she lay awake one night, in the comfortable bed provided for her by the Galbraiths, she decided that there was only one answer to Ailsa's query. She would write back and apologise that she had accidentally come away with the key. She would tell Ailsa that she was very sorry about this but she would of course bring it back when she returned home for her two weeks holiday at Christmas. Hopefully, Bernie thought to herself, she would then be able to explain the whole situation to Ailsa, at the same time making her promise never to tell anybody, least of all Archie.

As she handed her letter to the messenger next time he called at the Galbraith residence, the thought again crossed her mind that Archie would be very disappointed in her if he ever knew what she was now doing – she still could never imagine Archie ever breaking their pact and sharing their secret with somebody else, not even with Euan.

Or could she? How did she know that he had never done so? She hadn't set eyes on either Archie or Euan for ages now. They were living completely different lives. She might never see either of them again. And anyhow, why was she still worrying about this childish 'Seal of Promise' pact with a young man with whom she was not even allowed to be friends?

Eventually Bernie concluded that, as she wouldn't be returning to Eilean Shona until December, there was plenty of time for her to mull this over between now and then. In the meantime, she would think of some other places where they could hide this treasure, if that was what it was. She might even be able to bring it back to Glasgow with her. In the meantime, she would concentrate on being the very best tutor, or governess, or whatever it was that she was now employed to be.

* * * *

Bernie loved her new job, and it was very good to her. Fiona Galbraith had decided, as soon as she first saw Bernie, that she needed some smarter clothes. She took her shopping and ensured that she was fitted out with appropriate dresses for her position. Bernie soon learned that she belonged somewhere between the family itself and their maids and other domestic staff. She began to meet all sorts of interesting people as she took her charges to their friends' houses, or the Galbraiths' friends came to theirs. Typically, the family's friends were other business owners and their wives, and although Bernie was not supposed to converse with them, they frequently conversed with her.

One couple, the Kirks, were particularly friendly. He was a jeweller by trade and already had shops in both Glasgow and Liverpool, both of which provided him with immensely profitable custom. Mrs Kirk was always beautifully dressed, invariably displaying exquisite necklaces, brooches and other fine jewellery.

Every opportunity was taken by the single-minded businessman to promote the development of his enterprise, and one evening, when the Kirks were dining with the Hendersons, Theodore Kirk commented over the port – after the ladies had withdrawn – that he had noticed how the Galbraiths' new governess had just the right sort of head to show off jewellery to best effect. Sir Donald was greatly amused at this, and wondered whether they had overdone the port, but Kirk insisted that he was entirely serious. He rose from the table remarking that the girl was wasted working as a governess. One of these days he would have a word with her.

"Go on with you, Theo," was all Sir Donald would say, but afterwards he had to admit to himself that Bernadette Neish did have 'something about her'. He remembered the immediate impression that the girl had made when he and Anne had come across her on Eilean Shona in the summer.

* * * *

By now the MacDonell brothers had both progressed their careers quite rapidly. Euan had been promoted twice and was now a Captain in the 72nd Highlanders – the Duke of Albany's Own Highlanders, which had been formed as a British Army Highland Infantry regiment in 1778. He had given distinguished service during two tours of duty in Northern India but still found time to enjoy his shooting and fishing when he was home on leave. He occasionally reflected how he had originally been introduced to both these sports on that holiday with the Camerons at their Perthshire estate, while he and Archie were still at Harrow.

Archie, meanwhile, was now prospering as an up-and-coming Edinburgh lawyer – a 'Writer to the Signet' – and earning himself a fine reputation for his combination of expertise and hard work. His outgoing personality enabled him to make a great many friends and he was regarded in the Scottish capital's busy social circles as a highly eligible bachelor. On those occasions when he and Euan attended balls or other such events together, the daughters of Edinburgh's well-to-do families vied with one another for the brothers' attention. Antonia Farquhar and her younger sister Bridget, whose parents owned a castle and substantial estate in

Sutherland, were generally considered to be at the front of the queue but there were many other eligible young ladies for whom one or other of the MacDonells would be seen as the pinnacle of their ambitions.

Nevertheless, neither of the brothers showed any sign of wishing to commit to marriage just yet. They were enjoying life to the full, and they were also fully committed to their careers. They both still made the occasional visit to their parents on Eilean Shona, but these were now becoming much less frequent than their mother, in particular, wished them to be. Lady Elspeth yearned to see her two sons settle down, particularly Euan as the heir to the family's Moidart estate. But, as the years rolled on, there seemed to be little sign of any serious relationships developing.

That winter, when for a change both their sons were due to come home for Christmas, Lady Elspeth raised the subject with her husband.

"Alastair, you really must have a serious talk with Euan this time – well, with Archie as well, but certainly with Euan. He's going to be thirty next year and there are still no signs of any serious girlfriend on the horizon. My friend Mary in Edinburgh said she thought he was becoming very friendly with one of the Farquhar girls, but nothing seems to have come of that. Please, Alastair, do please take this opportunity to remind him of the responsibilities he's going to have in the future…"

"What do you mean, Elspeth? I'm not on my death bed yet. By Jove, I'm not even sixty. But yes, you're right, my darling. Of course, I'll speak with them when there's a suitable opportunity." The Laird said he was not going to be rushed into saying the right thing at the wrong time, nor, he added, the wrong thing at the right time. He smiled again at Elspeth, who shook her head and went back to her embroidery.

As it happened, he did speak to Euan – and also briefly to Archie – on this subject over Christmas, even though they only stayed at Eilean Shona for a few days. Euan had been invited to a shooting party soon after Christmas and Archie needed to get back to Edinburgh to take part in a prestigious Hogmanay ceilidh, to which one of his clients had invited him.

It was to be the last time either Alastair or Elspeth would have the chance to see Euan. On 31st December 1832 he died as a result of a terrible shooting accident. The news reached Eilean Shona the following day and the whole island mourned his loss as though they were all members of the family. Archie had received the news in the middle of the ceilidh, in the early hours of New Year's Day. He returned immediately to the island to be with his parents and sisters and to provide whatever support he could.

The whole community of Eilean Shona, and all throughout the whole Moidart estate, were shocked and shaken by the terrible news. Euan's body was brought back to be buried in the tiny churchyard beside the kirk, where he had been christened on a fine June morning just twenty-nine years earlier. His funeral was the most sombre occasion imaginable. The Laird and Lady Elspeth suddenly looked ten years older and both their daughters, Margaret and Annie, were in tears throughout. Their close family friends, the Camerons, who had hosted the fatal shooting party, had travelled over from Perthshire to attend. Local families, all those who had ever known Master Euan, seemed to be present.

It being the Christmas and Hogmanay season, Bernadette Neish was home and able to be there too, with her mother and sister. She scarcely recognised Archie, nor did he appear to notice her. Bernie had travelled to Fort William by coach on the day before the funeral, with her mother and sister, where she had spent most of her savings buying them each something suitable to wear. She herself had acquired a sombre dark coat and they all stood together at the back of the kirk and watched as Euan's coffin was borne by four of his fellow 72nd Highlanders officers, accompanied by Archie.

Father Thomas, long since retired from his clerical duties, led the prayers at the service. The Laird, still visibly shaken by the shock, spoke very briefly about the love that he and his wife and all their family had shared with Euan. He mentioned something about arranging a fitting memorial to their son, but was quite unable to say more. He was in tears just saying this much.

* * * *

Bernadette had sent an urgent message of apology to the Galbraiths as soon as she heard the news of Euan's death. She had been due to return to work in Glasgow two days later. Mrs Galbraith had replied to say how sorry they were to hear of her friend's death and had suggested she take an extra week to show her respect to her friend's family and the other mourners. What wonderful people these Galbraiths must be, said Bernie's mother. Ma Neish could not believe how much money her daughter was now earning, which had already enabled her to purchase some generous Christmas presents for her parents and sister, and now to pay for their shopping expedition to Fort William.

There was no reception after the funeral. Nobody expected to see either the Laird or Lady Elspeth for some while. They and their family would be accorded time and space to grieve. Neither was Archie to be seen after the service was over. He was straight back to Edinburgh, where he busied himself dealing with the inquiry into Euan's accident. A verdict of accidental death was delivered in due course. There were also many formalities to be attended to, ranging from the requirements of Euan's regiment through to the granting of probate and the administration of Euan's estate. His parents, still suffering terribly from the shock for some while afterwards, were at least comforted a little by the knowledge that Archie, now their heir, was well-versed in all the various legal requirements.

For all his leadership qualities, his delightful manner and his intellectual capacity, Euan had never been the most reliable of young men when it came to dealing with his personal correspondence. He was known to have forgotten family birthdays most of his life and to have frequently failed to reply to letters from friends, even when they included invitations to attend special occasions. It was not unusual to find him turning up to someone's birthday celebration without having accepted the invitation or given any indication that he would do so. Such was his warm and cheerful manner that his friends invariably forgave him.

Archie, however, was now to find that one particular exchange of letters, involving Archie himself, had been languishing in a drawer on Euan's desk – seemingly for a considerable period of time.

The letter in question related to the occasion, back in 1818, when the two brothers had walked to the spot near Samalaman, where the Seal of Promise had earlier been discovered. They were both schoolboys at the time, and during one of their holidays Archie had taken Euan round that way and shown him the strange hoard that he had previously discovered with Bernie Neish. Archie recalled that walk vividly and also that it was exactly seventy-two years after Bonnie Prince Charlie had been rescued nearby. It now appeared that, several years later, the brothers had had a further discussion about the discovery and Archie had written to Euan reminding him that he was going to look into the question of having the seal valued.

This letter was now sitting amongst a pile of correspondence, much of which appeared to have remained unanswered by Euan. However, in this case, it appeared that Euan had in fact written a reply to Archie but had never got round to dispatching it.

The two letters had been dated 9th January 1825 (Archie to Euan) and 24th February 1825 (Euan to Archie, signed but apparently never sent). In the first, Archie had written:-

"Dear Euan, I have been giving much thought to that conversation you and I had the other day while we were on Eilean Shona. It was interesting to hear you say you would welcome another chance to look at the seal which we uncovered on a walk all those years ago. I imagine it will still be lying where we found it that day, unless Bernie Neish has been back there again. I cannot imagine that she has, as I hear she is very busy teaching at the school these days. Anyhow, I think you said that one of your fellow officers is a bit of an expert on insignia and such things, so if you were able to get him to look at it, and give us some sort of opinion on it, I think that would be worthwhile. Other than sounding out your fellow officer, please keep this completely to yourself for the time being. However, I would be very interested to hear whether he would like to look at it. It would be fun to see it again and wonderful if it does turn out to be of value. I remain your affectionate brother, Archie."

And Euan's response, brief and to the point, had read as follows:-

"My dear brother, I am sorry not to have previously acknowledged yours of the 9th ult. I have spoken to Lieutenant Makinson and he would certainly welcome a chance to take a look at the seal. He was very interested in the story about how you first came upon it, and also the coincidence of the location being connected with such a significant historical event. Please let me know as soon as you have ascertained the present location of the seal and then I will see if we can arrange a date for Makinson to come and inspect it with us. I remain, etc. Euan."

After all the grief and sorrow attaching to Euan's sudden death, Archie experienced a strange feeling on reading this response from his deceased brother. It was wonderful to be able to read this belated, posthumous contribution from Euan, and typical of him to forget to dispatch it. But how frustrating to have missed the opportunity of taking forward his offer to obtain an expert opinion while Euan was still alive. It was now eight years since he had written that response. What chance was there of them still being able to trace this Lieutenant Makinson and to persuade him to take a look at the Seal?

No sooner had Archie come across this forgotten correspondence of Euan's, than he also discovered that his brother had not left a signed Will. Would this create any additional complications? Archie wondered.

Chapter Eight
Family Fortunes

Prior to Euan MacDonell's tragic death, a very happy 'Eilean Shona Christmas' had been enjoyed by all on the island. The weather had remained reasonably mild and, in addition to Euan and Archie, a number of other 'exiles' were also home for the festivities. Amongst these exiles had been Bernadette Neish, who now had so much to tell her mother and father, and her sister Ailsa, about her first few months working for the Galbraith family in Glasgow. Ma Neish had been amazed to see her elder daughter, so well-dressed and looking healthier and happier than she had ever seen her before. Even Mr Neish had perked up when he saw her and forgot all about his aches and pains.

Ailsa had also been delighted to see her sister, on several counts. First, she wanted to hear all about Glasgow, what it was like to live in a big city. She too had noticed the quality of Bernie's clothes and she asked her sister straightaway how much money they cost. Ailsa had thought that the two pounds she was paid each week for running Eilean Shona School was quite a good salary, but when she heard the prices of each of Bernie's garments, she realised what a different world it must be in Glasgow. Ailsa made up her mind that she should follow her sister there, but then realised how difficult it would be to leave her ma and pa. *How unfair life is for younger daughters,* she thought.

For the time being she was enjoying her position as the island's schoolteacher and she was able at the same time to fulfil her family responsibilities. Yet she realised now that she wouldn't wish to continue like this for too long. It was already beginning to feel like a trap.

Another reason for Ailsa's pleasure at seeing Bernie was the opportunity to show her sister some of the things she'd been doing with the children at school. She offered to take Bernie over to the school while it was closed for the holidays, a suggestion which Bernie readily welcomed. Of course, Bernie said, she would be very interested to see what the children had been doing since she left. And, she thought to herself, this was the obvious opportunity for her to hand over the cupboard key and share the whole Seal of Promise story with Ailsa, as she had now made up her mind she would.

Ailsa had already told her about some excellent paintings which the children had been producing, and a large map that they had made of the whole island. As she took Bernie over to the school, she mentioned the names of some of the children who contributed to these pieces of work, names which Bernie immediately recalled. She was delighted to hear of their progress and congratulated her sister on being so creative with her teaching. As they reached the school and Ailsa unlocked the front door, she said she thought it was good to try new approaches to teaching from time to time.

Bernie was much enjoying her discussion with Ailsa and, with nobody else present, she decided to broach the subject of the hidden Seal right away. "Ailsa," she said, "I've never told you this before, but you are the one person I know I can always trust."

Ailsa looked at Bernie, wondering what she was about to be told. "In that cupboard," Bernie continued, "you won't only find some French, and I believe also some Latin, text books. You will find something else that I hid in there." And at this moment Bernie produced the key to the cupboard and gave it to Ailsa. "Please open it, and you'll see what I'm referring to."

A very surprised and puzzled Ailsa duly unlocked the cupboard, which had proved such a frustrating mystery to her ever since she had taken charge of the school, and pulled out first the Latin books, then the French ones, and then a dirty old box. "Wha' on airth is this?" she asked her sister.

"Let me show you," Bernie responded, and forcing open the box for the first time for over three years, she extracted first the 'Seal of Promise', then a scroll which appeared to have been trapped behind the Seal, and then finally a very dirty glove. Ailsa was speechless for a moment, before stutteringly asking Bernie,

"W-wha' are they? And why are they here?" She thought for a moment that either she had gone mad, or Bernie had, or they both had. But she knew none of them had really gone mad. There had to be an explanation. Together they stared at each of the objects, before giving them a few more wipes and putting them back in the box. Bernie helped Ailsa return it to the cupboard, gave her the only key and suggested that they sit down for a while. It was a long story but, Bernie reflected, it was high time her sister knew how these strange old objects had come to be hidden in her schoolroom cupboard.

She told the whole story as best she could and Ailsa sat open-mouthed, listening to every word. By the time Bernie had finished she had so many questions she didn't know where to start. Why had she and Mr Archie re-buried their find in the first place? Why had they kept it all so secret? Why did they think it could be very valuable? What had she planned to do with it next?

As the questions occurred to her, more and more of her own thoughts entered her mind. Meanwhile, with this potential treasure sitting here in this schoolroom, Ailsa inevitably found herself wondering whether, over the next year or two, it could provide her with an interesting learning project for the children of the island to undertake. As the project developed, perhaps they could call upon relevant expertise from outside the island from time to time, and the children could work alongside them to piece together this whole, amazing puzzle. Maybe they could find out what kind of people used this sort of Seal – how old it was, what the scroll was all about, and whether the old glove belonged to anybody in particular.

In the process, Ailsa thought, they could learn how to be researchers, or historians, or designers or custodians, even museum curators? Who knows how many areas of expertise they could learn from this project, here in Eilean Shona's little school?

* * * *

Bernie and Ailsa talked for so long that they completely lost track of the time. They took the box out again, even Bernie looking at the contents as though she had never seen them before. She was fascinated by the scroll, which she hadn't really noticed before but which also looked very regal, with writing on it which was in a foreign language. Bernie thought that might be French. She peered again inside the box. Now they had managed to fully open it up, was it holding any other surprises? Each time she had seen this mysterious box, it seemed to pose more questions than it answered. Finally, they packed the treasures back into the cupboard and Ailsa locked it all up, retaining the key.

Eventually they set off back to the family's cottage, where they found their mother busily digging their small plot in readiness for re-planting in the spring. "Ye two ha'e been for a long walk, hae' ye been up Ben Nevis?" was all she said. She knew how much her girls enjoyed each other's company.

But they weren't finished yet. Bernie was just beginning to tell Ailsa that a nice jeweller called Mr Kirk had recently asked her if she'd be willing to model some of his newly-designed bracelets, earrings and necklaces.

"My word Bernie," their mother heard Ailsa exclaim, "and how much will he be paying ye for that?"

"Och, no very much," came Bernie's casual response.

Ma Neish could not contain herself at this. "Ye be careful ma girl in them big cities. I'll wager he be after more than jus' showing off fancy jewels," she warned.

But Ailsa smiled at Bernie and, out of their mother's hearing, whispered quietly to her sister,

"Go for it, Bernie, go for it."

Bernie had already decided to 'go for it'. She was due to meet Mr and Mrs Kirk at their shop in Glasgow on one of her afternoons off, as soon as she returned to the Galbraiths. Meanwhile Ailsa couldn't wait to start planning her pupils' prospective learning project.

* * * *

Archie had lost no time, after the funeral was over, in offering to deal with the legal formalities in relation to his deceased brother's affairs. Most of it was fairly routine and rather monotonous. But it had to be done. It was something of a distraction from the business of dealing with his own regular clients, but the partners in the Edinburgh practice where he worked were very sympathetic. Archie was not only a very able lawyer; he was also well-connected and he was seen as a potential senior partner once he had a few more years' experience behind him. His prospects now, as a significant future landowner, would surely stand him, and the firm, in good stead. So they happily allowed him additional leave to help sort out his late brother's estate and indeed to lend support to his bereaved parents.

Altogether it was a very busy time for Archie, particularly as the journeys he was obliged to make between Edinburgh and the island were inevitably very time-consuming – sometimes, especially in the winter months, occupying several days each time. Although for a while he aimed to return to the island at least once every month, by the following autumn his visits were becoming more spasmodic. He apologised to his parents – and his sisters, who were now shouldering the burden of sustaining their mother and father through dark and difficult days – for not being able to spend more time at home on the island. He promised, however, that he would take a full three weeks holiday at Christmas, recognising his responsibility to help see his parents, and the family and community as a whole, through the inevitably stressful anniversary of Euan's death.

* * * *

After Bernadette had returned to Glasgow in January, Ailsa had once again become immersed in the routine of running the Eilean Shona school. For a while she continued to concentrate on the creative learning projects, such as mapping the island, which she had recently been encouraging in addition to the essential skills of reading, writing and arithmetic, and the parish requirement to spend some time each day studying the meaning of various bible stories. There was no shortage of subjects to fill the children's working day. However, she was already giving some thought to investigating the significance of the hidden box and its fascinating contents. Alone at the school one evening the following spring, she decided to take the box out of the cupboard and have a closer look at each of the contents.

She began by cleaning the Seal, if that was what it was, as carefully and thoroughly as possible. Whatever it was, she soon formed the opinion that it was a magnificent piece of work. It did definitely seem to her to be some kind of individual Seal, which she imagined was used by a person of considerable influence to prove the authenticity of documents and letters which had been sent by them. It appeared to have been made out of some kind of resin, being of a very firm texture. And there were words engraved on its face, none of which she understood. She thought they must be Latin or some other foreign language. They were definitely neither English nor Gaelic, the only two languages that Ailsa knew.

Next she took a look at the scroll, which also seemed to be very official and perhaps of some importance. It contained a few lines, which as far as Ailsa could make out, were in yet another language. There was an elaborate signature at the bottom, with the name Louis appearing alongside other words. The document also carried what seemed to be a date. It read: "*Le 24 Octobre anno domini 1745*" and there was also the mark of a flower. What did this signify, Ailsa wondered?

And then there was the glove. Ailsa could not find anything notable about this, except that it was clearly very old and dirty but, if it was in some way connected with the Seal and the scroll, Ailsa reasoned that it ought to be examined by experts as well.

As she packed the three objects back into their box and returned this to the schoolroom cupboard, she pondered again whether they – Bernie and herself, and of course Mr Archie – were right to keep this all so secret. What harm could it do to share their story now with some expert from a University? Maybe Mr Archie should be asked if he wished to consult somebody in Edinburgh or Glasgow, or perhaps at St Andrews, where she understood he had studied. Perhaps she should ask to speak with Mr Archie next time he visited the island? Or maybe she should hold on and see what Bernie said when she next came home – she remembered her saying she had been granted some leave during August, so Ailsa decided she would wait and broach the subject with her then.

* * * *

By May, the Laird and Lady Elspeth were starting to get out and about again in the way they had done prior to Euan's death. They appeared to be making a great effort to restore a sense of normality to the island and, when the Laird announced that he would like to sponsor something special at this year's Island Games in Euan's memory, there was great anticipation across the whole community as to what this might be. The Island Games had proved a huge success each year that they had been held and it was generally agreed that it would be appropriate for Euan's memory to be permanently associated in some way with the Games.

The date announced for this year's event was Saturday 21st August and, by the middle of June, islanders could be seen in the evenings practising their running, their caber-tossing, their weight-lifting and other athletic skills in readiness for the big day. There was some discussion among them as to which of these events would be chosen to carry the prestigious award of a Euan MacDonell trophy. The Laird had already presented a trophy several years ago at the island's first highland games meeting – and it had been won, appropriately, by Master Archie as he was then known. Would a trophy named after Euan now be awarded for some other event, and, if so, which one would that be?

And then one day, they noticed the foundations being laid for a small building on one side of the sports field, and when three men arrived to start work from outside the island and some of the islanders were invited to earn money by joining the workforce, rapid progress was soon made with the erection of an elegant wooden pavilion. It was not large but it had clearly been designed by a trained architect and, as it started to take shape, it was easy to see that it would be sufficient to accommodate around twenty spectators, seated under a roof, with a changing area for competitors to the rear. It was a race against time but it was near enough to completion for it to be officially declared open by the Laird before the first race took place on 21st August.

There was a record attendance that day, for word had reached folk around the whole estate of Moidart and boatmen were kept busy all-day ferrying visitors across to the island. Archie had arrived on the eve of the Games, having travelled over especially from Edinburgh. He had heard from his mother that the Laird proposed to use the occasion to pay a special tribute to Euan, and then to name the building the Euan MacDonell Pavilion. Elspeth remarked that she thought her husband had found exactly the right way for their son to be remembered on the island, and Archie agreed wholeheartedly.

It was a beautiful, sunny day and the afternoon's Games attracted plenty of competitors. Many of the islanders recalled that Mr Archie was a former winner of the Laird's special trophy for the main event – the round-the-island race – and he was pressed by everyone present to take part again. He declared that he was neither dressed for running, nor fit to do so, but he gamely agreed to have a go. One of the household staff ran down from the House with some of his old running clothes and he became the first competitor ever to change in the pavilion. As he emerged, ready to run, he announced that his life in 'Auld Reekie' was not ideal preparation for running, a comment which was seen to be all too accurate when 'Mr

Archie', as he seemed to be generally known now that he was heir to the Estate, trailed in last of the ten runners. "At least I completed the course," he said, to everyone's admiration. He continued to be much loved and admired by the island population.

After the Laird had given a short, and again emotional, speech about Euan and formally named the Euan MacDonell Pavilion, Ritchie once again opened the bar as he had done for the Island Games every year since they first began. There were toasts to Euan's memory and many tears at the loss of such a fine young gentleman. Archie circulated among the islanders, as well as meeting many of the visitors from elsewhere on the Moidart estate, who were all anxious to meet the Laird's new heir.

As the afternoon gave way to evening, most of the visitors left to make their way home and eventually only a few of Archie's old friends remained, sipping ale or whisky as he recalled they had after the very first Island Games some years ago. Archie found himself sitting with Ailsa Neish and two of her friends, Kitty and Molly, all of whom he could remember from his childhood.

He noticed immediately how differently they treated him, now that they were all grown up and, of course, with him being heir to the Estate. They all now referred to him as Mr Archie and, although it was not in his nature to act in a superior manner to old friends, he instinctively allowed them to continue doing so. He was conscious that society expected certain conventions to be observed. After a while Kitty and Molly took their leave and Archie and Ailsa were left alone. "Mr Archie," Ailsa enquired, "have you heard from Bernie at all recently?"

"No, Ailsa, I haven't, I'm afraid, not for a long time now. Why do you ask?" Archie immediately thought of the times they used to spend together as teenagers and, inevitably, the 'ban' that his parents had eventually imposed upon them meeting.

"Oh, I just wondered. We haven't seen her ourselves since last Christmas, though she did stay on in the New Year because of …" Ailsa stopped abruptly, not wishing to refer to Euan's death.

"Aye, of course Ailsa, yes I saw you all as we were coming away from Euan's funeral; you were looking rather smart I seem to remember. I was sorry not to be able to speak to any of you, I'm sure you'll understand. How is Bernie, by the way?"

"Oh, she's fine. She has a wonderful job showing off clothes and jewellery in Glasgow these days. She writes letters to Ma and me, once every month if she remembers, and she sounds very happy. She was supposed to have been here these last two weeks but wrote to say she couldn't because she has been asked to take part in a parade of the latest styles of clothing at one of the big clothes shops in Glasgow. We're hoping to see her at Christmas but I doubt she'll be here before."

"So Bernie's in the fashion business now, is she?" responded Archie. "Sounds as though she's doing very well for herself. I have to say, Ailsa, I'm not all that surprised. Both of you were always so talented and it's so good to see young women like yourselves doing such interesting and useful things. You're leading the way, you know…"

He paused for a moment. "Did she…" he continued, pausing briefly again, "did she ever tell you that she and I discovered something rather exciting once? We never did much about it, but that was probably my fault. Funnily enough I found something when I was clearing Euan's old desk not so long ago and it made me think of Bernie."

There was a pause while Ailsa digested what Archie had just told her, and Archie remembered, rather too late, that he had promised faithfully to keep the Seal of Promise a secret between him and Bernie. Of course, he thought, he had eventually shared the secret with Euan hadn't he, so perhaps Bernie had done much the same with Ailsa. Or maybe Euan had spoken to Ailsa.

Ailsa, meanwhile, bit her tongue – she couldn't reveal to the future Laird that her sister had betrayed him. "Really?" she said after a moment's pause, "What did you find? I'd hate somebody to look at what's in my desk, especially the one where I hide the children's next test questions!" And then Kitty and Molly reappeared, and she said no more. The moment had passed.

* * * *

Bernie did make it home for the following Christmas, 1833. By this time, she was doing regular weekly demonstrations of how the latest jewellery should be worn, having been coached by Mr Kirk's wife, Ruth, herself a very attractive lady who was now in her late fifties. Ruth Kirk and Bernadette – as she was known to prospective customers – staged these demonstrations every Saturday in Mr Kirk's jewellery shop and the events proved so popular with the well-to-do Glaswegian ladies, and of such value to Mr Kirk in terms of sales, that she was offered a contract to continue doing so for the whole of the next year, every Saturday, at a salary of thirty pounds a month. Bernie had never known such riches – she was already being paid twenty pounds a month for being tutor to the Galbraith children, and both the Galbraiths and the Kirks were happy for her to combine the two jobs. With her combined income she would be able to buy even more generous Christmas gifts for her family in Eilean Shona this year, Bernadette reasoned, as well as starting to put some money aside for her own savings in case she never found herself a husband. Such a prospect may have been unlikely, with all the introductions she was receiving at the modelling events, but as she approached the age of thirty, she felt it wise to be prudent.

* * * *

Archie's conversation with Ailsa Neish after the Island Games had pricked his conscience and, on his return to Edinburgh, he decided to make fresh enquiries in the hope of establishing contact with this Lieutenant Makinson whom Euan had evidently spoken to about the Seal of Promise some years ago. He visited a library in Edinburgh and asked whether they had a register of officers, and former officers, of the 72nd Highlanders regiment. The librarian nodded and within a few minutes he was leading Archie towards a shelf containing a row of huge tomes which displayed the names of various Scottish regiments.

He carefully pulled out the latest volume marked, *"Officers of the 72nd Highlanders, the Duke of Albany's own Highlanders, 1778 to 1828."* It had been compiled to mark the 50th anniversary of the raising of the regiment. Archie was able to search through the names and soon found several Makinsons. The most recent was a Lieutenant Andrew Makinson, who was shown as having served for a total of twelve years after being recruited in the latter stages of the Napoleonic Wars. He had evidently retired from active service in 1826 and was now listed as resident in Musselburgh, East Lothian. This could hardly be more convenient, Archie felt, as this small town was less than a half-hour's coach ride from his own Edinburgh office.

No house address was given in the regimental register but Archie decided to visit Musselburgh the following week and make enquiries as to whether anyone knew of a Mr Makinson, a former army officer who had retired a few years ago. He would probably now be approaching the age of forty. On arrival in this pleasant little town, he first enquired of a coachman who said he recalled taking a gentleman of some similar name to an address on the Dunbar road but he couldn't be sure his name was Makinson. He offered a ride there, but Archie declined the coachman's offer for the time being, thanking him and wishing him a good day. Not sure where to look next, Archie noticed a church on the far side of the road and decided to see if there was anyone there who might know of a Mr Makinson, a resident of the town. Inside the church he found a parson who had just finished supervising a rehearsal of the following Sunday's 'Nunc Dimittis'. He happily offered Archie a friendly welcome.

"Excuse me, vicar," Archie began. "I am searching this town for a former regimental colleague of my deceased brother. His name is Makinson and I understand he has been resident in Musselburgh these past few years..." Archie's sentence tailed off as he noticed the parson beginning to smile.

"Sir, my own name is Makinson – Andrew Makinson," he replied, "and I was formerly commissioned Second Lieutenant, later Lieutenant Makinson of the 72nd Highlanders. I left the army when I received my calling and decided to read for a life in the church. I was ordained last year. How may I help you, sir, I wonder?"

"My word, what a coincidence," exclaimed Archie. "Reverend Makinson, my name is Archibald MacDonell and I believe you may have known my brother, Captain Euan MacDonell, who sadly died some two years ago. I have some correspondence mentioning your name in connection with an ancient Seal which I helped to find many years ago..." Suddenly there was a look in the Rev. Makinson's eyes which indicated to Archie that he recalled Euan's name and then, after a short pause, his eyes lit up and he replied.

"Yes, aye, I believe it was MacDonell who asked me if I would examine an old Seal with a Coat of Arms. Quite a long time ago now, I think. Let me see, must be almost ten years I should say." He paused for a moment. "Did you say your brother is deceased?" Archie nodded.

"That is indeed sad, sir. I remember our conversation well. Such matters have long held a fascination for me and I would have liked to have seen the Seal. We can learn so much from studying such relics of our history, you know."

Archie and the Rev. Makinson talked for a few more minutes before it was time for the church to be prepared for evensong. But Archie promised to bring the Seal, and a scroll which had been found with it, to Musselburgh some time, for the vicar to examine. As he left the church with a note of the Rev Andrew Makinson's home address for future correspondence – which was indeed on the Dunbar road – Archie was beginning to believe in divine intervention himself.

* * * *

Despite her busy life, holding down two demanding but very different jobs, Bernadette had never felt happier. She loved the three children in her charge, and they loved her. One or other of the three children, if not all of them, seemed to require her attention almost all of the time – if this were not for their tuition, it would be to ensure their safety and their entertainment. By the autumn of 1834, she realised it was nearly nine months since she had had any time to herself, other than on Sundays. Even then she was required to take the Galbraith children to church. Only on Saturday afternoons did she get a complete break from her governess duties – this was when she would make her way to Kirks the jewellers to prepare for the afternoon shows.

Bernie loved this work too. It was certainly a very unusual job, but Mr Kirk was successful because his approach was unconventional and she was not averse to being adventurous herself. Besides, she enjoyed the variety of styles which the Kirks were willing to try out in front of their clientele. There were always new styles for her to wear: if it were not fresh jewellery designs, then Mr and Mrs Kirk would generally produce garments that she had not seen before. Nor did Bernie mind parading these garments in person – she felt sure that this approach to promoting awareness of new styles would prove successful, and it was certainly proving popular. Week after week the Kirks' customers would turn out, and sit and drink tea, while exchanging the latest local news or gossip and observing the show. Bernie adored all this attention and the audience – mostly ladies, naturally – loved her. Some brought their husbands from time to time and they too seemed very fond of her. She was frequently asked if she would go to their homes to give private demonstrations to them and their friends, but always declined. That would not have pleased Mr or Mrs Kirk, nor the Galbraiths.

She did however occasionally wonder how long she could sustain her enthusiasm for this very demanding work. She was glad that she had asked both the Galbraiths and the Kirks whether they would mind if she took an extended holiday this Christmas. She was missing her family too, and wondered how everyone was coping on the island – she thought particularly of the Laird and his family, after the desperately sad loss of Euan.

Both the Galbraiths and the Kirks entirely understood Bernie's desire for a good holiday with her family this Christmas and Mrs Galbraith was her usual generous self, suggesting that she take at least three weeks to spend with her family at their island home. She offered to arrange comfortable travelling arrangements for Bernie, recalling the sadness that she and her friends must all have still been feeling when she last went home. She hoped that this time they would all be able to enjoy a happy and peaceful Christmas and New Year together. Bernie thanked Fiona Galbraith profusely, saying she was sure it would all be very different this time.

Upon receiving this kind gesture, Bernie wrote promptly to her mother (for Ailsa to read to her, she realised), informing her that she hoped to arrive home by 21st December and would be able to remain at home until 12th January 1835. She asked whether any of their family had any special requests for gifts, which she might find easier to purchase in Glasgow. There was no response until the day before Bernie was due to leave, when a short, hurried note from Ailsa arrived, apologising that they hadn't replied before and warning her that there had been an outbreak of cholera in the island, which had also affected much of mainland Moidart. The Neish family had not been affected as yet but several families had lost children and a few older residents had also died. The Laird had suffered himself but a doctor had visited him and a few other families and had supplied them with bottles of a potion which enabled them to recover. She really did not think this was a good time for Bernie to be coming home.

Poor Bernie was torn. Should she cancel the seat which the Galbraiths had kindly booked, and already paid for, on the special Christmas stage-coach to Mallaig – and also the trap that was due to meet her off the coach at Lochailort and take her the rest of the way to Eilean Shona? Or should she go ahead as planned? She soon decided that she owed it to her family, and to the island community that had been so kind to her throughout her childhood, to come home and do what she could to help. There was no doubt in her mind. She discussed the position with the Galbraiths and they understood and supported her decision entirely. They were even able to obtain a supply of calomel and opium from a physician they knew well in Glasgow, which she could take with her.

Ma Neish and Ailsa, who had been preparing for a quiet and sad Christmas, were astonished to find Bernadette on their doorstep late on the evening of Tuesday, 21st December 1834.

Chapter Nine
Responsibilities

Bernie had had a long and arduous journey from Glasgow but, tired though she was on arrival, she was elated to see her parents and sister once again. For a few minutes they hugged and kissed and exchanged greetings, Ailsa in particular being unable to believe that Bernie had gone ahead with the journey home despite all the inconvenience and the warnings about the cholera outbreak on the island. Fortunately, the whole Neish family had somehow avoided infection, Mrs Neish being convinced that her practice of boiling all the family's drinking water on the fire before touching any of it, had helped them to avoid the potentially fatal intestinal disease. Mr Neish, who still spent his days in or near his bed, had his own theory that the water also needed to be laced with the local whisky to remain safe. When Bernie went into the bedroom to see her father, he was busy putting his theory into practice.

Bernie had, needless to say, brought with her a variety of gifts from Glasgow, but it was the calomel and opium that her mother most appreciated. She would keep it in a safe cupboard in case there were any further signs of the cholera affecting them or any other families. Fortunately, no new cases had been heard of in the past few days, but you could never be sure.

It did not take long before Ailsa and Bernie sat down together on their own. Mrs Neish said she would leave them to it and, with a 'don't be too late, girls' as though they were still teenagers, she retired for the evening. The sisters' first conversation concerned the poor children, two boys and three girls who had all suffered such terrible deaths. Two of the girls were from the same family as one of the boys. They had all died in quick succession at the height of the epidemic. Bernie remembered teaching all but one of the five who had succumbed to the disease, and she had also known most of the parents and other families who had fallen victim to it. The two of them sat in silence for a few moments, both wiping away tears as they remembered happy, smiling faces that they would see no more.

Bernie then asked how the school was managing and Ailsa bravely brought her sister up-to-date on how they had coped, how school had to be suspended altogether for a month and how, even now, they were taking precautions to ensure that every child's family was following sensible precautions at home to protect themselves against the disease. The school had its own fire burning all day, every day, and every drop of water – whether it were for drinking or washing – had to be thoroughly boiled.

Eventually they moved off this gruesome subject and Ailsa shared with Bernie her latest ideas regarding the Seal of Promise hoard and how it still seemed to be an ideal project for the children to study. She carefully avoided telling Bernie of her brief conversation with Mr Archie after the Island Games but she did hint that she thought he might be interested to know that the mysterious treasure was now safely under lock and key, on Eilean Shona.

She added that she felt the Laird's family ought to be officially informed anyway. Its presence there was still known only to the two of them. Bernie nodded her agreement – she felt somewhat detached from the whole issue of the Seal these days, but their conversation reminded her that there were all sorts of unanswered questions which they really ought to be trying to answer. In the end Ailsa suggested that they should take the opportunity, while they were both on the island and Archie was too, to show him the Seal's secret location at the school.

"Would it not be sensible?" she asked, "if you and I went with Mr Archie to the school and showed him? I think he would be fascinated, don't you?" And Bernie, now remembering all the trouble and care they had taken to maintain the secrecy of the find, nodded her head slowly.

"Yes, sis, you're right, I think he would," she replied. "But will we be allowed to speak to him? And anyway, do we have to call him mister now?"

* * * *

The island's little church (the kirk) was fairly full that Christmas morning but there were one or two pews which, Bernie noticed, were empty or only occupied by two or three people. Everybody knew families which had lost some of their loved ones. Ailsa commented that there had been so many funerals that people had started to stay away from church. They couldn't face returning again to the site of their grief and sorrow.

But Christmas was a time to rejoice at the arrival of new life, the new young priest reminded all the worshippers, and to look forward to making the best of a new year and new opportunities. He felt sure there would be happier days in 1835 and beyond. As they filed out of church the Laird – now looking rather frail – and Lady Elspeth, together with Mr Archie and the Misses Margaret and Anne MacDonell, still observed the tradition of circulating amongst the island parishioners. It was not long before they came to the Neish family. "Merry Christmas to you all, and how are all your family?" the Laird enquired, as he did of every family to whom he spoke. And then there was a moment's silence before Lady Elspeth added, looking at Bernie, "Ah, you must be Bernadette. I am sorry, I hardly recognised you."

"Yes of course, my Lady," replied Bernie, dropping the faintest of curtseys. "Merry Christmas to you, my lady, and all your family. I do hope you are well? I am living in Glasgow these days but my mother and father kindly invited me to come and stay for the holiday season. It is so nice to be back in Eilean Shona."

Lady Elspeth smiled as she moved on to the next family. Mr Archie, however, paused and, allowing a moment for his sisters to move on ahead, raised his hat to Bernadette and Ailsa. "Excellent to see you both. You are looking very well, if I may say. We must catch up with each other's news some time. I shall be in touch." And with another touch of his hat, he smiled at both sisters, and at their mother, and moved on.

"What a lovely man he is, Bernie," whispered Ailsa to her sister.

Always has been, thought Bernie.

* * * *

Archie was true to his word and, two days later, a footman arrived from the MacDonell household to ask whether the Misses Bernie and Ailsa Neish would care to join Mr Archie and his sisters for a walk around the island the following morning at ten o'clock. He, Margaret and Annie would be happy to collect Bernie and Ailsa from their cottage at that time, if they wished to join them. The footman brought back to the Big House their immediate response that they would be delighted to do so.

Bernie and Ailsa were not simply delighted, they were astonished and flattered that such a formal indication had now been given that they were acceptable company for the Laird's son – and now heir – to keep. True, they were not exactly being invited to the Big House as his personal guests. However, after all these years, it did appear that, with a blossoming professional career in Bernie's case, and proven teaching capabilities in Ailsa's, their social standing was now deemed by the MacDonells to be worthy of being seen walking out with their son and daughters. It was a major step forward for the Neish family – one which certainly made their mother very proud.

* * * *

Low cloud descended over Eilean Shona the next morning but, true to their word, Mr Archie and his sisters Margaret and Annie arrived outside the Neishes' cottage at exactly ten o'clock. "Good morning, ladies," said Archie as Mrs Neish opened the door and asked if the family's visitors would like to come in.

"That is very kind of you, Mrs Neish, some other time perhaps. I suggest, though, that we should press on with our walk before the weather gets any worse. Those clouds look threatening if I know my local weather. We won't be out very long, Mrs Neish, and I will of course accompany your daughter's home."

"Well, now then ladies, in which direction do you wish to walk today?" Archie asked. This was just the opportunity that both Bernie and Ailsa were hoping for and they immediately suggested a route which would take the five of them in the general direction of the island's north coast, along a path that took them close to the school. Archie and his sisters happily agreed and the five of them set off. By the time they reached the school building, Archie's weather forecast had proved accurate and it was raining steadily. After exchanging glances with Bernie, Ailsa seized her opportunity.

"Mr Archie, and ladies, would you care to see some of the wonderful paintings the children did this year," she called out.

"What an excellent idea, Ailsa," replied Archie, as Ailsa unlocked the door and let them all into the school. "If you don't mind us all coming in here in our walking boots, this is indeed an excellent idea. I think we'll be better off inside here until the rain stops. My word," Archie continued, "it must be almost ten years since any of our family came to school here – I think you were the last to do so Annie, weren't you? About ten years ago, would you say?"

"More like twelve, Arch," replied his sister.

"Well, time does fly as they say," Archie went on, as they all gazed around the little one-room building, furnished simply with just four tables, around which it was clear that the children all sat for their classes – each, according to Ailsa, allocated a place according to their age. "But you've arranged it all in a much tidier fashion than old Father Tom used to – he had us all sitting in rows, I seem to remember. Well done, Ailsa."

"Not at all, Mr Archie," said Ailsa. "I think most of the reorganising was done by Bernadette, wasn't it, Bernie? While you were running the school?" Bernie said she couldn't remember.

"Anyhow," continued Ailsa, "this is how we arrange the children these days. Now I'm afraid I cannot offer you any refreshments today, as I normally try to do for any visitors. Of course, we are still having to take precautions to ensure we don't spread the disease. But we do have the paintings over here." And Ailsa pulled them all out, one by one, from behind a curtain. "We are hiding them behind here for their protection, pending an exhibition we're hoping to organise at next summer's Island Games."

"What an excellent idea," said Margaret and Annie in unison. "It would be great to have an art exhibition for people to enjoy during the Games. Perhaps it could be set up in Euan's pavilion." By this time, they were all poring over the paintings, about twenty of them ranging from landscapes and portraits to drawings of buildings and animals, and finally, her pupils' proudest achievement, their collective large-scale map of the island.

"You must be a brilliant teacher, Ailsa," they all said. "How do you do it?"

"Oh, it's not the teacher, it's the wonderful, talented pupils," came Ailsa's modest reply. "They all learn from watching one another, discussing things together, and of course competing with one another. I just watch, praise, and occasionally make a suggestion. It's all such fun, or was, until these past few months. Even then, I found that doing the painting offered a chance for the children to take their minds off the disease, until of course we were forced to close for a while."

With those remarks, Ailsa then invited Margaret and Annie to have a good look at all the paintings, as she had something that she and Bernadette would like to show Mr

Archie. She led Archie over towards the cupboard, unlocked it and carefully withdrew the Seal of Promise box. "Mr Archie, Bernie and I both thought you should know that we have been holding this here for its protection until there is an opportunity to have its contents examined. I hope you are happy for us to do so?"

* * * *

They were there for almost an hour, the five of them. Margaret and Annie were more interested in the children's paintings, although they did occasionally look across the room at the others, who were busy examining the three objects and the box which they occupied. Bernie and Archie had read one another's minds and immediately exclaimed, almost in unison with one another: "So much for our Seal of Promise!" Although they grinned at one another at seeing it all together once again, they each felt a pang of guilt that they had ultimately been unable to maintain total secrecy about the discovery they had made together as teenagers.

Archie had also been regretting, for some while, his inability to progress the whole matter of obtaining an expert opinion on their extraordinary find. But on witnessing how beautifully Ailsa had now cleaned and polished the Seal, both Archie and Bernie expressed themselves keener than ever to have it, and the scroll and glove, examined and valued professionally. They should not leave this any longer, they all agreed.

As they returned the box – with all the three items back inside it – to the relative safety of the school cupboard, and Ailsa locked the cupboard securely, Archie noticed that Margaret and Annie were closely examining and admiring one particular painting which, from their comments, they clearly considered to be an exceptional piece of work. This, he found, showed what appeared from the subject's hair and clothing to be a portrait of a young man. But he looked instead like an old man if you judged by the look of his face and hands and the way he was leaning sideways on a bed. "Is this your own work, Ailsa?" he asked.

"No," came her reply. "It was done by a young lad called Donald, the most talented young artist I have ever come across. He finished it just before he was taken ill. It's a portrait of his sick father, completed just two days before they both died."

In that case, that's something else that needs to be properly valued, thought Archie as he watched Ailsa lock the school door. And then he added, as they all stood there,

"That painting needs to be kept under lock and key too." They were all rather quiet as they began to make their way back across the island. They had begun to contemplate the responsibility they were carrying for some unique, and potentially priceless, treasures.

* * * *

Archie was in touch with Bernie and Ailsa again the very next morning. He would like them to come up to the house that afternoon, bringing with them both the Seal of Promise items and the painting by Donald, so that they could discuss the appropriate way forward with his mother and father. The footman indicated that three o'clock would be a suitable time – tea was invariably served to Lady Elspeth's guests a little after three. This left Bernie and Ailsa with plenty of time to go and collect the relevant items from the school and prepare to show them to Archie's mother and father.

They needed something suitable in which to carry everything up to The Big House. Bernie immediately thought of her old knapsack, which she knew to be the right size as she had carried the Seal of Promise box in it when she made her solitary expedition to retrieve it from its original site. She was sure it must be somewhere in the cottage but, when she and Ailsa looked, it was nowhere to be seen. After they had explored what they thought was every corner, Ailsa suggested their father's bedroom. They could hear him snoring, it was mid-day and he usually slept for a while around this time. The girls crept quietly into the room, anxious not to disturb him but desperate to find the knapsack. And there it was, next to a pile of clothes beside his bed. Picking it up off the floor and preparing to apologise for disturbing him if he awoke, they noticed that it was crammed full of mostly empty whisky bottles.

"Wha' are ye doin'?" their father suddenly screamed. "Them's mine, leave them alone."

"Och, Pa, 'tis only the bag we're after. Ye can ha'e it back this evening," they told him. And, giggling to themselves, Bernie and Ailsa carefully removed all the whisky bottles and arranged them in a neat and tidy row, just out of their father's reach on the far side of the room.

* * * *

The Seal of Promise box fitted neatly into the knapsack, just as it had done a few years earlier. Meanwhile Ailsa had borrowed two dishcloths to protect Donald's painting from the elements. Their mother, who had been over to her friend Betty's house most of the day, would no doubt have found something more suitable but Bernie and Ailsa couldn't wait till she returned. By a quarter to three they were making their way over to the Big House. On arrival, Ailsa hesitated for a moment as to which door they should use. "The front door, silly," said Bernie, now quite used to being treated as 'family' by wealthy Glaswegian households. "The back door is for servants and tradesmen," she said, but Ailsa wasn't so sure.

Their dispute was settled by a maid opening the front door and welcoming them with a cheerful, "Good afternoon, ladies, would you come in please? May I take your coats?" Bernie was sure she was about to address them as 'madam' but was relieved that she didn't. She and Ailsa were feeling a little out of their depth already. Bernie handed over her coat but kept hold of the knapsack. The maid took both the girls' coats away and they were shown into the drawing-room, where they waited a couple of minutes – just long enough to start worrying about how they would present their exhibits – before

Lady Elspeth entered the room, followed by the Laird and Mr Archie.

"How very good of you to come and see us," Lady Elspeth began, looking at Bernie and then at Ailsa. "Archibald tells us you have some interesting exhibits you helped him find. He tells me you've been looking after them very carefully and now want us to arrange a valuation. Is that right, Archie?"

"Well, sort of, Mama," replied Archie. "Actually, I think it was more a case of Bernadette finding the box and the Seal inside it, and then Ailsa looking after it at the school and discovering the other things that were in it when she cleaned out the box, they were in. All I did was just try and make sure Bernadette didn't fall over when we first found them – the sort of thing I seem to have spent my life doing, eh?" With this he grinned at Bernie, who started to relax and smiled back.

"Well, anyway, do sit down," continued Lady Elspeth. "They'll be bringing the tea in shortly. Now then, I gather you've brought the Seal with you and some other things which you think might also need to be valued. Is that right, Miss Neish?"

Bernie and Ailsa took this as a signal to start opening the knapsack and the old box, and extracting the Seal for everyone to see. Bernie carried it across the room to the Laird.

"This is the Seal itself, my lord," she said as she placed it on a side table in front of the Laird. Meanwhile Ailsa took the scroll over to Lady Elspeth.

She immediately exclaimed, "This must be from a King of France, isn't it? Yes, I'm sure it is. Look at the fleur-de-lis, and the signature – Louis Quinze. What does it say? I should be able to read it. I used to do French with Ma'mselle. Archie, this really is interesting. I know your grandfather Lord Moncrieffe will be interested. Alastair, we must look after these things. And of course have them valued. Who do they belong to, I wonder?"

"I wouldn't know," replied the Laird. "But I suppose if these two young ladies and Archibald found them, and on our estate, then it's up to us. Or perhaps it should all belong to the crown? Archie, this Seal looks pretty genuine to me. What else did you find, did you say there's an old glove there?"

"Well, yes, Pa, there is, but it's very old and dirty I'm afraid," replied Archie. And as Bernie passed him the glove, he added. "But it's all part of the same hoard, I suppose. Papa, would you mind if we kept all these things here for the time being, under lock and key? I do think we should take responsibility for their safe keeping. With all due respect to Ailsa, I think they'll be a lot safer here than they can be at the school."

Before her husband could respond, Lady Elspeth offered her opinion. "That sounds sensible to me, Alastair. We can easily keep them with all your medals and other valuables for the time being. But I think you were saying, Archie, that you were in touch with a man who had corresponded with Euan about all this before..." She stopped suddenly. Neither she nor the Laird could yet talk easily about the loss of their elder son.

"Yes, Mama, that's right," said Archie. "We have tracked down somebody who seems to know a great deal about these things. His name is Makinson and he was in the Highlanders with Euan, that's how we traced him. Lives over near Edinburgh, a place called Musselburgh, these days and he's become a vicar. I've been over to see him and he does seem interested in seeing what we've found. So what I'm suggesting is that, if we all agree that these things are worth investigating, then we start with him. I would be more than happy to travel over there with Bernadette and Ailsa and show them to this chap for him to have a look. If he hasn't got all the answers, I'm sure he'll help point us in the right direction." Archie paused for a moment, conscious that his parents were digesting the idea of him taking the Neish sisters across to the other side of Scotland. He realised that a few years ago he would not have been allowed to cross the island with them. And then he added: "You see, Pa, Ma, we need to start somewhere. We all think what we've discovered is unique and could be of some historical importance."

The Laird and Lady Elspeth looked across at one another for a moment but it was finally agreed that this needed to be done. They couldn't delay matters any longer. Archie promised to arrange a coach to take him, Bernie and Ailsa, with their treasures, over to Edinburgh so they could visit the Rev. Makinson together and see what he made of them. He immediately wrote a letter to Makinson, requesting an early date on which he could receive the three of them and inspect the hoard. "We can give this to Machray now to take over to the messenger tonight," he added. And while Archie was writing his letter to Makinson, Lady Elspeth went straight to her writing desk and wrote a brief letter to her father, telling him too about the remarkable collection of items that Archie had helped to find.

"Machray can take this one too while he's about it," she added.

"Now then, after all that, how about a dish of tea?" Lady Elspeth asked Bernadette and Ailsa. "And, by the way, did I hear you say you also have a painting by one of your pupils? I would love to take a look at that…"

* * * *

As they left the Big House and made their way back to their cottage, Bernie told Ailsa she hoped this Rev. Makinson would be able to see them before 12th January as she was expected to return to her duties with the Galbraith family on that date. They had always been so kind and generous, especially with regard to her holidays, so she wouldn't want to have to ask for any more time away. She needn't have worried. A reply to Archie's letter came swiftly enough from the Rev. Makinson, explaining that although he was fully committed until after the Epiphany, he would be delighted to receive Archie and the Misses Neish at his home in Musselburgh on the 8th of January if that were convenient for them. This suited Archie well, as he had recently been invited to a meeting with the partners of Anstruthers on the 9th, which he was anxious to attend.

He duly made arrangements for the three of them to leave for Edinburgh early on the 6ᵗʰ. He knew of an excellent coaching inn near Loch Earn where they could break the journey and arrive fresh in Edinburgh by the following afternoon. There were spare rooms in his town house in Edinburgh's new town, where they were welcome to stay in preparation for their visit to Andrew Makinson in nearby Musselburgh. He would also arrange their return transport – they could take a coach which went via Glasgow, where Bernie could alight in good time to re-join the Galbraiths. Ailsa was pleased with this too – she could take the opportunity to see a little of Glasgow before travelling on back home.

Bernie's old knapsack was once again pressed into service for transporting the Seal, scroll and glove and the old box in which they were still being kept. The journey to Edinburgh was uneventful, a snowfall that had been predicted by local residents totally failing to materialise. They arrived on schedule and immediately made their way to Archie's house, where they were able to deposit their overnight bags and the all-important knapsack before setting off to look round Edinburgh. Neither of the girls had previously visited the Scottish capital and as they walked between the Castle and Holyrood Palace, they experienced for the first time a true sense of Scotland's great history. Later that evening Archie took them for a meal nearer to his house and they continued to marvel at the way in which the city had managed to blend the old and the new.

Next day they set off early for their appointment with the Rev. Makinson in Musselburgh, where they received a warm and enthusiastic welcome from their host. He had clearly been looking forward to seeing what they had to show him and he was not going to be disappointed. Archie had asked the staff at Eilean Shona House to give the Seal a really good polish before they left and it positively sparkled in the morning light. "They've done a much better job of cleaning it than I ever did," observed Ailsa.

Andrew Makinson began by examining the intricate engravings on the Seal and carefully copied down the words displayed around its perimeter, which read, *"JACOBVS SECVNDVS DEI GRATIA MAGNAE BRITANNIAE FRANCIAE ET HIBERNIAE REX FIDEI DEFENSOR."* He promptly translated the Latin into English for his guests' benefit, as, "James the Second, by the grace of God, of Great Britain, France and Ireland, King, Defender of the Faith." Makinson was clearly very knowledgeable when it came to historical treasures. He then pressed his hand on the face of the Seal and lifted it to feel its weight. Looking first at Archie, and then at Bernie and Ailsa, he told them that it certainly appeared to be authentic. He asked them again to explain exactly where it was found and Archie and Bernie took him through the whole story, Archie pointing out that he hadn't yet looked at the scroll.

"I'll come to that shortly," Andrew Makinson replied. "Before that, I'd like to try out the Seal." And he got up from his seat and picked up a candle, some paper and some sealing wax which he had placed on a shelf ready for use. He folded one part of a sheet of the paper and then lit the candle and heated the wax, pouring some of it onto the paper so that it covered both the edge of the folded section and the unfolded part. After waiting for it to start solidifying he then took the Seal and stamped it onto the drying wax so as to leave a permanent impression from the Seal as well as sealing the join of the paper. After a few minutes, there it was – the stamp of James II's Great Seal of the Realm applied to the paper like a sealed envelope. Bernie looked at Archie, and then at Ailsa, and back at Andrew Makinson, and they all said,

"Can we have a closer look?" And they stared for two or three minutes at the writing on the wax, and at the Seal itself, finally asking if they could take the waxed and stamped paper with them.

"Of course, it's your Seal," Makinson replied, handing it to Bernie, "unless someone claims that it constitutes treasure trove, I suppose. Shall I look at the scroll now?" he asked. They took this out of the box and, as they were doing so, he asked them to confirm that this was the actual box which had been buried and in which both the Seal and the scroll had been kept. Archie confirmed that this was indeed the case – it was only the glove that they couldn't be sure had been in the box when they discovered it. "You might need to do some tests on the glove at some stage, so take care with it if I were you," Andrew Makinson warned.

Meanwhile he had untied and unrolled the scroll and was reading and translating the writing on it, which he agreed certainly appeared to have been signed by King Louis XV of France. This of course was in French. It carried the mark of the fleur-de-lis and read as follows:-

"*Moi, Louis de France, confirme par la presente que je soutiens de tout coeur, ainsi que celui de mon royaume de France, notre plus fidele cousin, Charles Edouard Stuart, l'heritier legitime de son pere, James Francis Edouard Stuart, roi de l'Angleterre, l'Ecosse et d'Irelande. Compte tenu de ma main, ce vingt-quatre octobre, anno domini 1745.*"

Again he translated. "I, Louis of France, confirm by this deed, that I give my whole-hearted support, and that of my kingdom of France, to our faithful cousin, Charles Edward Stuart, the true heir to his father, James Francis Edward Stuart, king of England, Scotland and Ireland. Given over this my hand, this twenty-fourth day of October, in the year of our Lord, 1745."

Andrew Makinson looked again at the box, and the Seal and the glove, and back at the scroll. "Well, it certainly is quite a find for you to have made. You may have happened upon something of real historical interest here. I am not professionally qualified in these matters and, if you ask me, I think you should really be taking them to the British Museum, and perhaps also to a good professional jeweller if you know of one. I am sure the British Museum will be interested, and they should be able to tell you whether it would be regarded as treasure trove and therefore belong to the Crown. As far as value is concerned, I expect each item will influence the valuation of the others, and the fact that the Seal and the scroll were evidently placed together in the box may also affect their valuation. No doubt there will be all kinds of theories as to why these items were buried in the ground." He paused for a moment and then simply added, "I am really glad you came to show them to me. I am only sorry I cannot help you further, but do keep in touch please, and let me know what it is that the experts advise."

With that the Rev. Andrew Makinson thanked them all for taking the trouble to visit him with such an interesting discovery. Archie told him that, on the contrary, they should be thanking him. Reaching into the pocket of his coat, he took out a bank note and gave it to Andrew Makinson. "Please accept this belated contribution to your church's Christmas collection, vicar. You really have been most helpful."

Archie, Bernie and Ailsa took their leave and set off back to Edinburgh. If they had not already appreciated it, they were certainly now conscious of the responsibility they were carrying.

Chapter Ten
Peer Pressure

As they boarded the carriage back into Edinburgh, Archie informed Bernie and Ailsa that they would need to wait until the following morning for a safe and comfortable coach to Glasgow. They had spent rather more time than he had expected in visiting the Rev. Andrew Makinson and he did not advise two such attractive young ladies to join an afternoon coach between the two cities, especially with valuable possessions and particularly at this time of the year, when much of their journey would take place after dark. Instead he suggested that, if they would like to join him for the evening, he would be delighted to take them to the newly-opened Edinburgh Caledonian Club for dinner. He was only sorry to be having to leave them to travel to Glasgow without him, owing to the meeting he had to attend at his firm's office tomorrow morning.

During the evening he told the girls a little about Edinburgh's business community and how rapidly it had been growing in recent years. Companies like the Scottish Widows insurance company had started up in the past twenty years and been so successful that they were now not only expanding their operations in Edinburgh, and investing in property in the city's prime business district, but were also starting to open branches in other cities like Glasgow, Aberdeen and Dundee. He mentioned that the salaries being paid to some of their most successful managers were thought to exceed two thousand pounds a year. Bernie and Ailsa gasped. Bernie had thought that her own total income of seventy pounds a month was extremely generous, and she was only achieving this by taking a lucrative second job on her day off every week. As for Ailsa, she was still only earning two pounds a week. Archie regretted for a moment that he had ever mentioned any details of Edinburgh salaries and hurriedly changed the subject.

"What do you think Theo will make of the Seal?" he asked Bernie. "I can't imagine," replied Bernie, reflecting for a moment on what she had heard and seen in his shop.

"I suppose it will depend on what kind of mood he's in. He can be very critical at times and I just hope he decides it will attract the kind of interest that we all think it might. If he does, it seems he can be very influential. I've already noticed how he seems able to set the market prices for rare jewels arriving in the country for the first time. I would guess that our very unusual treasure might be a bit like that." Ailsa looked open-mouthed at her sister – she hadn't realised how much Bernie had learned about business and commerce since leaving home. She was starting to sound like a business woman, not a governess.

"I do think we need to make the most of the mystique surrounding our particular treasure," agreed Archie. "From what you say, I think Theo sounds like exactly the right kind of dealer to help us achieve that."

* * * *

They were up early next morning for Bernie and Ailsa to take a coach to Glasgow. Archie escorted them to the coach terminus, where they found a mass of coaches and carriages of different sizes with their horses all fed, watered and harnessed ready for whatever journey was required. Archie led the girls down the line before selecting a coachman whose face he recognised.

"Good morning, I believe you brought me back from my island a few months ago. Very comfortable journey I recall. Now would you care to take my two sisters to Glasgow please," he said, brandishing a five-pound note.

"Very good sir, thank you very much sir," replied the coachman, pocketing his best fare for some weeks. "Let me give you a hand up, ladies." And he helped Bernie and Ailsa up into a well-sprung seat in his carriage and lifted their overnight bags and knapsack into the coach beside them as Archie watched, calling out, "Safe journey, sisters," much to their amusement as he waved them farewell.

As the coach rolled away through Edinburgh's fine residential new town, Bernie turned to Ailsa and just said, "If only Ma and Pa could see us now."

And Ailsa simply replied, "The way you're going, sis, you're going to have to get used to this."

* * * *

Archie was left with an empty feeling in his stomach as he made his way back to his town house. He had so enjoyed having Bernie and Ailsa to stay with him and the visit to Andrew Makinson in Musselburgh could not have gone better. However, he now needed to turn his attention to his professional work, conscious that his meeting that morning was with the senior partner of the firm, Sir James Anstruther, and probably one or two of the other partners. He hurried back home so he could have a wash and a cup of his favourite coffee before making his way to the office. As he opened his front door, he noticed a handful of letters lying on the doormat inside. He would have a look at those this evening, he decided.

There was also plenty of business correspondence on his desk at the office, which had piled up while he was away. He spent much of the morning attending to this, mainly enquiries from clients regarding the various issues pertaining to the Scottish heritable property law on which he was generally considered to have become very knowledgeable of late. At half-past eleven he was summoned to his meeting, which he was surprised to find was attended by four other partners in addition to Sir James. He was welcomed to the meeting by Sir James and invited to take his seat.

"You are probably wondering why we have asked you to join us this morning, MacDonell," Sir James began. "For some months we have been reviewing our partnership and the volume of clients we now seem to be attracting. The load upon each of us has become almost intolerable. I myself was only able to take two months' holiday last year and very few of us have been able to take more than three months. MacKenzie here missed the grouse season altogether last summer. Meanwhile we have noticed that you are earning considerable fee income for the practice through your expertise in heritable property and related matters and we would like to offer you a partnership in Anstruther and MacTaggart on terms which we have set out in this contract." Sir James passed a document comprising several pages of script across to Archie, who started to read it. "No, don't try and read it now, MacDonell, please take it away and read it carefully, but we all hope and trust that you will deem it an honour to join the partnership and will play your full part in taking our firm forward to a great future."

The partners talked pleasantries around the table for a while, following which Sir James offered to take Archie to his club for lunch, which Archie happily accepted. The two of them talked over lunch about the rapid growth of Edinburgh's professional and financial services companies and the opportunities for further expansion. "I was sorry to learn of the sad death of your brother, by the way. A shooting accident, was it?" said Sir James. Archie grimaced and nodded. "Does that mean you're now heir to your father's estate?" Sir James enquired.

"Yes, as a matter of fact I am," replied Archie, wondering how much of a factor this was in their choice of him as the next new partner in the firm.

Thanking Sir James again for the offer, and the lunch, Archie took his leave and left the office early that afternoon to make his way back to his house, taking with him the contract he had been offered. He would read it carefully tonight and give it his consideration. It was a pity he hadn't received the offer before he left for the holiday season, as that would have given him the opportunity to seek his father's advice, and indeed his mother's. As he opened his front door, he remembered there were a number of letters waiting for him to open. Perhaps he should take a look at these before he did anything else.

* * * *

As he sorted through the envelopes Archie immediately noticed, to his concern, one bearing his own mother's unmistakeable hand-writing. His mother never wrote to him these days, not like she did when he first went away to Harrow. What could be the matter, he wondered? He immediately tore this open, fearing perhaps his father's health again. He'd only left them last week, he thought for a moment, as he started to read. It was dated 6th January, the day he had left the island with Bernie and Ailsa, and was the shortest letter he had ever received from his mother. It read as follows:-

'My dearest Archie, I learned today that you will be receiving an important letter from your grandfather, Lord Moncrieffe. Please accept his generous suggestion. It would give your father and myself both great pleasure and pride. Your ever-loving mama'.

Archie searched through the other letters. He had no idea what his grandfather's handwriting looked like but there didn't seem to be anything that looked like a personal letter. He looked through them all once again, and then noticed that the last one had a mark on the envelope representing the portcullis of Parliament. It was also tightly sealed with somebody's personal Seal. *Just like the Seal of Promise*, Archie thought, as he opened it and read:-

My dear Archibald, I trust you are well. I understand from your mother that is the case. It is my pleasure to inform you that I am recommending you for a Peerage. We have for some

149

little while lacked adequate Tory representation amongst the sixteen Scottish Peers who, as I am sure you are aware, carry the onus placed upon us under the terms of the Act of Union of ensuring that the Parliament of Great Britain adequately represents Scottish interests. With your standing as a Writer to the Signet and now as heir to your father's Moidart estate, you are peculiarly well qualified. I should therefore be obliged if you would write to me by return post and advise me of your acceptance. Baron Moncrieffe of Aberfeldy in the County of Perthshire.

Archie read the letter twice and then wondered what he had done to merit such an extraordinary pair of offers as he had received that day. He was quite unable to sleep at all that night. He was honoured to have been offered a partnership in the law firm to which he had given so much of his time, and for which he had burned so many candles studying over the years. It was exactly the position for which he had been striving. And now, by a remarkable coincidence and on the very same day, he was even more honoured to have been offered a peerage too. Which did he want to accept, he wondered? Could he take both? And, he reminded himself, now that they had lost poor Euan, he was also destined to become the Laird of Moidart and Eilean Shona one day. It was all too much.

Meanwhile, he couldn't altogether stop wondering how Bernie and Ailsa had got on at Kirks the jewellers in Glasgow. Had they arrived safely? Had Kirk agreed to look after the Seal hoard? Was he able to arrange the insurance? Archie tossed and turned all night and eventually, at five in the morning, reluctantly abandoned any thought of sleeping. He rose, put on a clean shirt and walked across the new town of Edinburgh to the office where he had the previous day been offered a partnership. A night watchman answered the door and let him in. "You're early this morning, sir," was the extent of his greeting for Archie.

Archie pulled a sheet of paper from the drawer of his office desk and wrote a short note marked, 'Strictly

Confidential' and addressed to Sir James Anstruther. It read as follows:

"Sir, I was honoured to receive your kind offer yesterday to join the partnership of Anstruther & MacTaggart. I am minded to accept but, privately, I have to tell you that I also received an indication yesterday that I am being considered for appointment to the House of Lords as one of a very small number of new Scottish peers. I do not wish to accept either of these prestigious positions without very careful consideration, nor without discussion with my family. For this reason, I should be grateful if you would allow me leave of absence from the office for the next two weeks. I hope, Sir James, that you will understand my position and that you will be happy to grant me such leave in these circumstances. I remain, sir, your obedient servant, Archibald MacDonell."

Archie sealed his letter to Sir James Anstruther and placed it in Sir James's mail box outside his office. He then walked out on to the street and made his way to the coach terminus. Standing at the very spot from which he had bidden farewell to Bernie and Ailsa the previous morning, he waited only a few minutes for another of the new coaches in which the girls had themselves travelled. "To Kirks the jewellers, Glasgow, please," was the instruction he gave to the coachman.

Six hours later his coach rolled into Glasgow and made its way to Kirks. He was pleased that the coachman knew the location of the shop, even more so that he mentioned how all the well-to-do people in Glasgow knew of it. "It's famous, sir," he said, as they pulled in to a spot a few yards from Kirks' front door.

"I'm told they stock the most beautiful, exotic and fashionable jewellery, and the shows they do with a model on Saturday afternoons bring all the rich ladies out. I've had plenty of good business myself from them, sir. They say the model is only a poor crofter's daughter from the isles, but she's certainly making a difference to Kirks. There, here you are sir, that will be two guineas, sir, if you don't mind."

"What, only two guineas, all the way from Edinburgh?" came Archie's response. "Look, here's three pounds and may I wish you a good day. You have certainly made my day," he added as he strode up to Kirks' front door.

The doorman who the previous day had swiftly opened the jewellers' front door to Bernie and her sister, now peered cautiously at Archie. "Can I help you, sir?" he enquired as he opened the door a few inches on the chain.

"Oh, yes please. I've come to see Miss Bernadette Neish and her sister."

"That's what they're all saying now. Sorry, sir, I'm under strict instructions..." The doorman's voice tailed off as Bernie herself appeared behind him, calling out,

"Och, Archie, wha' are you doing here? Come on in." Archie entered with a forgiving nod to the doorman, and he and Bernie embraced one another for several seconds while staff and customers looked on in amazement. "Well," she repeated, "what are you doing here?"

* * * *

Bernie led Archie through to a small changing room at the rear of the shop, which, she explained to Archie, was her base every Saturday when she gave her demonstrations of how to wear Kirks' glamorous jewellery to greatest effect. When Archie finished staring around him, she asked him for a third time, "Well, my dear Archie, what ARE you doing here?" She realised too late how familiar she was being with the son of her Laird. And then she realised that he was indeed very dear to her. Meanwhile Archie was going through the same thought process.

"Bernie, I've got so much to tell you. Can we go somewhere? Where's Ailsa? What happened about the Seal?" The questions all came pouring out.

"Archie, what do you mean, you've got so much to tell me? We only saw one another yesterday, and the day before, and the day before that. Anyhow, yes, and I've got plenty to tell you. Can we go somewhere quiet? I've actually finished here for the day, so shall we go across to the coffee house? I can tell you everything there." And Bernie held onto Archie's arm as they walked out of the front door of Kirks together, to the doorman's astonishment.

* * * *

"Ailsa's gone home," she said as they crossed the road to a quiet, friendly little coffee house. "She was worrying about her mother and Mr Kirk was so thrilled to see our Seal and everything, that he kindly arranged a carriage to take her home. He's done that for me once or twice. Yes, Theo was amazed at what we've brought. He thinks the hoard as a whole is worth a fortune. He's arranged the insurance on it and, wait for it, he's asked me to go to London where he's opened a shop now in a place called Hatton Garden. He wants to put the Seal and the scroll and the whole hoard on display and he wants me there to speak about it and tell our story. He also wants me to do a few modelling sessions there each week. It's a brilliant idea, Arch. So I'm going to London, I'm so excited!"

Archie suddenly felt deflated. He was tired after all his own excitement, after his journey, and now, after the joy of being reunited with Bernie, he was going to lose her to London. But he couldn't help but be pleased for Bernie. She was developing a new career; he certainly mustn't stand in her way. And then he thought again. Isn't London where the House of Lords meets? Of course it is, he realised. Perhaps they could meet up in London sometimes. He didn't feel quite so tired now.

"Bernie, I've got exciting things to tell you too," he said. And he took her through the extraordinary day that he had just had.

"So which are you going to do?" she asked. "Will you be a lawyer in Edinburgh, or a Lord in London? I know which I'd prefer," she said, with a grin that extended right across her face.

"You don't get to choose," Archie replied. "I'll tell you in good time. I haven't even spoken to my father yet, although I gather Mama had something to do with it. Or her father, my grandfather, did."

"Is that how it works?" asked Bernie.

* * * *

They sat and drank coffee, and then they just sat and held hands. Bernie was so happy for Archie, and Archie was equally happy for Bernie. He had made up his mind now to accept the peerage. Maybe his aunt in Dorset Square would put him up while he sorted himself out with somewhere to live. "That's all right for you," said Bernie, "I don't have any aunts in Dorset Square. Or anywhere near London," she countered.

"Don't worry," he assured her. "We'll find somewhere for you before long, I'm sure. And anyhow, forget about all that," he added. "That's all in the future. More to the point is where are we going to stay tonight?"

"Well, I've got my bed at the Galbraiths. In fact, I'd better be getting over there or they'll wonder whether I've already left for London."

"So you've told them already, have you? I'll bet they'll be sorry to see you go."

"Yes, and I'll be sorry to leave them, and of course their lovely children. It's been like having my own family, which I've never had. I'm thirty now and all I've done is teach and look after other people's bairns. By the way, there's plenty of room at the Galbraiths, so if you ask nicely, I'll try and persuade them to let you stay there as well. Come along, my Lord, we'd better be going."

Chapter Eleven
New Challenges

The Galbraiths welcomed Archie as though he was their own son and thanked Bernie for bringing him back with her. It took a few moments for Bernie to explain how she had come to be spending the afternoon in Glasgow with the Laird's son from Eilean Shona, but by this time the Galbraiths had got used to Bernie doing extraordinary things. They were only sorry that her latest career move was taking her down south. The children would all miss her terribly. "Oh, I'm not going to disappear completely," she told them. She would be back to give them some more of those horrible spelling tests, she assured them.

They had arrived just in time to join the Galbraith family for dinner. A maid had promptly laid extra places at the table and Archie was placed between Fiona Galbraith and her young son Donald, now aged eleven, while Bernie sat with Iain Galbraith and the girls, Isobel and Hannah. By this time the grown-ups had all shared a wee dram, which Archie found was helping to revive him. He did not let on that he had had no sleep at all in the past thirty-six hours.

Before long the conversation turned to their friends the Kirks' rapid expansion of their jewellery business. Iain Galbraith had known Theo Kirk since they were teenagers and said he could tell all along that Theo would do well for himself. He was always on the look-out for a chance to make a profit. It didn't surprise Iain that Theo had spotted the opportunity presented by the discovery, all around the expanding British empire, of many fine and rare jewels. Communities like the tobacco barons of Glasgow and the cotton and shipping magnates of Manchester and Liverpool could not resist the power of distinctive jewellery in attracting and adorning their womenfolk. It was no coincidence that Glasgow and Liverpool were the first two cities in which Theo Kirk had opened up shops, nor that he was now in the process of opening a third, in the heart of Hatton Garden, the hub of London's jewellery trade. At this point Bernie, anxious to bring the children into the conversation, asked them, "What are all you children going to do when you grow up?"

Isobel was the first to answer. "From what I've seen, I think I'd like to be a jewellery model, like you, Miss Bernie."

"Sorry, that job's taken, Izzy, you're too late," came Bernie's rapid response. Isobel looked downcast for a moment, but then countered with,

"Well, in that case I'll be the jeweller." Bernie, for once, had no answer.

Hannah also wanted to be a model, but she thought she'd like to wear the latest dresses, not just the jewellery. And Donald wanted to be a ship owner. He had seen the wonderful ships that sailed day after day in and out of the River Clyde. The children all had ideas about what they wanted to do. Was this Bernie's influence on them, Archie couldn't help wondering? And then finally he yawned – to his acute embarrassment, in front of these very kind hosts, he yawned a huge gaping yawn.

"Archie's tired," said Bernie, coming to his rescue. "You've had a busy couple of days, my love, haven't you? Would you mind, Mrs Galbraith, if we retire?" And, for a moment, Archie then wondered whether he was going to be shown to Bernie's bedroom. It was not to be. He soon found that another room, at the furthest end of the corridor, had been hastily prepared for him while they were dining.

* * * *

Archie fell asleep as soon as he hit the bed and slept soundly all night until he experienced a strange dream in which he and Bernie, in the rough clothes in which they had

156

attempted to cope with Shona Craig all those years ago, were being welcomed into the House of Lords and someone was asking him if he would like a cup of tea. He was hurriedly trying to remember the correct procedure for accepting a cup of tea in the Lords, when he realised it was one of the Galbraiths' maids who was kindly bringing him his morning tea tray. He pulled himself together, tried to remember where he was, and how he had got there, and then enjoyed the very pleasant China tea on offer.

He was back to his normal self by the time he came down to breakfast – a splendid array of porridge, kippers, salmon and various delicacies that he didn't immediately recognise. He supposed that the well-to-do in Glasgow enjoyed the best of both local Scottish fare and also food such as fruits and exotic spices which were brought into Glasgow on the trading ships. There was plenty of it too, perhaps rather more than the family could ever be expected to eat themselves, but happily consumed as 'left-overs' by the ever-hungry house staff. Clearly this was one of the attractions of being 'in service', particularly for girls from some of Glasgow's most deprived districts.

Archie decided that he would make his way to Kirks for a short while that morning before picking up a coach to take him home. It would be a good opportunity to introduce himself to Theo Kirk and have a word with him about what approach he thought they should take with the Seal hoard. As he got up from the breakfast table, he complimented and thanked Fiona Galbraith for her generous hospitality and wished her and her husband a good day. And then he turned to Bernie and asked whether she was ready to leave. All he received in return was a rather sullen, "No, not today."

As he boarded his coach back into town, Archie wondered quite what he had said or done – or maybe not done – to upset Bernie. But in the meantime, he had things to do, which could not wait. He would still go straight to Kirks and introduce himself, perhaps he might also be able to find a small gift for the Galbraiths for their kind hospitality while he was there. And then he must make haste back to Eilean Shona. The conversation he needed to have with his mother and father, and also with his sisters, could not wait much longer.

Bernie had a private meeting arranged with Theo Kirk that morning, which was why she was not able to accompany Archie back into Glasgow. Theo had asked her to meet him at his home so he could discuss details of her London contract and confirm her salary details with him. Bernie had never been to the Kirks' home and she was bowled over when the coach turned into the long sweeping drive of their beautiful Georgian mansion. If this was how jewellers lived, then she was certainly going to stay with the trade.

Theo was at the door himself when she alighted from the coach and he welcomed her with a warm embrace, explaining that his wife Ruth was away for a few days. He showed Bernie through to the morning room which looked straight out onto a spacious lawn, behind which all she could see were woods. It was all very private and secluded. Theo invited her to take a seat on the sofa and then picked up a carefully scripted contract and sat down beside her to talk it through.

Bernie was glad she had chosen to wear a well-buttoned blouse and full-length skirt that morning. Theo started to go through the proposed contract with her. Bernie wasn't really listening. She heard him say 'flexible hours' and 'higher salary for her personal performance' as well as 'the excitement of London life'. He was proposing to be in London every other week so that he could combine his business interests there with his responsibilities in Glasgow and Liverpool. He would purchase a flat in a desirable part of the City for her exclusive use. He would not expect her to bear any of the costs of maintaining this apartment.

All Bernie could think about was how she could keep Theo at bay whilst not losing the opportunity of landing this prestigious and lucrative role in the capital. "We'll come on to your actual salary in a moment," he said, as he reached over and touched one of her pearl earrings. "These, my dear, were one of the first pair we stocked when I first opened my shop in Glasgow. They are simple but beautiful and they look lovely on your perfectly formed head." He moved right across her as he added, "and as you have yourself blossomed into the most beautiful lady I have ever known…"

At this point Bernie cut him off, moving away to the other end of the sofa and then standing up and straightening her clothes. "Mr Kirk, I am very willing to work for you as your shop assistant or your prime promotional manager or model, here or in London, provided the terms are attractive to me. But I am not willing to be your lover, still less any man's mistress when his wife happens to be out of the way. Would you please give me the remaining details of the professional offer you are making to me, before I write to Mrs Kirk regretting that for reasons she would not wish to hear, I am no longer able to continue working in her husband's business."

For a moment she wasn't quite sure where those words, and her tone, had come from. Was she back in Eilean Shona School, bossing the young children and teaching them a lesson? Whatever it was, it seemed to have had the desired effect on Theo Kirk, who now looked shaken and less than five foot tall.

"Of course, Bernie, er Bernadette, I quite forgot myself. I'm er sorry, I do apologise. I promise I won't ever do that again. Now, as to your salary, would a hundred pounds a month be acceptable to you in London? I do understand your—"

"One hundred pounds?" responded Bernie, cutting Theo off. "That won't go very far in London, from what Lord MacDonell has told me." She paused for a moment, wondering whether she had jumped the gun referring to Archie's title. But Theo was now only concerned with his own reputation.

"Well, would two hundred, no, three hundred pounds a month be acceptable?"

"Three hundred pounds is fine, Theo, with good quality living accommodation as you were saying earlier. That will be fine. Did you want to complete that contract now?" And so Bernadette Neish was signed up to work as principal fashion and jewellery model and adviser to Kirks, the Jewellers, Hatton Garden, for a salary of three hundred pounds a month, with all her living expenses covered in London and three return carriage journeys a year to her home in Eilean Shona thrown in for good measure.

* * * *

Archie, meanwhile, had arrived at Kirks and asked a man on the front desk if Mr Kirk was available for a brief word about the Seal hoard his friend Bernadette Neish and her sister had recently brought in. "Oh, yes sir," came the reply. "I know the items you're referring to. I'm afraid they're all under lock and key and nobody can touch them without Mr Kirk or Miss Neish's approval. I'm afraid neither of them is in this morning, sir. Is there anything else I can help you with this morning, sir?"

"Well, yes, as a matter of fact there is," replied Archie. "Those delicate, very pretty flower vases over there. I wonder if you could send, er, I think that one there – I wonder if you could send that to a Mrs Galbraith for me this morning – I'll give you the address – with the following message: 'With most grateful thanks for an excellent evening and overnight stay, from your uninvited guest'. I think that will be all."

Archie then picked up his bag, paid for his purchase, and set off in search of the next stage-coach to Fort William. He hoped it would reach there that evening and that he would be home by tomorrow afternoon. He had so much to discuss with his parents.

* * * *

Bernie escaped from Theo Kirk's house without any further alarms and as she boarded the coach to take her back to the Galbraiths, she congratulated herself on having escaped with her dignity and her London contract intact. She didn't want to lose the patronage of Theo Kirk, who for the time being held all the keys to her future career, but she hoped that from now on her relationship with him would be purely professional. She felt confident that would be the case.

160

She now needed to confirm her notice arrangements with Fiona Galbraith and when she went to speak with her, she was pleased to find her alone in the drawing-room, carefully unwrapping a parcel which had been sent to her by Kirks. What could this be? Who at Kirks would be sending something to her today, she was wondering? It wasn't her birthday... By this time, Fiona Galbraith had finished unwrapping a beautiful cut glass flower vase and was reading the message which accompanied it. "With most grateful thanks for an excellent evening and overnight stay, from your uninvited guest," she read out aloud.

"He really is such a gentleman," she said, looking Bernie in the eye.

* * * *

Archie's journey home, though long and arduous, went according to plan. He was able to sleep well at the coaching inn near Fort William, and was beginning to recover from the excitements and stresses of the past few days when he finally reached Eilean Shona. It was three o'clock in the afternoon, time for the winter sun to disappear beneath the rocks looking over towards Farquhar's Point and the Ardnamurchan peninsula beyond. His parents had not expected him back in the island so soon after his Christmas and New Year stay, although letters had of course been exchanged regarding his grandfather's kind offer of a seat in the Lords.

His mother in particular was thrilled to see him back home. They had so much to discuss, she said to him, still unaware of the offer of a partnership in Anstruthers' legal practice, not to speak of the developments in his relationship with Bernie. "We must have a good talk with your father," she said, "as soon as we can. He's still not very well, I'm afraid, and we eat early these days so he can retire to bed afterwards."

Tea was brought into the drawing-room by Gertie as soon as Archie's bags had been unloaded off the trap which had met the ferry boat. Alastair MacDonell greeted Archie without getting up out of his chair, saying how tired he looked after the coach journey. Archie refrained from commenting on how weary his father looked. The three of them sat for a few minutes, talking of the weather and the lengths of these winters.

And then Archie brought them up to date. He had duly received Lord Moncrieffe's kind letter and of course he was minded to accept. "By the way, Mama, thank you so much for writing in the way you did," he added. But he had also, on the very same day, received a formal offer of a full partnership in Anstruthers, who were now expanding fast on the back of the rapid growth of Edinburgh as a business city. He also mentioned briefly what a useful conversation they had with Makinson, Euan's old army friend, regarding the Seal of Promise hoard and that Bernadette had told him how highly Theo Kirk, the Glasgow jeweller, valued that whole hoard.

"Oh, so she's shown it to him now, has she?" said Lady Elspeth. "When did she do that?"

"She and Ailsa took it straight there the next day while I was at my partnership meeting in Edinburgh, and I called in to see her and Theo Kirk on my way home. She kindly arranged with the Galbraiths, who she works for, for them to give me dinner and a room for the night before I boarded my coach yesterday. They have been so impressed with Bernie."

"I think you have too, my son, by the sound of things," commented the Laird. "Don't blame you. She's a remarkable woman, that Bernadette. I've heard nothing but good when it comes to her — and her sister too, what's her name?"

"Ailsa, Papa," replied Archie.

"That's the one. What those two have done with our little school is amazing, so good for all our youngsters. Nothing short of excellent, I've heard."

"Yes, well, Papa, of course the school was all your idea in the first place, but I agree that the Neish sisters have done a good job; and yes, Ma, I do hope to keep in touch with Bernie," admitted Archie. "You're right, I am quite sweet on her, but I'm not sure how she feels about me. Anyhow, what I wanted to talk to you both about are these offers I have — I'm being asked to become a peer and a partner at the same time."

"Well, you can't refuse a peerage, especially not after all my papa has done to arrange it," intervened Lady Elspeth.

"Yes, of course, Mama," said Archie. Whereupon Margaret and Annie entered the room, having come back from a tea arranged by Ailsa at the school to raise money for the families affected by the cholera outbreak last autumn.

"Hello, darling brother, how lovely to have you back here. What's happened?"

"Your brother has just heard that he's going to be made a Lord," explained their mother. "And now we're also hearing he's being made a partner in his law firm. Hasn't he done well, girls?"

"He certainly has. Well done, Arch," replied Annie. "Isn't it funny how things happen in two's?"

"No, Annie, that's not right," her sister Margaret corrected. "Things happen in threes, not twos." And with that they made their way through to the dining-room for their early evening meal.

* * * *

Alastair wasn't the only one who retired early to bed that evening. Archie did so too. He was relieved to have heard his parents' reactions to recent events, especially his father's relaxed attitude to his relationship with Bernie. But in the middle of the night he heard his mother calling from his parents' bedroom.

"Archie, Margaret, Annie, come quickly all of you. Your father's had another of his attacks. I don't know what to do. Will that mixture help? Are you all right Alastair?"

But Alastair clearly wasn't at all right. Margaret ran straight down to fetch Ma Neish, who they had heard was good with sudden attacks. She came hurrying up to The House, carrying one of her husband's half-empty bottles of whisky and some of the cholera mixture that the Galbraiths had given Bernie. But it was too late. Alastair had had another attack, in the arms of his beloved Lady Elspeth, and he would breathe no more. He had died at the age of just sixty, proud husband and father, and a popular and successful Laird of Moidart and Eilean Shona. Archie would now have to be a Laird, as well as a lawyer and a Lord.

* * * *

Alastair would not have wanted a big funeral but it was difficult to avoid giving him one. After some lengthy discussion Lady Elspeth decided that, as her husband had been Laird of Moidart and not just Eilean Shona, they should hold it at Mingarry rather than in the tiny island kirk on Shona. The church at Mingarry was not large but it would accommodate many more mourners than the local kirk.

It was also agreed to delay the service for a few weeks to avoid the worst of the winter weather for those travelling – this would also enable Alastair's wide circle of old friends from around the country to make the journey, including the many fellow Lairds from around the Scottish Highlands with whom he had maintained regular contact. Many of the island residents would also wish to be there, of course, but a fleet of coaches and traps could be arranged in order to transport them there and back home afterwards.

So the service took place at Mingarry, twelve weeks later. In the meantime, Alastair's death was reported in the local newspaper and in The Scotsman and The Times. There followed a stream of letters of sympathy, which Lady Elspeth found difficult to read. They brought home to her just how much she was going to miss her husband, although they appreciated she would continue to have the support of her son Archibald and her daughters. One so-called acquaintance upset her even more by revealing that they were unaware she had also lost Euan, saying how she would no doubt gain strength from his support as Alastair's heir. After this Lady Elspeth found it difficult even to open some of the large pile of letters on her desk.

Archie's role in all this was crucial, and it was not easy for him. He found himself having to open all his mother's mail and check there was nothing too distressing for her to see. He soon decided he now had no option other than to base himself on the island for the foreseeable future. He wrote immediately to Lord Moncrieffe, saying how honoured he felt to accept his very kind offer of the peerage, but informing him that as his father had died, he needed to stay at home to support his mother, at least for the time being. He also wrote to Sir James Anstruther to inform him of his father's sudden death and apologise for his unavoidable absence for a while. And naturally he also wrote to Bernie, at the Galbraiths' address, to inform her.

All three wrote back immediately. Moncrieffe, who naturally wrote separately to Lady Elspeth as well, said how shocked he was and urged Archie to stay at home with his mother as long as he could. He and the other Scottish Tory peers should be able to handle the situation in the party in these circumstances. Sir James wrote in similar vein. He noted that Archie would now want time to spend with his family, and to adjust to the extra calls on his time, but he felt sure his partners would fully understand the additional burdens that would now fall upon Archie. He sent his condolences and those of all the firm's partners. And Bernie had also written to say she would be back on the island as soon as she possibly could. She sent her regards and sympathy to Lady Elspeth and all their family, and she looked forward to meeting the new Laird. Her final comment made him smile, for the first time in days.

* * * *

The funeral service at Mingarry was so well attended that most of the contingent from the island had to stand throughout the service. Apart from those reserved for family and very close friends at the front, every pew was fully occupied at least half an hour before the funeral was due to begin.

The service was conducted by a priest from the local area and Father Tom was once again called out of retirement to lead the prayers. The coffin was borne into the church by four of the Laird's longest-serving staff – Ritchie, Brown,

Machray and Mackay – and followed by the family. Archie escorted his mother, who was bravely fighting back tears, and they were followed up the aisle by Margaret and Annie who both wept throughout the service. Behind them came Lord Moncrieffe with his elder daughter, Lady Elspeth's sister Lady Hermione. Moncrieffe and Lady Hermione had travelled up from London in the stage-coach and planned to stay for two or three days. Lady Elspeth was pleased that they were willing to do so, but wished it could have been in happier circumstances and at a better time of year. Despite delaying the funeral as long as they could, many of the older mourners were shivering in the icy March wind.

Archie was invited to deliver the eulogy and he spoke movingly of his father's achievements. No laird could have done more for the well-being of the community into which he was born. Archie paid tribute to 'a wonderful husband, father and Laird'. One of his first initiatives for Eilean Shona had been to establish a free school for all the children and, thanks to a succession of excellent and devoted teachers, a whole generation of young islanders had been given the best possible start in life. He had also insisted on creating a playing-field on the island, which had led on to the establishment of one of Eilean Shona's greatest traditions, its own version of Highland Games, known locally as the Island Games 'if you could notice the difference'. There was a chuckle from the congregation at this, and another when he admitted that his father's generosity in arranging for Ritchie to set up a free bar every year at the Island Games had 'cost some of us the last vestige of any dignity we ever had'.

He finished by paying a special tribute to his mother, Lady Elspeth, who had not only been the rock around which his father's life had revolved for so many years, but had also helped to create an immensely strong sense of community leadership way beyond their own family's activities. He knew from talking with many of today's mourners from mainland Moidart how much his parents were both admired all across the district.

After the service was over, tea and sandwiches were served in the nearby manse, where the family were overwhelmed by the generosity of personal tributes and happy memories recalled by men, women and children from all over Moidart. Archie stayed close to Lady Elspeth throughout the reception, conscious that the ordeal was not yet over for her. Everyone seemed to want to say a friendly word or two about her husband, and there were many people whose names she did not even know but whose lives had apparently been touched by this very caring Laird.

Archie could not help hearing these kind, personal tributes, nor could Bernie and Ailsa and their mother avoid listening when waiting in line while others spoke to Lady Elspeth or Archie. When it was their turn, Lady Elspeth said – looking straight at Bernie – how delighted she was that they had all been able to be here. She added that she looked forward to catching up again soon. Bernie, who had only managed to return home the previous day, resisted the temptation to give Archie a big kiss, realising just in time that it might not be appropriate at this particular time. But it was apparent that she was very proud of Archie's own tribute. He was going to make a brilliant Laird himself – she knew that now, if she hadn't known it all along.

* * * *

Lord Moncrieffe and his elder daughter Hermione stayed at Eilean Shona House for three nights and Elspeth was glad they did. It was the first time they had all three been together for years. Fortunately, the weather picked up the next day, with the gulf stream kindly bestowing its favours once more in the shape of a mild west wind. Moncrieffe announced at breakfast that he and Hermione would like to see as much of the island as possible, and perhaps meet a few of the local community.

An obvious starting-point was the school, so they and Lady Elspeth set off in that direction after breakfast. They were almost there when Moncrieffe asked whether it would come as too much of a shock for the children if they just walked in uninvited. Lady Elspeth didn't think that would be a problem but she went on ahead and crept quietly in at the back of the class. She hadn't seen the school at work for a long while and was amazed to find not just one Miss Neish, but two, both hard at work helping some twenty children who were all busily writing, or drawing pictures, to record personal memories of the late Laird. They could not have arrived at a better time, Ailsa told Lady Elspeth, and Bernie agreed that it would be lovely if Lord Moncrieffe and Lady Hermione could come in as well and see what the children were doing.

So in they came and Ailsa began by introducing her elder sister Bernadette, who explained that she had been in charge of the school herself for a few years but had handed over to Ailsa when she moved to Glasgow to take up a position in the jewellery trade. She enjoyed helping her sister whenever she was at home on the island. Lady Hermione was particularly interested in the reference to jewellery and stopped to speak with Bernie, while Ailsa introduced Lord Moncrieffe to each of the children in turn.

One child, a boy called Angus, was near to completing an excellent portrait of the late Laird, drawn just as he recalled seeing him, riding a horse on the beach and splashing through the shallow sea. Moncrieffe asked Angus how long he had been drawing pictures and was told by the boy that he had always done it, he couldn't remember not doing it. Now eleven years old, young Angus had decided he was going to be a great artist. He had studied the paintings of Gainsborough and Constable and learned from their work.

Lord Moncrieffe congratulated Angus and told him to keep at it. He then moved on and spoke to a young girl called Bess who had written a beautiful paragraph about what Laird Alastair had done for the island. In it she said he had thought a lot about the young people and given them places to learn and play, which they never had before. Some of the smaller children needed a bit of help with talking to these important people but Ailsa said afterwards how pleased she was that they had come. It was a great experience for the children, and much better that the visitors had just turned up. If they had known in advance that they were going to have visitors coming to ask them questions, the children wouldn't have been themselves. They would have been much too nervous.

* * * *

That evening, over a light supper, Archie asked his mother, and his grandfather and aunt, whether they had enjoyed their day. They evidently had, and the visit to the school had clearly been the highlight. The existence of the school was itself a tribute to Alastair, not only in the sense that it had been his initiative in the first place but also that, for an island the size of Eilean Shona, it was quite an achievement to have been able to maintain such an excellent school for so many years. Lord Moncrieffe said how impressed he had been with Angus's portrait of Alastair and Lady Elspeth had been touched by the little essay by Bess. The girl was correct in saying that Alastair had thought a great deal about helping the young people of the island.

After all the stress and distress she had endured in recent weeks, Lady Elspeth now seemed to be almost back to her old self. With the weather still mild, she enquired of both her father and sister what else they would like to do while they were here. Lord Moncrieffe said he would be interested to talk a little more with the schoolteacher Ailsa about how she approaches the task of teaching so many children of different ages simultaneously. He had gathered that the other young lady who was helping her was only doing so whilst she was home for the funeral service, but Ailsa herself must have developed techniques which could be of interest to educationalists more widely.

Hermione added that the lady who was helping out – was her name Bernadette? – was interesting to talk to as well. Apparently, she had been in charge of the school for some while and was now specialising in exotic jewellery in Glasgow and London. Archie smiled to himself to hear them singing the praises of the Neish sisters and couldn't help but look in the direction of his mother.

"Well, why don't we ask Ailsa and Bernadette to join us for supper tomorrow," suggested Lady Elspeth to Archie's surprise. "You're quite friendly with them, aren't you Archie? Would you like to invite them up?"

"Certainly, Mama. I'm not sure quite how long Bernadette is planning to stay but I'll get a message to them in the morning and see how they're placed."

"Tell them not to dress up," Lady Elspeth added.

* * * *

Archie managed to get a message to Bernie before she and Ailsa went off to open up the school next morning. He had her reply within an hour. It was her last day before leaving tomorrow to return to Glasgow, but she and Ailsa would be delighted to join Lady Elspeth and the family at The Big House that evening. She had much enjoyed talking to his Aunt Hermione the previous morning and would be delighted to meet Archie's grandfather too. They would come in their teaching clothes unless they heard to the contrary.

Despite all that had happened over the past few years, Ma Neish was still totally taken aback to hear that her daughters were now being honoured with an invitation to dine at The House, not just with Mr Archie and his mother and sisters, but with his grandfather and aunt too. If ever there was a sign that things were serious between Bernie and Archie, this surely was it. And what with him now being Laird? What would happen if her daughter married the Laird? Would that be allowed? Ma Neish had grown up at a time when, with the clearances still commonplace over much of the highlands, Lairds were so feared that you never ever spoke to them without a curtsey or a doff of the cap, and then only when you were directly addressed by them.

Ailsa and Bernie were both rather excited too. Perhaps surprisingly, Ailsa was the more nervous of the two of them. Bernie already felt in many ways to be on equal terms with

Archie, despite the huge gulf in their social status only a few short years before. But Ailsa, who had as a child often felt left behind by Euan and Archie in view of the age difference, still looked up to Archie as though he was her superior. Which of course he was, she realised. However, there was no such fear or inferiority as far as Bernie was concerned, just love and respect for Archie, for all that he stood for and all that he had already achieved in his thirty odd years.

The dinner went very well. Lady Elspeth, having insisted that nobody dressed up, had put on one of her new 'mourning' dresses out of respect for her husband's memory, of course, but also out of courtesy to her sister Hermione, who she knew always dressed for dinner. Archie and his grandfather wore what they would have done to meet for lunch at a club, and Margaret and Annie, who their mother insisted should join them, were instructed to 'dress down' so as to put the Neish sisters at ease. They needn't have worried. At Bernie's suggestion, she and Ailsa had discarded their teaching clothes and were wearing much the same as they had to Archie's father's funeral – again out of respect for the late Laird. Bernie also decided, at the last moment, to wear a rather beautiful diamond-set bracelet in rose gold, which Theo Kirk had recently given her 'by way of a peace offering' as he had put it. She felt this cheerful piece would help to offset the funeral attire, as well as being a discussion point with Hermione with whom she had enjoyed talking the day before.

Lady Elspeth had arranged for the staff to wear their dining-room uniform, so the evening had a feeling of much greater formality than originally indicated. This was typical of Mama, Archie observed. He also realised, as did Bernie herself, that it had suddenly become a kind of test – carefully designed, albeit at short notice, to examine Bernadette's ability to cope with the kind of occasion which Lady Elspeth expected a future Lady MacDonell would need to be able to handle.

It was certainly quite an experience for Bernie, and for Ailsa as well, of course. Bernie was placed between Lord Moncrieffe, on her left, and Hermione on her right. Lady

Elspeth presided, at the head of the table, with her father to her right and Ailsa on her left. Archie was at the other end, between his aunt Hermione and his sister Margaret. The eight of them, six ladies and two gentlemen, never ran short of conversation. This ranged from the work of the school – and how both Bernie and Ailsa had been able to succeed as teachers with no experience other than having been pupils themselves – through to the extraordinary range of fine jewellery now reaching the shops in Britain's great cities. Lord Moncrieffe spoke of the recent Reform Bill, concerned that any diminution in the power of the great aristocratic landowners would eventually weaken the nation. Archie, looking across the table at Bernie, said he agreed with his grandfather but there were many who wouldn't. He was treading carefully so as not to prejudice his imminent ennoblement.

At the appropriate point in the evening Lady Elspeth invited the ladies to join her in the drawing-room and they withdrew accordingly. This left Archie and Lord Moncrieffe alone with the port. "Shrewd observation of yours just then," said Moncrieffe. "I'm sure you're right. You only have to look at what happened with the American colonies. And once we give way, where will it end? The nation will be run by people who haven't been bred to lead. This is why we need people like yourself, Archibald – bred to lead, but at the same time benevolent towards the people and with an appreciation of the way the world is changing. Now that young lady of yours, Bernadette is her name, right? She's what we want to see. Knows both sides of the fence. What do you think?"

Archie was thinking hard, but the port was starting to work its effect on him, coming as it did on top of the fine wines that had been served during the meal.

"Well, Grandpapa," Archie began. "You're right about Bernadette. She's a climber, you know. Nothing's too much of a challenge, though our Shona Craig nearly was, some years ago. No, I think it's good for people to be ambitious, Grandpa, like you must have been." And then Archie stopped, not quite sure whether he was talking about rock-climbing, or politics, or what. Perhaps he should not have asked about his grandfather's ambitions.

"Yes, my boy. I was always ambitious, as you call it. I always wanted to do my best for the nation. We were a warring nation then, you know, not like we are now. Always at war we were, with France or the colonies, in America or India or wherever. Now no-one wants to take us on, not since Waterloo. By the way, have you met Wellington yet? Don't worry if you haven't. I'll arrange it when you're next in town. Still the grand old man, you know."

And so they talked, over more and more port, about momentous topics such as the reform of government and Parliament, the role of the British Empire in the years ahead, and the impact of the corn laws and the great challenges facing landowners. "You're a landowner now, my boy, never expected it I don't suppose, but be careful, what I say is this, don't let them change anything, not anything. That's what I say."

* * * *

Eventually the butler, Ritchie, intervened to say that Lady Elspeth was saying good-bye to her guests and wondered whether Lord MacDonell wished to escort them home. Archie looked around the room for a moment, wondering to whom he was referring, before realising that it was he who was being asked to take Bernie and Ailsa back to the Neishes' cottage.

"Why, of course, Ritchie," he eventually responded. "Grandpapa, my Lord Moncrieffe, would you excuse me?" he added, before lurching across the room and out into the hall, where Bernie and Ailsa were being helped into their coats – their Fort William coats, he noticed – and thanking Lady Elspeth for a lovely evening.

"Ah, there you are Archie," his mother said. "I'm sure Bernadette and Ailsa will appreciate you walking them home. Thank you for coming, ladies. You've helped make it a lovely evening for us. Just what I needed, at a time like this."

As Archie manfully endeavoured to steer a steady course towards the Neishes' cottage, with Bernie on one arm and Ailsa on the other, he announced to them both that he was sure they had all passed the test. Well, the two of them certainly had, and he hoped he had too. *It had certainly been a test,* Bernie thought to herself, *but one that she had much enjoyed.* She wouldn't mind doing that again, some time. As for Ailsa, she had found Lady Elspeth and Lord Moncrieffe's suggestions for future school projects very helpful. She would be looking for new topics now that Bernie was returning to Glasgow.

Tactfully, Ailsa slipped back into the cottage with a quick "Good night, Archie" while he and Bernie embraced. Not sure when they would next be together, they held one another for quite some while. Neither of them wanted the evening to end.

Chapter Twelve
London Calling

Although the time that she had enjoyed with her father and sister and her own family – all together for a few days for the first time for years – had helped her come to terms with her husband's death, it was still some weeks before Lady Elspeth had recovered her confidence enough for Archie to feel he might now be better employed pursuing his other challenges. After all, neither his partnership in Anstruthers' law firm nor the seat he had been offered in the House of Lords would wait for him for ever.

By the end of March, Archie had received letters from both Lord Moncrieffe and Sir James Anstruther politely enquiring after his mother's health and inviting him to join them to discuss their future commitments. So, somewhat reluctantly, Lady Elspeth told him without any further ado that the time had come for him to return to his other commitments and start showing his face in both Edinburgh and London.

Promising to be back on the island by early summer, Archie therefore set off at the beginning of April, with his mother and sisters kissing and waving him good-bye on the jetty by Castle Tioram and still waving across the water as he boarded the coach that would eventually take him to Edinburgh. A meeting with Sir James and some of his other partners had been provisionally arranged for 11th April and they looked forward to welcoming him back. Meanwhile another letter had arrived from Lord Moncrieffe to say that his elevation to the peerage had been confirmed and he now simply awaited notification from Archie as to when he would be able to attend the House for his formal ennoblement. There was work to be done on a draft Bill to ensure that no undesirable modifications were made to the Heritable Property legislation, so it might be helpful if the two of them could meet with other Scottish Tory peers before the end of April. And Bernie had exchanged a number of letters with him, in which she told him that she was now back in London working full-time in Kirks' lovely Hatton Garden shop and couldn't wait to see him and show him where she was living and working.

* * * *

The meeting in Edinburgh, with Sir James and other partners in Anstruther & MacTaggart, was a happy enough occasion. The partners again extended their condolences to Archie at his father's sudden death but were pleased to learn that his elevation to the peerage was now confirmed and that he would be formally ennobled by the end of the year. Archie told them he didn't yet know the precise date. Sir James then announced that he had a proposition to put to Archie, now that they had a chance to speak together as partners. He suggested that Archie be listed on the firm's formal documentation as an 'Associate Partner'. This would allow him to attend partners' meetings when he was free to do so, and obliged him to refer to Anstruthers any legal work which was introduced to him in return for a percentage of the fees derived from such work.

In other words, they wished to use Archie's name and connections in return for a percentage of the fees. These, they no doubt reasoned now that he was to serve in the House of Lords and had also inherited a substantial estate in Scotland, might eventually amount to a considerable sum. Archie would have the right to review the terms of his associate partnership and terminate the agreement at any time, should he wish.

After some discussion this was agreed by all parties. The arrangement suited Archie well – it would enable him to maintain his involvement in the legal profession, and in the Anstruther partnership, without the time commitment he was previously being expected to make. Now that he had inherited the Moidart estate, with all the income which that generated, and would also be entitled to fees whenever he attended the Lords, his relatively modest Anstruthers income should be sufficient for him to maintain his life style, and to contemplate marriage. He would of course wish to keep the Anstruthers arrangement under review, but this was readily understood by the other partners. They were understandably keen to have the title 'Baron MacDonell of Moidart' displayed on their letters and were happy to pay the price for doing so.

* * * *

Bernie was delighted to receive Archie's latest letter, which was sent from Edinburgh, telling her of the outcome of his discussions with Anstruthers and that he was now expecting to pass the next few weeks in London. He would call to see her at Kirks in Hatton Garden as soon as he arrived. He also needed to present himself at the House of Lords for a meeting with other Tory peers and to attend to whatever formalities and briefings were necessary to process his ennoblement. He hoped that she was enjoying London and that the work in the Hatton Garden shop was suiting her.

She wondered whether to write back but then realised he would have left Edinburgh by the time it arrived. Nor did she know of an address that would reach him in London. She would just have to wait and hope that it would not be too long before he appeared at Kirks. Meanwhile she would continue to give her daily demonstrations of how to wear necklaces, brooches, earrings and other jewellery to best effect.

There now seemed to be an endless supply of rare, if not unique, precious stones and the shows took place every afternoon at two o'clock. In addition, she had also been asked to give a short presentation, twice a week, to customers who were interested in the mysterious Seal of Promise hoard, which, she was now well used to explaining, she and a boyfriend of hers had accidentally discovered in a remote corner of Scotland almost twenty years earlier. The hoard itself was now exhibited under glass in the presentation room at Kirks and there were often as many as fifteen or twenty interested observers listening to these presentations.

Archie duly arrived at Kirks, fresh from a night in Brown's Hotel, Piccadilly, after a long journey from Edinburgh which occupied the previous six days. In preparation for both his reunion with Bernie and his first visit to the House of Lords, he had gone to the trouble and expense of visiting a tailor who was well-known to him in Edinburgh and had purchased two day suits, and a morning and an evening suit, all of which were then loaded onto the coach by his tailor with help from the postilion who was driving the post chaise coach he had hired for the journey. The night at Brown's enabled him to sleep well on his arrival in London and to appear fresh, well-groomed and tidily dressed when he reached Kirks' very smart-looking Hatton Garden shop.

It happened to be a morning when Theo Kirk had assembled his full team for a review of the shop's performance for the previous month. Sales had been rising week by week ever since the shop had first opened the previous autumn. Bernie's influence had been noticeable since she had returned to work at the end of March, with a number of significant purchases being made by customers immediately after attending one of her regular demonstrations.

But the last two weeks had been flat. Theo was concerned that the 'Bernie effect', as he called it, was beginning to wear off and that it might be time to give her a different role, perhaps one where she was less conspicuous to customers. Her apparent absence might make her admirers beg him to bring her back into the front of shop, he reasoned. Bernie herself, not for the first time, strongly disagreed with Theo.

So it was unfortunate that this, of all days, was when Archie, Lord MacDonell of Moidart, arrived at Kirks front door asking to see Miss Bernadette Neish. "I'm sorry, sir, I'm instructed not to admit any further customers until two o'clock. If you have come to attend Miss Neish's daily demonstration, I regret to inform you that this has been cancelled today as Miss Neish is indisposed."

"Indisposed? What do you mean, indisposed?" said Archie. He was not pleased. In fact, he was furious. Archie, Lord MacDonell, was once again being thwarted by a Kirks doorman, but on this occasion, he was not to be defeated. He could not believe that Bernie could ever be 'indisposed'. She would work till she dropped if she had to. Taking one of a set of new visiting cards from his pocket, Archie presented it to the doorman and asked him to kindly pass it to Mr Theodore Kirk. He would be returning to his hotel, Brown's, where he was to be found for the remainder of the afternoon.

* * * *

Archie did not have to wait long at Brown's before a tearful Bernie appeared, having been passed Archie's card by an exasperated Theo Kirk. Theo had grown tired of his star employee's demands and had reminded her that this was his shop, not hers, however much the customers may have visited the shop because of her shows. In the aftermath of the altercation between them, the doorman had presented Archie's card to Theo, who at first did not recognise the name on the card: *"Baron MacDonell, Laird of Moidart and Eilean Shona."* Only on a second look did the mention of Eilean Shona ring a bell. Wasn't that the place where Bernadette had come from? Theo was relieved – here was his chance to calm the waters – he would send Bernie off for the rest of the day and give himself some thinking time with regard to her future.

Less than half an hour later, Bernie was walking into Brown's Hotel, having seen the whole episode rather differently. She was still adamant that Theo had singled her out and blamed her for falling sales. He took her for granted and just assumed that his sales would go on rising every week just because of her shows. Well, that wasn't fair and she… At this point a porter welcomed her to Brown's and asked, "May I help you, Madam." And at almost the same moment, around a corner, into the entrance hall, stepped a handsome, well-dressed, smiling Archie also enquiring,

"Or perhaps I may help you, Madam?"

"Oh, I'm so sorry, Archie, my darling. I'm so sorry," she sobbed. "You couldn't have arrived at a worse time. I'm so sorry, it's not your fault Archie..."

"That's good to know," Archie replied, still grinning from ear to ear. "Come on, let's go and sit down and have a drink together," he suggested and immediately called for the barman. It was good to see the human side of Bernie again.

Seeing Bernie like this reminded him of that episode all those years ago, when she had found herself marooned on Shona Craig, he told her, and she nodded her head and smiled. That was the only other time he could ever remember seeing Bernie in tears. Once every twenty years – that wasn't a bad record for an artistic performer, he teased.

And soon they were in each other's arms and Archie was offering her, even directing her, to join him in partaking of a 'not so wee dram' – a glass of the single malt 'Laphroaig' whisky, so well-known and such a favourite tipple, not just throughout the western highlands but evidently in London too and no doubt even beyond.

As it happened, Theo had told Bernie to take the rest of the week off. He would tell her regular audiences that she was indisposed and that she was expected to return next week. Archie was pleased to hear this, on two counts. It would give her time to recover from the altercation with Theo; and it would give him, Archie, time to enjoy her company.

The beneficial effect of the whisky was soon being felt. Bernie said not one further word about Kirks and wanted instead to ask Archie all about his plans. First, however, she asked after Lady Elspeth. How was she doing? In her own mind, Bernie was now suddenly back in Eilean Shona, where her heart belonged. So she was pleased to hear Archie assure her that his mother had seemed much stronger. He told her she was more content now and had been ever since their memorable evening with his grandfather, aunt and everybody. Bernie smiled immediately at the memory of that very special evening, only a month or so ago but it now seemed like years, when she and Ailsa had been made to really feel part of the MacDonell family.

"Archie, I'm feeling so much better now. Let me show you where I'm living these days, over in Fleet Street. I've got a lovely flat, amongst all the lawyers and newspaper writers and other such inhabitants. All paid for by Kirks under the terms of my contract."

"Yes of course, Bernie darling," replied Archie, "I would love to see it. But remember, it won't be your home any longer if you break your contract." And with that, he took her by the hand to the front door of the hotel and waited for the porter to hail a carriage. "To Fleet Street, please."

* * * *

They drove across from Piccadilly past Charing Cross and into the Strand, Bernie telling Archie of the places she had already visited in the few weeks she had been in London. She had been taken one night to a play in the Haymarket and had never seen such wonderful acting ever before. The Strand soon led into Fleet Street and in no time at all they were outside the building in which she had been provided with her rooms. They climbed three flights of stairs, Archie commenting that these would be helping her to maintain her slim physique and that he could do with this kind of exercise daily himself. And then there they were in her 'home', as she called it. "For the time being, of course," she added. Archie couldn't help noticing that one window looked out over to a church with a strange, tiered steeple, and he asked Bernie what that was.

"Oh, that's my church," she replied. "It's called St Bride's. I've been going regularly, every Sunday. The vicar is very nice, and so are all the other worshippers. When I get married – if I ever do – that's the kind of church I'd like to be married in. Warm and friendly," she added, before glancing at Archie, who steadfastly ignored what she had been saying.

181

"And over there," he pointed, gazing out of another window into the distance. "That looks like part of a much larger church. Is that the famous St Paul's Cathedral?"

"Of course it is, silly," was her reply.

"What do you mean – silly?" he responded, slightly irritated at this description of him. "I've hardly ever been to London, not since Ma and Pa sent us to Aunt Hermione's that time. I'm not a well-travelled Londoner, like you are now."

"You mean, after a whole month living here?" she said. But she had to admit she still didn't know her way around most of this huge city.

"Well, I'd certainly like to see a bit more of St Paul's Cathedral," said Archie.

"Oh, that's no problem," she explained. "It's only a short walk from here out on to Fleet Street and over up Ludgate Hill," and she took his hand and led him out of her front door.

As they neared Sir Christopher Wren's majestic masterpiece, Archie asked whether she thought it would be possible to enter the sacred building at this time of the day. "It's only five o'clock," she said. "I expect they'll be preparing for Evensong. Shall we go in?"

In they went, and she was right. Sidesmen were busy arranging the prayer books and two clergy were checking the altar and making sure the bible was open on the lectern. Suddenly the organ started up, making them jump for a moment. But they stayed for the service and admired the choir's rendering of an extract from Handel's Messiah. There was something about the occasion which made them both think of marriage and, on the steps outside, as they turned to admire the gracious architecture, Archie suddenly said how amazing it would be to be married at St Paul's. And there followed an exchange for which they had both longed, ever since they were children playing together.

"Oh, so are you going to get married?" asked Bernie.

"That depends on whether she says yes," he responded.

"And who may I ask is 'she'?" she enquired, squeezing his hand.

"Oh, just someone who's just shown me her bedroom. Someone I've known for a little while."

"Not me then."

"And that is just where you are wrong, my dearest Bernie. Of course, it is you. Will you, Miss Bernadette Neish, please do me the honour of becoming my wife?"

"You should be on one knee, sire, I believe that is the age-old tradition."

And so, with the rest of St Paul's congregation filing away down the steps of the great Cathedral, Archie, Lord MacDonell of Moidart and Eilean Shona, went down on one knee and begged Miss Bernadette Neish, daughter of the crofter Ken Neish and his wife Mary, to be his lawful wedded wife. And she said, "Yes, My Lord, I will, but we will have to be married at St Bride's. That is now my parish."

* * * *

It was indeed her parish and, for three consecutive Sundays, their 'banns of marriage' would require to be read by the Vicar of St Bride's to his congregation, announcing the proposed marriage of Archibald Alexander Moncrieffe MacDonell, bachelor of the parish of Acharacle and Eilean Shona, Invernessshire, and Bernadette Mary Neish, spinster of this parish, and requiring anyone who knew 'cause or just impediment why these two persons may not be joined together in holy matrimony', now to declare it or else forever hold their peace.

As they made their way, hand in hand down Ludgate Hill and back towards her flat, Bernie said, "That's settled then, is it – can we do it this summer, here in London? It would be lovely if we could, Archie. I don't ever want to be apart from you again, and, with you becoming a member of the House of Lords, you're going to need to be in London now, aren't you?"

"Yes, my love, I am. But please don't tell my mother that. Not yet, anyway."

* * * *

Bernie wanted Archie to spend the night with her but he was adamant. It would be very damaging to his reputation, in Parliament especially but also in professional circles, if he was exposed as having slept with her outside of wedlock. Besides, it would not look good if she were to have a little 'bump' on the day of her marriage. So Archie returned to his room at Brown's Hotel, for the sake of his reputation. Bernie asked him how much that was costing him – the other half of her bed wouldn't have cost him a penny, she pointed out.

In any event, he told her, he would soon be needing his own house in London and, if they were able to arrange their wedding before the end of the summer, they could be living there together by then. This prospect encouraged Bernie and she suggested they should start looking for a suitable property straightaway. "Do you have enough money to buy somewhere suitable?" she asked, suddenly aware that there were important practicalities to be considered.

"No, darling, I've never got enough money for anything, let alone a decent house in London," he told her, "but don't worry your pretty head with such matters. We'll manage," he said, but he did wonder what the cost of having somewhere fit for a Peer of the Realm might be. The sooner he paid a visit to the Lords, and picked Lord Moncrieffe's brains on these practical issues, the better, he decided.

"I think tomorrow I shall go to the House of Lords and introduce myself," he said to Bernie. "Would you like to come? You're not expected at work this week, I think you said." Archie wasn't sure whether ladies were allowed into the Lords but, if not, they would find somewhere she could spend her time – an art gallery, perhaps – while he paid his first visit to the Palace of Westminster.

"Och, tha' wid be an honour, Your Lordship," she replied, teasing him by reverting to her Gaelic dialect, as she liked to do from time to time. She knew that he would be embarrassed if she did so at the Lords.

"Maybe I should just go on my own," he said.

* * * *

He did go on his own, and it was as well that he did. Bernie had decided she would start looking for small town houses reasonably close to both Hatton Garden and the House of Lords, which were not too expensive. She thought it would be good if she had some suggestions to put to Archie by the time she re-joined him in the evening, at Brown's. Archie had said that by then they would have been engaged for twenty-four hours, and high time they celebrated their engagement with a decent meal together. He would book a table for the two of them. He hoped that by then he would know more about how things would work for him in the Lords.

He realised that, having no official appointment, he would be at the mercy of the gatekeeper when he arrived at Westminster. He decided to go early in the morning, and he took with him the three letters he had received so far this year from Lord Moncrieffe. Hopefully these would serve as some kind of introduction if this were needed. He arrived outside the members' entrance at nine o'clock and found a friendly doorman standing alone. "I'm Archibald MacDonell," he announced to the doorman, "and although I don't—"

The doorman bowed to him. "Good morning, Lord MacDonell, now if I remember, sir, you are on the list for formal ennoblement later this year. Is that right, sir? A Scottish Peer, of course. How may I help you, sir?"

"Well, I've been travelling. Just come down from Scotland and I wondered whether Lord Moncrieffe is expected in the house today. He is my proposer. Happens to be my grandfather too."

"Oh, that's good, sir. Always best when seats stay in the families that know their way around. Now, yes, here we are sir," said the doorman, who had by now introduced himself as 'Chilvers'. "Here we are, yes we're expecting Lord Moncrieffe at 12 o'clock. He's booked in for luncheon with two guests. May I suggest, sir, that if you would like to meet with Lord Moncrieffe, that if you were to return at around half-past eleven, I will arrange a table in the bar for you to speak with his Lordship for a short while before his luncheon."

Archie duly returned, at a few minutes before eleven thirty, and was shown through to the bar. Coffee was brought to him and a moment later Lord Moncrieffe appeared.

"Archibald, how marvellous. I'm so pleased to see you. How's your mother? Do tell me all the news. I'm afraid I have luncheon today with Bobby Peel and a young man with a funny name – Dizaley or something – otherwise I'd have asked you to join me. But what about tomorrow? How would you be placed for lunch here then? I think Arthur's going to be in tomorrow, usually is on a Thursday, so I'll introduce you. I think I promised you I would, didn't I?"

"Yes, sir, that would be splendid," replied Archie, conscious that there were going to be exciting times ahead for him here. "Yes, Mother was much better by the time I left her a week or so ago. I think Margaret and Anne are helping to keep her spirits up and she was so pleased that you and Aunt Hermione were able to spend a few days with us. That helped her a great deal. And, though I would ask you please, Grandfather, to leave me to give her the news myself, I have some good news for her. Well, I hope she'll regard it as good news now."

Lord Moncrieffe interrupted his grandson, and shaking him by the hand, said, "Don't worry, my boy. If it's the good news I think it is, I'm sure she will be pleased. Is there a marriage on the agenda?" And Archie simply nodded.

"Now I haven't told you, Grandfather, have I?" he said with a smile.

"Ah, here are my guests. Bobby, may I introduce my grandson, Archibald. He's on the list to be ennobled this year. Archie, this is Sir Robert Peel, the former prime minister. And this is Mr Dizaley, no doubt a future prime minister."

"Archibald," said Peel, giving Archie a friendly handshake by way of welcome. "Now then, you must be MacDonell. Welcome to the party, young man. Another Scottish member, that's excellent. You're following in a fine tradition, as no doubt your grandfather will have told you. Dizzy, have you met our newest recruit to the Lords?"

"A pleasure to meet you sir. My name is Disraeli, Benjamin Disraeli. I'm new to Parliament myself, and I'm only in the lower house. You, sir, will have the advantage of me. But I trust we will work closely together."

With that, Lord Moncrieffe took his distinguished guests through to the House of Lords dining-room for luncheon, and Archie took his leave. It would be his turn tomorrow. In the meantime, he would enjoy a much more relaxing and enjoyable meal tonight, with his fiancée.

* * * *

"How was your day, my darling," he said to her as soon as Bernie's coach delivered her to Brown's that evening.

"Well, as a matter of fact, it was rather interesting. I've been exploring and I've found that there are some rather nice new houses about to be auctioned. Next Wednesday, I think they said. They're in a road called Chancery Lane, which is very near to Hatton Garden and not that far from Westminster either. They look really nice, they seem to all have three storeys, and they say most of the people who are interested in them are lawyers or something like that, so you should feel at home, my dearest. And how was your day? Did you meet anybody interesting?"

"No, not really, well, not until a few minutes ago. I saw Grandpapa for a short while and we're going to have luncheon tomorrow. He couldn't entertain me today because he had a chap called Robert Peel with him, who has just finished being Prime Minister. And another man called Dizraley – I think – who he said might be Prime Minister in the future."

"That's amazing, darling, I thought you must have been joking – they must have been very interesting. And who was it you met a few minutes ago that you did find interesting, may I ask?"

"Oh, that person – that was the most beautiful girl in the world, who is going to be the Lady MacDonell of Moidart and

187

Eilean Shona by the time summer is over. Provided the Vicar of St Bride's church doesn't receive any objections from his congregation."

* * * *

Chilvers, the House of Lords doorman, was on the lookout for Archie the next day and suggested he take a seat in the bar exactly as he had done the day before. He noticed that Lord Moncrieffe had reserved a table for three and had been allocated one in the top corner of the members' dining-room – an area which was reserved for very senior members. Chilvers said he thought the other guest might possibly be somebody very distinguished indeed, though he hurriedly added that he was not of course suggesting that either Lord Moncrieffe nor he, Lord MacDonell, were anything less than distinguished. Chilvers was doing his best to extricate himself from the hole he had just dug for himself. Meanwhile Archie was wondering exactly who his fellow guest must be. His grandfather did seem to be remarkably well connected.

At that moment Lord Moncrieffe appeared, accompanied by several officials and then, limping slightly, there came the Iron Duke, the hero of Waterloo twenty years ago – the man whose leadership had finally put an end to decades, perhaps even centuries, of war with France.

"Archie, as you are about to be ennobled, you must first meet His Grace, The Duke of Wellington. Arthur, would you like to meet my grandson Archibald, the future Lord MacDonell of Moidart. Archie has agreed to take the Tory whip and will bolster our Scottish representation at just the time we need it most."

"How interesting," said Wellington, "that is indeed interesting. Robert, where are we sitting today? Oh, usual table, that's good. Now, where was I? Oh yes, you're from Moidart, eh? Now I saw in The Times the other day that somebody in Moidart has found the missing undertaking by Louis Quinze – the one we knew he gave in favour of the Pretender and everybody had denied ever since. We knew all along that the French king had promised support for the Jacobites and then denied it. Thank goodness he did, mind, but it showed how duplicitous those French kings were…"

By this time Moncrieffe and Archie were looking at one another, and Archie was dying to tell the Duke that it was he, and his future wife Bernadette, who had found the document. Moncrieffe kept raising his hand to Archie as a signal to let the Duke finish. Eventually he did and Lord Moncrieffe, who Archie now found was 'Robert' to his close friend 'Arthur', was able to explain his grandson's role in the discovery. And then Archie was left to describe how it had all happened.

Somehow, he managed to do so in no more than two or three minutes. He finished by informing the Iron Duke that the whole hoard was now on display in Hatton Garden, at the jewellers Kirks, and that he would be more than pleased to accompany the Duke there and introduce his fiancée Bernadette Neish and her employer Theodore Kirk, who were these days giving occasional presentations on the subject to interested observers. However, by this time he wasn't entirely sure the Duke was listening to him.

"I expect, Arthur," repeated Lord Moncrieffe, "you might welcome the opportunity to see the Louis XV letter and the other things that were found with it. They include what they claim was a surviving Great Seal of James II and also what I guess was one of the Stuart kings' souvenir gloves. But, from what you say, it may be that the scroll carrying King Louis' undertaking is the most significant item."

As they sat enjoying their luncheon, with Lord Moncrieffe doing his best to introduce a variety of different topics for discussion – like the latest position on the Corn Laws and the concerns over King William's health – both Wellington and Archie kept wanting to return to the subject of the Louis XV scroll and the Seal of Promise. "Tell me again, young man," the Iron Duke was saying. "In an old bible box, did you say? Well, that is interesting, I've heard it said that a Catholic seminary was used as a store for some of Charles Stuart's possessions during the uprising. I don't suppose we'll ever know the full story." And Archie promised him that he and his fiancée were still trying to piece together what could have happened. It really was so strange to find such treasures where they did.

When he re-joined Bernie later that afternoon, Archie kept her guessing who could now be her next audience when Theo welcomed her back to work. She never did guess, and Archie was more than a little disappointed at Bernie's reaction when he finally revealed that it was none other than the Duke of Wellington, and that he had wanted to talk about nothing else all through their lunch. "The Duke of where?" she asked.

Chapter Thirteen
For Richer, for Poorer

Archie had emerged from having lunch with his grandfather and Britain's greatest military leader, totally inspired on a number of fronts. Clearly, he was now in a position, preferably in the company of both his grandfather and his fiancée, to approach Theo Kirk and suggest a new 'distinguished guest' who they might like to invite to a private presentation on the Seal of Promise hoard. This he would discuss carefully with Bernie, so as not to steal what he felt really ought to be her trump card.

He realised that he would first have to explain to her exactly who this great national hero was, but he was determined to pursue the matter. In particular he was fascinated by the angle that the Duke had kept taking on the Louis XV scroll. Perhaps it would be best to suggest, through his grandfather who was evidently very close to the Duke, that a private meeting with Theo and perhaps the British Museum experts should take place first.

Archie had also felt inspired by the whole aura of the House of Lords and now simply could not wait to be formally introduced and to take part in a debate. Before leaving that afternoon, he had enquired about the procedure – when it would be likely to take place, what would it be appropriate for him to prepare beforehand (for instance a maiden speech) and whether he was allowed to invite guests to witness the ceremony. He was informed that he would be notified in writing in due course.

Archie asked if he might be allowed to collect his correspondence from the House, as his home address was several hundred miles away and he would not be returning there very often in the foreseeable future. Fortunately, this was agreed and the doorman Chilvers was instructed to hold on to all mail addressed to Lord MacDonell, who would call to see if there was anything for him, at least twice a week. In the event there was a thick envelope awaiting his collection early the following week, enclosing various questionnaires which he should complete as soon as possible and pages of 'Information for Candidates for Ennoblement'.

In the meantime, Archie was concerned to make sure he kept two very important ladies fully in the picture. These were of course his mother and his future wife. He wrote a long, happy letter to his mother, praising her father – his grandfather – for all the help and kindness he was showing both to him and to Bernie.

He saved to the end of his letter the happy news that Bernadette had graciously accepted his formal proposal and that they wished to marry in London, at St Bride's Church, which had now become Bernie's weekly place of worship. He added that, thanks to his grandfather, there would be a reception afterwards at the House of Lords, and he and Bernie hoped that a service to bless their union could take place at the Eilean Shona kirk two weeks later.

Archie hoped that these arrangements would meet with his mother's approval and would be grateful if she could arrange for the happy news to be conveyed to Mrs Neish on their behalf. All those from the island who wished and felt able to attend the service in London would be invited, as would many of Archie and Bernie's friends from elsewhere, including some of his old chums from Harrow and St Andrews. Bernie read his letter through several times and only wished to add that she wanted to send her love and thanks to Lady Elspeth and her daughters for their friendship and support. Like Archie, she was keen to spend more time back on the island as soon as they felt able to do so.

The following week a letter from Lady Elspeth arrived at the House of Lords – the address Archie had given her – congratulating Archie and Bernie and wishing them long life and every happiness together. She knew that Archie's grandfather must be delighted, as no doubt Aunt Hermione would be too. They had much enjoyed meeting Bernie earlier in the year. The Neishes were thrilled too, she added.

Bernie had followed up with her own letter to Ailsa, saying how happy she was and how she hoped Ailsa would be her maid of honour. The 29th July was their proposed date for the marriage – the church and the House of Lords dining hall were apparently both available that day – and they would only switch to a different date if there were found to be a clash for any of the essential participants. This seemed unlikely now – Grandfather Moncrieffe was definitely available to attend that day and had booked the House of Lords for them; Lady Hermione had been notified; and the only other people who they obviously wanted to be able to attend were Ailsa and her parents.

This was going to be a busy summer for both families, what with all the travelling involved as well as all the arrangements for the wedding itself. Lists of people to be invited needed to be drawn up at as early a date as possible, so there was time for the invitations to be sent out and for replies to be received and numbers counted. The House of Lords staff were magnificent in this respect, removing much of the burden of recording the acceptances and apologies received and ensuring that numbers remained manageable. There was a capacity limit of two hundred for the reception, which was similar to that at the church.

St Bride's Church wardens were also helpful in every way, and even made a suggestion that one of their parishioners, a well-known local confectioner named William Rich, could supply one of his trademark St Bride's wedding cakes, with tiers like those on the church's steeple. This amused Bernie and, as they probably would never see a cake like that ever again, they decided to accept the suggestion. It would make an interesting talking-point for guests.

* * * *

Meanwhile both bride and groom had other distractions which took their minds off the wedding arrangements. Bernie still had to patch up her quarrel with Theo Kirk. Fortunately, Theo was excited to hear of the interest shown by the Duke of Wellington in the Seal of Promise hoard and for the time being seemed happy to have Bernie back and playing a prominent role at the shop. But their personalities were beginning to clash more and more frequently and the news of her forthcoming marriage did not seem to have greatly pleased Theo, even though she did drop the hint that Archie was looking for an attractive diamond engagement ring. She hoped he was, anyway.

As for Archie, he had to play his own part in the organisation of his introduction to the Lords. This would not now take place until October, as His Majesty was not expected to be available for the ceremonial Opening of Parliament until then. However, the House of Lords administration still required the full names of all the future Lord MacDonell's invited guests no later than the end of June. Archie was limited to no more than five such guests, including his wife (if any).

This apparently simple task proved almost more trouble than agreeing the invitation list for the wedding but, in the end, he agreed with Bernie's suggestion that Lady Elspeth, Margaret and Annie should take precedence, followed by Lady Hermione and Bernie herself. She told Archie she would try to remember on the big day that she was merely his wife (if any). They assumed that Grandfather Moncrieffe would attend in his official capacity as sponsoring Peer. Archie said it was a shame that Ailsa could not also be invited but Bernie told him not to mention it. Anyhow, she would be far too busy to take another week or so away from school at that time, nor would she be able to afford all the travelling expenditure after also coming to the wedding.

* * * *

It was a glorious summer in London that year and the happy couple passed long evenings together, taking walks in the beautiful parks which had, with great foresight, been created in central London to help avoid the city becoming an urban jungle. Regent's Park was one of the latest to be created, named in honour of the Prince Regent and located quite close to where Archie's Aunt Hermione lived in Dorset Square. Archie remembered staying there when he and Euan came with some of their Harrow friends, all those years ago, and he paid his aunt a courtesy visit as soon as he had an opportunity, to bring her up to date with all their news.

On hearing that he was living temporarily at Brown's Hotel she insisted that he stay with her until his own house was ready for occupation. He had by now been successful with his bid for one of the new properties which Bernie had found in Chancery Lane and they hoped to be able to move in there immediately after the wedding.

Dorset Square was also fairly convenient for Bernie to visit after work and Aunt Hermione, who had lived alone ever since losing her husband at Waterloo, welcomed her company and of course that of Archie whenever they cared to call. Often, she would provide them with a light supper after they had had a walk in the park and she enjoyed being able to catch up with their news on a regular basis. She was intrigued to hear from Archie one evening that her father's friend the Duke of Wellington was taking an interest in the Seal and Louis XV scroll that Archie and Bernie had dug up in Moidart. Her husband had of course fought alongside the Iron Duke and she showed them some of his medals, including two that he had won in the last few days of his life, awarded posthumously for his bravery at Quatre Bras and at Waterloo itself.

"I haven't spoken to Arthur – the Duke – for quite a few years I'm afraid, but Father meets him regularly for lunch at the Lords," she said one evening when they were talking about him over supper.

"Yes, Auntie," replied Archie, "I found him very interesting to listen to when Grandpapa invited me to lunch there. A really great man, and he did seem seriously concerned about the Louis Quinze letter and its implications. He spoke as though he thought it showed the French in an even worse light than people realised, implying that they were willing to carry out a full-scale invasion of England in '45 on the back of Charles' rebellion. I got the impression listening to the Duke that he still thinks they are capable of such aggression, even after the hammering they were given at Waterloo."

"Do you know, Archie?" asked Bernie. "I think I'd like to suggest to Lord Moncrieffe that, if he were able to bring the Duke to see us at Kirks, Theo and you and I could have a closer look at it all with him and see what else he says."

"I think Father would love to do that," said Hermione. "Would you like me to suggest it to him?"

* * * *

Whether or not she remembered to ask her father, nothing further was heard on this subject until after the wedding. Needless to say, there was soon little time to think about anything apart from the wedding, which was now firmly arranged for 2.30 pm on Friday, 29th July. Bernie had somehow managed to make peace with Theo Kirk, without mentioning the name of the Duke of Wellington, and rather belatedly Archie informed her that he would like to choose an engagement ring for her and at the same time look at wedding rings. This process took some while in itself, but when they arrived in the shop, carefully arranged on one of Bernie's days off duty, they found Theo laying out a magnificent selection of his finest diamond and gold rings, all carefully arranged on a tray for their inspection.

Bernie just could not make up her mind. Despite now having worked for almost two years in Kirks, either in Glasgow or here in London, she had never quite appreciated the allure of beautifully cut diamonds to the full. She tried on several, one after another, before asking Archie to choose for her. Archie hesitated, looking carefully at two in particular and asking Bernie to try each of these on her finger. She did so, looking lovingly at them both and back at Archie, before finally choosing another – a simple, solitaire ring with a brilliant cut diamond set in gold.

Theo, looking on, was effusive in his congratulations at her choice and immediately offered Archie a generous discount. Bernie turned away, so as not to see the price. She could not imagine what her mother would have said. She had never had a ring in her life. But they hadn't finished yet. Out came a selection of gold wedding rings and, by the time they finally left Kirks, Theo was at last beginning to think that this Bernadette Neish, who had both thrilled and exasperated him for the past two years, really had been very good for him. He and his wife would accept their wedding invitation after all.

* * * *

Ironically, in the middle of what had continued to be an excellent summer, the day of the wedding itself was somewhat grey, with intermittent rain. Nevertheless, the church, decorated with summer flowers, looked wonderful as Elspeth and Hermione arrived together to inspect. They had offered to support the somewhat overwhelmed Mary Neish, mother of the bride, but both Bernie and Ailsa had said they would be fine as they prepared to change in her flat nearby. Meanwhile Archie, his best man Hugo – an old friend from Harrow – and several of his other school, University and legal friends who he had press-ganged into acting as ushers, were all assembling in the nearby Fleet Inn. They were all in traditional Scottish dress, which startled a number of passers-by. Suddenly they noticed the time and all but Archie and Hugo left to begin their duties showing guests to their seats. Groom and best man allowed themselves one more glass of the local brew before nervously following on, to be greeted inside the church by the Vicar of St Bride's, a cheerful and genial priest who immediately expressed delight that they would be trying out one of his friend William Rich's cakes at the reception in the House of Lords.

Soon the church filled up. Bride and groom had agreed in advance that, apart from those in the leading roles, they would ignore the new fashion of seating the bride's guests on the left and the groom's on the right. "There wuid nae be many on my side," Bernie had indicated, although as it turned out she had under-estimated the number who had boarded the stage-coaches specially arranged to bring guests down from Eilean Shona and Glasgow. In addition to several of the generation of children she had taught at school, now most of them in their late teens, there were the Galbraith family and the Hendersons, with one of their sons, and of course there was also Theodore Kirk and his wife.

The organist played extracts from Handel's Messiah as well as a selection of traditional highland tunes. And then there she was, the beautiful sparkling bride, Miss Bernadette Neish. Archie could not help but turn his head to watch her, majestic in her beautiful pale, hand-embroidered wedding dress, almost pure white in line with the new fashion. She was on the arm of Sir Donald Henderson, in her father's regrettable absence. He had stayed at home to toast his absent daughter's health in private, much to his wife Mary's displeasure but his daughter's relief. Sir Donald, understanding as ever, had said he would be honoured to give Bernie away. He would also be happy to say a few words at the reception, if required.

Ailsa, looking just as beautiful as the bride herself, helped Bernie to straighten her dress and then the Vicar began. It all went like a blur, as far as both Bernie and Archie were concerned. There was a hymn, "Love divine, all loves excelling," and the vicar spoke of the importance of the sanctity of marriage, and what an excellent and most welcome parishioner the bride had been since she settled in the City of London. And then suddenly they were being asked to make their vows. The vicar turned to Archie and asked,

"Archibald Alexander Moncrieffe, wilt thou have this woman to thy wedded wife, to live together after God's ordinance in the holy estate of Matrimony? Wilt thou love her, comfort her, honour and keep her, in sickness and in health;

and, forsaking all other, keep thee only unto her, so long as ye both shall live?" And Archie, just about recognising his full name, said quietly,

"I will."

And then it was Bernie's turn:

"Bernadette Mary, wilt thou have this man to thy wedded husband, to live together after God's ordinance in the holy estate of Matrimony? Wilt thou obey him, and serve him, love, honour and keep him in sickness and in health, and, forsaking all other, keep thee only unto him, so long as ye both shall live?" And Bernie, looking Archie full in the eye and smiling happily, said,

"I will."

The vicar now asked, "Who giveth this woman to be married to this man?" and Sir Donald Henderson, standing in for Ken Neish, stepped forward with his hand on Bernie's elbow for a moment, then left her to it and withdrew. And this was the signal for Archie and Bernie, each in turn, to promise to have and to hold their spouse, from this day forward 'for better for worse, for richer for poorer, in sickness and in health'. This done, they had given their vows and in a moment they would be declared Man and Wife. They held hands, they exchanged rings, they held hands again. Archie and Bernie were man and wife, for ever. For better for worse, for richer for poorer, in sickness and in health.

They hardly heard the rest of the service. Their thoughts were all now on the future, their life as man and wife. The vicar spoke again and the choir sang an anthem, but they kept looking at one another. And then they were out in the open air, down the little alley onto Fleet Street and into their carriage, to the delight of all the guests, and off up Fleet Street into the Strand and on into Whitehall, and so to their reception at the House of Lords.

Lord and Lady MacDonell, of Eilean Shona and Moidart, were 'at home' to welcome their guests to a Reception to celebrate their Marriage.

* * * *

Needless to say, the Reception was magnificent. At the outset the guests were served coffee or tea and invited to watch the bride and groom cut the splendid tiered wedding cake. Bewigged House of Lords flunkies brought endless trays of food around the room, including generous slices of the cake, and the House of Lords wine flowed freely. After a while a Serjeant-at-arms called for silence, commanding those present to 'pray silence for Sir Donald Henderson, who will propose a toast to the health of the bride and groom'.

Bernie thought for a moment that this could have been her father, and shuddered at the thought. How fortunate she had been that day when she happened to meet Sir Donald and Lady Henderson when they had lost their bearings on a visit to the island. Her mind wandered on, to the happy days with the Galbraiths and Kirks to whom the Hendersons had introduced her and to all the other events which had brought her miraculously to this day. She must indeed be thankful for all her good fortune.

And then she heard Sir Donald himself recalling that same lucky day, that visit he and his wife had made to Eilean Shona, a few years ago, when they were lost and happened to ask a young teacher the way to the pier. That teacher, he was saying, was in the process of walking two young children safely home and was so helpful that they thought she was just the person their daughter needed as her children's tutor. After that, Bernadette had progressed through her personality, courage, determination and charm, to where she was today. Meanwhile her husband, shortly to become a Peer of this Realm, had himself progressed in his own profession to earn himself a partnership in a top Edinburgh law firm. Their union today brought together talent and influence, charm and authority. He had no doubt those qualities would lead the couple to great success and happiness and he wished them well in all their endeavours. He invited those present to join him in a toast to the bride and groom and there was rapturous applause as Sir Donald took his seat.

And then Archie got to his feet and, in much lighter vein, recalled some of the adventures that he and his wife had shared, including that unforgettable occasion when Bernadette had got herself trapped on the top of Shona Craig. He thanked her for her love and affection – 'and for various other hairy episodes since then!' And he thanked Mary, known to all as 'Ma Neish' and Bernie's father Ken – in his absence – for helping and allowing Bernie to develop her sense of adventure and ambition. It was just a pity that her father had not been able to share in this very special occasion, but maybe it was just as well for the sake of the House of Lords whisky supply!

He finished by thanking his grandfather, Lord Moncrieffe, for sponsoring not only this wonderful Reception but also his forthcoming ennoblement, and he proposed a toast to 'our very generous host, and my beloved grandfather, the Earl of Moncrieffe'.

There were no further formal speeches but plenty of spontaneous calls for toasts and, as the evening wore on and the pipers started to play, the Scottish dancing began. Archie and Bernie took to the floor first, of course, but were very soon beckoning to others to join them. A mixture of Scottish and English dress filled the room and the dancing continued until late in the evening. Eventually, with a broad smile on his face, Lord Moncrieffe announced that Lord and Lady MacDonell would shortly be leaving for their first night as a married couple, from the St Stephen's exit onto Parliament Square. This was the signal for the guests to make their way, through the great Westminster Hall, and out onto the street where a magnificent four horse carriage awaited. It was the beginning of what Archie and Bernie hoped would be a long and fruitful life together.

* * * *

The service at St Bride's and the House of Lords reception were only the first part of their wedding celebrations. There was still a service of blessing to be held in Eilean Shona's kirk in less than a fortnight's time, with a reception at the Big House. And then there would be the annual Island Games. But none of this was in the minds of either bride or groom as their carriage took them across London to Piccadilly and back to Brown's Hotel, where only a few weeks earlier Bernie had arrived in tears and left hand in hand with Archie on her way to receiving his proposal of marriage on the steps of St. Paul's Cathedral. This time they arrived hand in hand and did not leave for three days, much of which was spent in bed together. "You needn't worry about me sporting any bumps, now, my darling," she said. "I'm hoping for quite a number of bumps, and will hopefully present you with bonny bairns." And she threw her arms around her husband's neck and wouldn't let him go until he had more than made up for all those years of celibacy.

* * * *

They travelled home to Eilean Shona by stage-coach, arriving back on the island ten days after their marriage in London. Word reached the island when they were approaching Castle Tioram and the people of Eilean Shona all dropped what they were doing and made their way to the pier to welcome the happy couple home. Ailsa had returned three days earlier and had suggested to the children at school that, in readiness for the return of Archie and Bernie, they might like to draw pictures or write 'Welcome Home' messages on old sheets or pieces of clothing. They all rushed to get these messages of greetings and hurried down to the pier. Several of the adults were there too, and they were all singing Gaelic songs of welcome to the new Laird and his even newer Lady. And then, as Archie and Bernie stepped off the ferry-boat onto the pier, there was a spontaneous rendering of 'Should Auld Acquaintance' and prolonged cheering such as had not been heard on Eilean Shona for many a long year.

As soon as they stepped ashore, Archie and Bernie went round speaking to every child, and every adult too, thanking them for their good wishes and reminding them that next Thursday afternoon they would have their Eilean Shona blessing service with a reception afterwards in the ballroom at the Big House. They hoped that every one of them would come and join them.

The following day a letter arrived from Lord Moncrieffe, addressed to Lord and Lady MacDonell. He began by saying he hoped that by the time they received this they would have had a chance to recover from the excitement of their wedding day and what, he was sure, will have been a tiring journey back to the island. He had important news. The Duke of Wellington had written to ask him to inform Archie and his wife that some archaeologists from the British Museum would shortly be visiting Moidart. They wished to carry out some excavation to ascertain whether any further items had been buried in the same area.

They should, incidentally, also be able to advise upon the question of legal title to the hoard – there was a possibility that this might need to be offered to the Crown. They were likely to arrive in the next week or two and Robert Moncrieffe said, "His Grace would be most grateful if they could be accorded appropriate hospitality and assistance in their search." He finished by asking Archie to pass on his love and very best wishes to his mother. He hoped she and her daughters were all well and that they too had recovered from all the travelling.

"What are we supposed to do to help?" asked Bernie as soon as Archie had finished reading her the letter. "As far as I know you are not exactly an archaeologist and I certainly am not."

"Are you sure?" Archie responded. "Then what were we doing digging up that box and its contents twenty years ago?"

"Yes, well, I see what you mean," admitted Bernie. "Well, I suppose we could take them to the right spot and show them just where and when we found them. But we couldn't really discuss our find as it's all locked up under glass in Theo's shop in London. For all I know the Duke of wherever-he-is could have been and looked at it, or told the Museum people to do so, but I doubt whether Theo would let them take it away." She paused for a moment and then added, "Though I hope he does recognise that at the end of the day it all belongs to you and me, not him."

They decided they had better offer whatever help they could to these people, which presumably included providing them with hospitality at the Big House for the duration of their stay. "Will Lady Elspeth be happy with that, Archie?" she asked.

"She may well not be, Your Ladyship, but it's not up to Lady Elspeth any more. You, my dear, are the Lady of the House now," replied Archie.

Oh dear, this is going to take some getting used to, thought Bernie.

* * * *

The archaeologists did not arrive for another three weeks, which was a great relief to the whole household as it allowed the promised blessing of their marriage to take place, including the evening ceilidh which was never going to offer any visitors anything resembling a good night's sleep. By this time the archaeologists had themselves written to Archie, specifying the purposes for which they wished to dig and requesting that he and, if possible, his wife accompany them to the site on the first day to ensure that they were at precisely the right location. They gathered that it was the two of them who had, as children, originally uncovered the hoard. They would also like to explain, in the strictest confidence, exactly why they considered this was now so important.

* * * *

The Service of Blessing was conducted by Father Thomas McNaughton. He said he was delighted to be asked to officiate but warned that they should bear in mind he was now almost eighty years old and hadn't been involved with a marriage ceremony for many years. However, it would make a pleasant change for him, as for the past ten years he had only been invited to take funeral services!

He asked if he could call in at the Big House and speak with the happy couple earlier that day. Bernie, still not accustomed to her new position, duly consulted her mother-in-law Elspeth before confirming to Father Tom that he would be most welcome to come and see them that morning. Elspeth had actually replied, somewhat tartly Bernie felt, that it was no longer for her to decide these matters although she appreciated being informed.

Needless to say, the kirk was packed for the occasion. This wasn't a marriage service but it certainly felt like one, with the Laird and his Lady standing before the altar and repeating the vows they had made the previous week. Father Tom said some prayers and gave a friendly, very informal address which seemed to Archie and Bernie to be more like a collection of stories about their activities as small children in his class. Inevitably he recalled the episode on the rock which had terrified islanders of all ages, not least himself and his cousin Margaret McTavish. He concluded that they were always likely to remain friends after that adventure, although he had never imagined that they would be on quite such friendly terms as they were now.

The festivities commenced in the Big House immediately after the service ended, with the ballroom dressed for the occasion and a duet of pipers all set up for a long evening of Scottish dances. There was no formality at all – Bernie and Archie had let it be known that everybody must come, in whatever clothes they wished. The emphasis was on 'everybody' and Bernie told her mother and father that they both had to be there this time. The Big House whisky was wonderful, she promised her father, and for once there was no excuse for him not coming. She would come and get him herself if there was any nonsense. The Big House was only a couple of hundred yards away, she reminded them.

So the whole island was there, even quite small children for a while, arriving at around five o'clock. And there were no speeches, just plenty of food and drink of both the hard and soft varieties. And the bottom layer – the largest layer – of the

St Bride's wedding cake was there to be consumed. "It will all be thrown away if there's any left," Bernie told everybody.

They danced their reels and Archie and Bernie, still known to most of the guests as exactly that – Archie and Bernie – heard their health being toasted again and again. And the father of the bride gave them the moment of the evening. He got out of the chair that Bernie had put him in – telling him to sit still and stay quiet – and started to dance a jig, whisky bottle in hand. He danced for a minute or two, twice almost falling over, before collapsing back into his chair and enjoying the applause.

All around the room, islanders who had been brought up on stories of the highland clearances, and to fear their Laird as they feared their God, and always to curtsey or doff their cap, were tonight hugging the Laird's Lady – and even the Laird himself. Ken Neish even tried to hug Lady Elspeth. She retired to her bed shortly afterwards, relieved that there were to be no further celebrations of her son's rather protracted marriage ceremonies.

Chapter Fourteen
On the Scent

For better or worse, that year's Island Games had been arranged for the second Saturday in August, which would have been fine for everybody had it not been for the happy couple's Service of Blessing – and more particularly the ceilidh that took place after the service – being held on the second Thursday. This meant that those Games competitors who stayed at the ceilidh right through to the small hours had barely twenty-four hours to shake off their hangovers before they would be lining up for the races.

The Games had continued to grow in popularity, taking place every August on a Saturday afternoon and attracting not just those who lived on Eilean Shona or had family connections there, but a growing number of keen athletes from elsewhere in Scotland. The more the merrier, Archie had been saying as he prepared to host his first Games since becoming Laird earlier in the year.

There were a number of new events this year, in addition to the traditional sixty-yard dash, the five-times-round-the-island endurance test, the caber-tossing and high jumping of previous Games. This year there was to be a three-legged-race, children's somersault and handstand competitions, and even a ladies' race. Ailsa Neish had suggested these events to the informal organising committee some months earlier in an effort to involve the island's children, but was now slightly regretting doing so as they left her to do all the organising herself when it came to the day of the Games. But she had to acknowledge that, as their schoolteacher, she did have the advantage of knowing all the island children so she was the obvious candidate to oversee the junior events.

The afternoon started with the men's sixty-yard dash, a race which held mixed memories for Archie as he had tripped over while leading it at Eilean Shona's very first Island Games many years before. By now he had modestly forgotten how that experience had helped him win the round-the-island race, later that day. He hoped, now that he was Laird, that he would be allowed just to watch from the side-lines, perhaps presenting some prizes but otherwise just relaxing and 'presiding over the occasion'. He felt sure that he would be prevailed upon to say a few words later in the day but he did not want to make an exhibition, still less a fool, of himself in this his first year as Laird. He knew that, on an island this size, any such mishap would be talked about for ages afterwards.

Bernie, however, was not impressed with what she called his 'cowardice'. "Come on, Archie, show them you can still do it. Or if you don't, I'll run for you, and show them which of us is the good sport."

"All right then, you run," was Archie's instant response and then, remembering that there was to be a ladies' race this year, added, "Go on, go and run in the ladies' race, if you want to be a good sport."

So that was settled. Bernie approached her sister just as she was collecting names for the 'Ladies' sixty-yard dash' which would be run later in the afternoon over the same course, with all its humps and bumps including the one that had defeated Archie all those years ago. And Ailsa's reaction was predictable. "Really, sis, do you really want to run that race? Remember what happened to Archie, his first time? I'm sure you do. But it's up to you, I'm sure it will be popular if you do go in for it."

By the time the Ladies' Race was due to take place, word had got round that 'Lady Bernie', as she was already being fondly called, was one of seven entries for the race. At thirty, she found that she was the oldest competitor by some years, the others comprising four teenagers – one of whom was only fourteen – and two twenty-somethings, both of whom were mothers who had been urged by their young children to have a go.

In the traditional amateur spirit of these Island Games, the grown-ups just took off their shoes and ran in their bare feet. Bernie, who had spent most of her childhood without any shoes of her own, felt perfectly at home doing so. They lined up at the start, facing the bumpy track which she well remembered causing Archie to stumble. She had her strategy worked out. She had noticed that, as usual, no lanes had been marked out so she would steer her course between the two most prominent mounds. Ailsa, acting as starter, called out, "Ready, steady, go," and they were off – the ladies, with their skirts swirling in the summer air, battling it out with the younger girls. Bernie had an early lead but one of the teenagers, Alice, overtook her. And then, just before the winning line, young Alice stumbled on the mound and fell straight into the path of Lady Bernie. Bernie quickly grabbed her hand, and the two of them crossed the line together. It was declared a 'dead heat', but young Alice would always remember Lady Bernie's spontaneous sporting gesture, right on the winning line.

* * * *

The Island Games were once again followed by a free bar and informal outdoor ceilidh, following the tradition established by Archie's father. Archie had no wish to lose anything of his father's most popular island traditions, particularly those which related to young people, sports and other outdoor pursuits which had helped do so much to maintain the community spirit throughout Alastair's years as Laird. Everyone had their own memories of Games Day, not least Archie and Bernie themselves.

One or two of the islanders went so far as to enquire of Archie, during the evening, whether he had had a chance to consider a suitable memorial to his father. They appreciated how he had had his hands full ever since his father's sudden death but wondered whether he had considered something such as an extension to the school, which they thought would be appropriate given that the school, which had been Laird Alastair's brainchild in the first place, had grown so much in recent times that it was very crowded for the children when they were all in the old cottage at the same time. Archie thanked them for the idea and decided he would discuss it with Bernie, and of course with Ailsa, who continued to provide such an excellent elementary education, available to every child on the island from six years old to fourteen.

Needless to say, both Bernie and Ailsa supported the idea and within a month work had commenced on the construction of a new school building, close to the existing one but as a separate entity so as to allow two separate age groups to be taught independently from one another. Manpower for the construction work was readily available once the harvest had been gathered in, and the men who undertook the building work were only too happy to earn extra shillings for their labour. So the brand-new building would be ready by the following spring. Arrangements were made for 'The Alastair MacDonell School' to be officially opened by Lady Elspeth in memory of her late husband, in the presence of the Lord and Lady MacDonell, on the first day of the new summer term. Meanwhile Lady Elspeth suggested that, amongst other features, it would be good to include a memorial, somewhere within the new building, to the five former pupils who died in the cholera outbreak three years or so ago. Perhaps young Donald's dying portrait of his dying father could be displayed within it by way of a tribute to all those poor families.

* * * *

Over the following few months Archie and Bernie received a number of visits by the British Museum archaeologists. Their first visit, which eventually took place six weeks after it was originally expected, had been purely exploratory but it was interesting for Archie and Bernie to see how these experts set about their task. To save time they all rode out to Samalaman on this occasion and, once there, the archaeologists – by name Wilson and Gordon – took great trouble to locate the precise spot where the box had been buried. After all this time it was difficult for either Archie or Bernie to be absolutely sure of the exact position, but after several minutes of debate, and of trying to re-enact Bernie's fall and Archie's gallant attempt to save her from injury, they settled on a spot on the side of a small bank, just a few feet from the solitary dolmen-like stone. They agreed that it was on a bank just like this one that Bernie had slipped, and could not see any other bank nearby that looked anything like it. Wilson and Gordon duly measured its precise location in relation to the stone and took a reading of the position of the stone, commenting that whoever buried the box had probably chosen this spot so that they could return sometime later and easily locate it.

Wilson then pointed to the existence of an old chapel, now long since deserted, but which appeared from its condition to have been inhabited within the last hundred years. They noted its precise position too, and its dimensions, and stated that they might need to return with an expert on ecclesiastical buildings to gather further data regarding this chapel. It was possible, indeed quite likely, that an inhabitant of this building could have had something to do with the burial of the box.

Wilson and the ecclesiastical buildings expert came twice more over the following twelve months. Eventually, on the second of these visits they reported to Archie and Bernie that, following further research, they now understood that the old chapel had served in the late eighteenth century as a seminary for the training of Catholic priests, having previously been used for many years as a secret location for celebrating Mass. They wondered if there were still any elderly priests in this part of Scotland who might have information, or better still any memories, concerning this establishment. At this Archie and Bernie looked at one another and both of them immediately said, "Father Tom, maybe?" It was agreed that Father Tom should be approached and the archaeologists were astonished to find that, by the very next day, Archie had been able to persuade the elderly retired priest to meet the

British Museum representatives. Archie offered to bring them over to Father Tom's cottage but he said he would prefer to call at the Big House. "Would tomorrow morning be convenient?" Tom asked.

Bernie asked Gertie to serve coffee on Father Tom's arrival and she, Archie, Lady Elspeth and the two archaeologists, who both had pens and note-books at the ready, were all in the morning-room to greet him. Tom must have thought he was facing the Inquisition. But his evidence was like manna from heaven for the hungry archaeologists. He mentioned straightaway that he had undertaken part of his theological studies at the Samalaman seminary and had spent most of his life serving as a Catholic priest in Moidart, much of it in this western part of the district. He had seen the old Laird, Angus MacDonell, and then the recently deceased Alastair, and now Archibald, all inherit the estate and it had been his pleasure to serve the church throughout this time. He did not recall ever seeing any notice taken of the dolmen-like stone until now, though he was aware of its existence and its approximate location, and he recalled that it was visible, though some hundreds of yards distant, from the seminary.

Father Tom added that it was interesting that the items which the Museum were investigating were all found buried together in or near a sturdy box, and he wondered whether this might perhaps be one of the kind that had traditionally been used as a bible box. It was also most interesting that the items could all have identifiable links with the Stuarts and the Jacobite uprisings. He would have liked to have seen the box and its contents himself but, if it were all now being kept in London, he assumed that would not be possible. He rarely travelled far these days.

Father Tom had stayed almost two hours before the Museum representatives decided they had received all the answers that they were likely to obtain from him at this stage. Wilson said he rather doubted whether they would be able to bring the relevant items back to Moidart, as it would be difficult to persuade the jewellers' shop in London where they were now being kept to release them. At this, Bernie, who had remained silent but fascinated throughout the discussion, intervened.

"Actually I think we might be able to persuade Theo Kirk, the jeweller in question, to release them so we can bring them back up here for Father Tom to see – and for that matter for any other people in this area who might be able to throw some light on the subject. I am currently employed by those jewellers, though they haven't seen much of me recently, and it is through me that they have come to be taken to London and displayed for our clients and other invited guests to view and discuss."

"In that case, Lady MacDonell," replied Wilson, "I think we might wish to explore with Mr Kirk the possibility of having them returned, on your authority of course, Madam." Turning then to Archie, he added, "I take it, Lord MacDonell, that the area in which the box was found is now part of your estate, having formed part of your late father's estate prior to his untimely death?"

At this both Archie and Lady Elspeth nodded. "Yes, that is definitely the case," said Archie, adding that there had never been any doubt that the Lairds of Moidart owned the land on which the hoard had been found. It had been part of the MacDonell estate for several generations, in fact.

There was a pause while Wilson made a few notes. Bernie then added that as they were also the people who originally discovered it all, surely they should be entitled to have it relocated to their estate as and when they required. She was not aware of any contract which entitled Theo Kirk to hold on to it if the owners wished it to be returned.

"I think that's right, Madam," replied Wilson. "But we may still need to clarify whether the legal title officially resides with the Crown."

* * * *

In the meantime, while the British Museum archaeologists pondered over the evidence they were assembling, the date of Archie's long-awaited formal ennoblement was fast approaching. He, Bernie and Lady Elspeth, Margaret and Annie had all needed to make their travelling arrangements and Lord Moncrieffe had written to Archie to ask whether they had considered joining one of the splendid new steam-driven 'locomotive' trains, at least for part of the journey. They were said to be much faster, more reliable and more comfortable than any of the traditional horse-drawn carriages, coaches or post-chaises. Robert Moncrieffe also mentioned in passing that he had now persuaded the Duke of Wellington to go with him to look at the Louis Quinze letter and other exhibits at Kirks' jewellers but perhaps it would be better if they waited until he, Archie, and of course Bernadette, were in town and available to accompany them. Maybe they could discuss this when they all meet up at the House of Lords on 14th October, he suggested.

Archie and Bernie seriously considered the idea of travelling on a steam train for their journey south, before eventually concluding that they didn't know enough about them to be taking such a risk. Having been given several months' notice it would not be a good start to Archie's career in the Lords if he were late for his inauguration. Maybe some time in the future they would be able to travel on one of these new locomotives. They certainly sounded as though they would save travellers a considerable amount of time in the future.

They still went back to London a week ahead of Elspeth and the girls, for a number of reasons. First, they wanted to see for themselves how matters had progressed with the Chancery Lane house. Surely that should be ready for completion now, so Archie could instruct one of his legal colleagues to set the purchase process in motion. For the time being they could live at Bernie's, or rather Kirks', flat in Fleet Street. Bernie was also anxious to see that the flat was still in good order and was relieved to find Mrs Hudson, the caretaker, in good spirits and pleased to see 'Miss Neish' return. Bernie made Mrs Hudson's day by calmly informing her that she was not Miss Neish any longer. She took pleasure in casually mentioning that she was Mrs MacDonell now, and introducing her husband 'Mr MacDonell'. For some reason she felt more comfortable delaying the news of his elevation to the peerage until after Archie's formal ennoblement, but the news that they were married needed to be shared with Mrs Hudson to avoid the possibility of any awkward questions being asked.

As it turned out, such were the delays over the purchase in Chancery Lane that it appeared they would need to stay at the Fleet Street flat until the end of the year, or even longer. *At least*, Bernie thought to herself, *they would be able to show their faces again at St Bride's Church for a few more Sundays, and would have a chance to thank the vicar for conducting their marriage service in such a friendly manner.* She and Ailsa had been brought up always to thank people whenever they could – you never knew when you might need their help again in the future.

Another reason for returning to London ahead of Elspeth and the girls was to enable Bernie to visit Kirks' and apologise to Theo for the length of their 'honeymoon'. On her arrival at the shop Bernie was surprised to find Theo quite amenable towards her, despite her having been away so long. Perhaps by now he understood that Bernie's outburst earlier in the year was due to her domestic uncertainties and her anxiety to know where things were going with her and Archie. She had to admit that she must have been behaving in a very tetchy and immature way around that time. Maybe she and Theo would now be able to reach a mutually acceptable agreement as to whether, and for how long, her role at Kirks could continue, given her new status as a married woman.

When they did finally discuss this matter, Theo freely acknowledged that even if she only made occasional appearances from now on, he would wish to continue the connection and to be able to use her name, perhaps with a painted portrait, to demonstrate that the Lady MacDonell wore exclusively Kirks' jewellery. Bernie thought she detected some anxiety in Theo's attitude but was so taken with the idea of a painted portrait that she decided to take him up on that suggestion. Meanwhile Archie advised her that, if she were to agree to such an arrangement, she should ensure that she was paid really well for the use of her name and image – he had by now heard that Anstruthers were attracting new clients through their use of his name and title and had begun to wonder whether he was being adequately compensated for this.

Archie was also glad to be back in London well ahead of the date of his ennoblement, for he was becoming increasingly conscious of the need to meet up with Lord Moncrieffe. Not only had he still not attended any of the Scottish property law debates but he was also unsure of the arrangements for the ceremony itself. He wondered too when they might be able to have a further discussion with the Duke of Wellington, preferably in private at Kirks, where they could perhaps bring the British Museum researchers into the discussion as well. He was conscious that they needed to bring Robert Moncrieffe and the Duke fully up to date with regard to the ongoing investigations carried out on the site and the subsequent discussion with Father Thomas McNaughton.

With only a few days left before his big day at the House of Lords, Archie decided to speak first to his grandfather Moncrieffe, while Bernie went and had her catch-up with Theo Kirk. Both these meetings proved fruitful. Moncrieffe told Archie that there had still been no debate on the Scottish property legislation and suggested that was probably just as well for now. He also confirmed that everything was still in order for the ennoblement, although Elspeth and her girls had not yet arrived in London. They were going to stay with Hermione.

As far as Wellington was concerned, he couldn't wait to be shown the Louis XV letter and the other things with it. He thought he was now, at last, on to something which had been concerning him for years. Despite a promise which the French had given after their defeat at Waterloo, they had still never agreed to withdraw their commitment to support Stuart rule in Great Britain, stating categorically that no such commitment had ever been made. Meanwhile, Wellington had heard, there were direct descendants of the Stuart kings still going around the continent offering to champion a further uprising, even a full-scale invasion. No wonder these people wanted to rule England now that it was unquestionably the world's most powerful country, Wellington said. He had spoken to Peel and Melbourne but neither of them wanted to even think about it. Apparently, they were adamant that some German Prince was soon going to be put forward as a future husband for Princess Victoria, and with the King in such poor health, Victoria could become Queen at any moment. They may be more concerned with the question of the succession but he, Wellington, was still not happy that the French, and Catholic, claims had been adequately quashed. Yes, he added, he did want to see the documents, and the sooner the better.

* * * *

Archie and Bernie also lost no time in approaching Theo Kirk to discuss the situation on the Seal of Promise exhibits. For obvious reasons they had to ask him to maintain total secrecy with regard to Wellington's concerns. Archie strongly recommended to Theo that he should invite Lord Moncrieffe to bring the Duke to Hatton Garden as soon as he was available to do so. It would be helpful, if they wouldn't mind, if the British Museum representatives were invited at the same time, so that all relevant information could be shared on a confidential basis, between these parties only of course.

Theo was somewhat hesitant but eventually agreed to send a letter to Lord Moncrieffe inviting him and the Duke of Wellington to view the exhibits at such date as they wished, preferably one morning. He mentioned in his letter that Lord MacDonell would of course also be invited to attend and that Lady MacDonell, who still enjoyed a contract of employment with Kirks, would be present too. He did not have to wait long for a reply. Robert Moncrieffe responded later that week to confirm that he and Arthur Wellington had met up for another of their customary lunches and they agreed that the sooner they saw the evidence the better. They looked forward to visiting Kirks on 15th October – the day after Archie MacDonell's formal ennoblement.

* * * *

Lady Elspeth, Margaret and Annie arrived in London on 10th October and were driven straight to Hermione's house in Dorset Square where they would be staying until after Archie's ennoblement on the 14th. Lord Moncrieffe, realising that Hermione would not have been included amongst Archie's guests, had decided rather belatedly to invite her as his personal guest, so they would all be able to enjoy the occasion together. Secretly he had told her that Arthur Wellington would also be present. Arthur had been impressed by young Archibald and felt sure he would be an asset to the Tory party in due course. He would be delighted to associate himself with Archie's ennoblement. But neither of them had made any mention direct to Archie of their roles at the ennoblement, and Archie had only found out through Chilvers that Lord Moncrieffe and the Duke had been listed as his two official supporters for the forthcoming ceremony.

Meanwhile the British Museum researchers were beginning to piece together the evidence they had recently collected. They had found Father Thomas immensely helpful and might wish to meet him again at a later date. His memories of life at the Samalaman seminary in the eighteenth century could help to throw further light on possible reasons for hiding the King James' Seal and the French King's undertaking in such a way, and in such a place, that they could readily be found at some later date by anybody in receipt of a few simple directions. They were keen now to bring the box itself, with its contents (including what they now imagined would turn out to be a typical Stuart souvenir glove) back to the island so that it could all be shown to Father Thomas. Meanwhile they mentioned that their legal people had been in touch with the Crown agents who had said they did not wish to make a claim to any part of the find. They recommended that it remain in the custody of the Museum, or at such other place as the Museum and Lord and Lady MacDonell mutually agreed.

* * * *

Archie had never felt more nervous than he did on the morning of his ennoblement. He changed his mind three times as to the shirt and jacket he should wear, despite Bernie assuring him that nobody would notice either of these once he was in his ermine and wearing his hat. As for Bernie herself, she had found a new dress in a shop in Oxford Street which she adored and she was going to wear it, together with the diamond-set bracelet which Theo had given her as a 'peace offering'. She smiled at the memory of Theo's clumsy attempt to have his way with her. How different things were now! Today was going to be the proudest day of her life and as she prepared herself that morning, she decided that this was exactly what she would like to wear for that portrait which Theo was planning, perhaps with a rather wonderful diamond necklace which was currently on display at the Hatton Garden shop.

They had agreed to meet up with Elspeth, Margaret and Annie inside the members' entrance to the House of Lords at ten o'clock, over an hour before the ceremony was due to begin. Archie was still paranoiac about arriving late for this, of all occasions. Chilvers was on the door, as usual, and wished him and all his guests a happy and successful day. They were then shown through to the waiting room and offered coffee. Three other newly elevated Peers were also being formally ennobled at this ceremony and each had their own quota of guests, so the room started to fill up as introductions were made and polite conversations embarked upon. Meanwhile the ticking of a rather noisy grandfather clock attracted their attention, and added to the suspense, whenever these conversations stalled. *The time did seem to be passing very slowly,* Archie thought. And then suddenly they saw Lord Moncrieffe arrive, and then the Duke of Wellington, and everybody went quiet again. They both walked straight past the family group and on towards the chamber to take their seats, and soon all the Peers that were attending this session were to do likewise.

Suddenly it was time for the proposed new Peers to be led through to the 'robing room' and for their guests to be escorted to the strangers' gallery from which they would be able to observe the ceremony. In the robing room Archie found himself being helped into his new Parliamentary robe and a funny hat. Neither garment seemed to fit him particularly well but he supposed he just had to take what he was given and make the best of it. This was the last time Archie had any time to stop and think that day. From then on, the time seemed to rush by. All of a sudden, he was being called to come forward and join his two supporters, led by someone called Black Rod and the Garter King of Arms, apparently in accordance with a centuries-old custom. Archie had not been told officially who his two supporters were to be and he feigned surprise, whilst of course being delighted, to find his grandfather and the Duke of Wellington standing there beside Black Rod. They, he now understood, were his official supporters and they too were in their Parliamentary robes and hats, both looking as though they had performed this function many times before. Archie was then led solemnly towards the Woolsack where he had to hand over a Writ of Summons which had been written for him, and which was now handed to him by Lord Moncrieffe as his principal supporter.

They then all moved to the Table of the House where a clerk read out Archie's formal 'Letters Patent of Creation' and he was required to take his Oath of Allegiance and sign something called the Test Roll. And then, as a new Baron, he was taken to his appropriate place for a Peer of that category. Archie was ready for the next bit. He had been warned by his grandfather that he would find this part of the ceremony rather comical. And comical it certainly was, for he was now required – not once, nor twice, but three times – to solemnly sit down, put on his hat, stand up again, doff his hat and bow to the Lord Chancellor. And then, as if he had still not accorded the Lord Chancellor sufficient acknowledgment, he was required to shake hands with him as they processed back out of the chamber.

* * * *

The ladies looked on in awe and amazement at the whole ceremony. Bernie could not believe what she had seen. She might be sitting in something called a 'Strangers Gallery' but nothing was ever quite so strange as the procedure they had just witnessed. She supposed that the various customs had evolved over the centuries and nobody had ever wanted them to be changed. Anyhow, she now really was so, so proud of Archie – her beloved Archie, who had rescued her off a rock all those years ago and was now definitely, completely, formally the Baron MacDonell of Moidart and Eilean Shona. They would never, they could never, ever forget this day. Lady Elspeth, growing up as the daughter of an Earl, had had some knowledge of what to expect but neither Margaret nor Annie could quite believe what they had just witnessed, any more than Bernie could. Bernie wondered what on earth her own parents would have made of it all.

Before long they were all being shown through to the members' dining-room, where Archie had been entertained a few weeks earlier by his grandfather and been introduced to the Duke of Wellington. He now realised why Lord Moncrieffe had invited them to lunch together a few weeks earlier – it had been the opportunity for Archie to be introduced to his second supporter. It had all been very carefully planned, and very thoughtfully too, Archie had to concede.

They all sat together for their lunch now. Lord Moncrieffe had Elspeth and Margaret either side of him, whilst the Duke sat with Hermione on his left and Bernie on his right. Archie was between Hermione and Annie. The Duke noticed Bernie's delightful diamond bracelet and asked where she acquired it. Upon hearing that it had been obtained from Theo Kirk, he immediately commented that he and Robert

Moncrieffe were going to meet Mr Kirk the next day. So it was not long before the conversation turned to the Seal of Promise, and particularly the Louis XV letter. "Och, 'tis nae a very long letter, sir, just a couple of lines to promise the Bonnie Prince he had the support of all of France." She enjoyed reverting to her highland accent in the company of the Duke, who appeared similarly to enjoy listening to her.

"That's exactly what I want to see, my dear, exactly what I want to see." He looked forward to renewing her acquaintance and meeting Mr Kirk and the British Museum people 'on the morrow'.

* * * *

They assembled in Kirks at ten o'clock the next morning. The shop was closed to customers all that morning but Theo, Bernie and Archie, and two of Theo's staff, were there by nine to prepare for what they recognised was a vitally important meeting. The glass case in which the Seal, the scroll, the dirty glove and the old box were exhibited, had been cleaned and polished, awaiting inspection by the Duke of Wellington, and by Lord Moncrieffe and the representatives of the British Museum. At Bernie's suggestion, they also had with them the sample sealed envelope which the Rev. Andrew Makinson had insisted on producing to illustrate the operation of the Seal.

The visitors all arrived punctually at ten and Theo began by welcoming them all to his 'emporium', taking the opportunity to impress his very small but extremely influential audience with the range and exceptional quality of all the jewellery and other valuables he stocked. Many of the items were believed to be unique. He went on to mention that he had originally employed Lady MacDonell in his Glasgow shop and now did so here in London, subject to her commitments as the Lady of Moidart, the district in which she and her husband had, as children, originally uncovered these fascinating items. He then suggested that his guests take time to examine the items displayed in their case and ask any questions that they wished. Finally, he introduced the two gentlemen from the British Museum, who he hoped might have some answers as well as no doubt some further questions.

It was to be a long morning. The Duke said little to start with, but was evidently listening and thinking. The Museum representatives spoke of their interesting site visit and a particularly useful discussion they had had with an elderly priest called Father McNaughton. They would like Father McNaughton to see the whole display and particularly the box, as he had trained for the priesthood in a now somewhat derelict seminary which was by far the nearest building to the site of the discovery. If the box were found to be similar to those used in the seminary as bible boxes, that would suggest that the items had probably been buried by someone connected with the seminary for future recovery and needed to be preserved. They therefore recommended that, once they had completed all their own inspections at the Museum, the collection be housed in Moidart – perhaps at Eilean Shona House which now conveniently belonged to the very people who had made the discovery. At that stage a further discussion with Father Thomas, with the exhibits on view, might be very productive and they confirmed that the Museum would cover the costs of transporting and insuring the items if they were to be taken back to Moidart. Finally, they were happy to report that they had now received written confirmation from the Crown official, the 'King's Remembrancer', that the Crown was content for Lord and Lady MacDonell to retain the collection on condition that it was exhibited, for at least part of every month in the year, either in the British Museum or at such other place as the Museum and Lord MacDonell agreed.

The Duke of Wellington had listened carefully to every word of this. He refrained from mentioning that he was a trustee of the British Museum himself but the Museum staff were aware of that and knew his influence was immense. Meanwhile, the Duke was becoming ever more confident that the scroll in particular could become an object of some significance to diplomatic relations between France and

Britain, whenever such relations were next called into question, which with the French now constantly in revolutionary mood he feared could happen at any time. He thanked Mr Kirk for displaying the hoard so elegantly and showing it to them that morning, but suggested that, if Archie and Bernadette MacDonell agreed, it should now be taken to the British Museum for a short while to enable it to be inspected by appropriate diplomatic officials before it was returned permanently to Eilean Shona. Before leaving, the Duke took another look at the wording of King Louis of France's undertaking – "*Je soutiens de tout coeur, ainsi que celui de mon royaume de France...*" His whole-hearted support and that of his kingdom of France for the Catholic rebel, indeed! How did that not amount to an undertaking to support an act of aggression?

Archie wrote to the Rev Andrew Makinson as promised that very evening to tell him the outcome of the meeting. Meanwhile Bernie agreed to sit, the following week, for her portrait to be painted wearing a diamond necklace, with matching diamond earrings set in white gold, a gold oval brooch, a gold bracelet and her own engagement and wedding rings. "Will I get to keep them all?" she cheekily asked Theo.

"Of course," replied Theo, much to her surprise. "I wish to state, alongside the portrait, that Lady MacDonell acquires all her jewellery exclusively from the Kirk Emporium, Hatton Garden."

Chapter Fifteen
Back Home

The Seal of Promise exhibition was duly collected by the British Museum later that week and transported to the Museum's laboratories with a great deal more protection than it had enjoyed when it had been carted around Scotland in Bernie's old knapsack. Archie and Bernie wondered what scientific secrets the laboratory tests might reveal – they had heard that experts were now able to check the age of certain objects but they wondered just how accurate this could be.

They now simply needed to wait until Bernie's portrait had been painted before they could begin their return journey to the island. They so looked forward to returning to Eilean Shona. For a few days they would be on their own, with just the household staff for company. Lady Elspeth and her daughters were remaining in London, having accepted Hermione's kind invitation to stay on for a while after Archie's ennoblement. Hermione planned to take them to various places of interest, including the British Museum and Madame Tussaud's brand new display of waxwork sculptures which had recently opened at the Baker Street Bazaar.

Bernie had to sit a day longer for her portrait than she had expected but she could hardly complain when Theo honoured his promise to present her with the jewellery she had worn for the sitting. She wondered how he could afford to be so generous. The only disappointment was that neither she, nor Archie, felt the artist had captured her best features. The painting showed her as a rather serious lady, more a middle-aged matron than the lively, happy thirty-year-old beauty who had recently married into the aristocracy. The more Archie looked at it, the more disappointed he was and the more he felt it was a painting of the jewellery rather than a portrait of the lovely young lady who sat for it. Maybe that was what Theo wanted but it was still irritating that it was so unflattering.

They left with mixed feelings but, as she travelled home to Scotland with necklace, earrings, brooch and bracelet all carefully and securely hidden in her baggage, Bernie had to admit that she had certainly been well remunerated for all that she had done for Kirks the Jewellers.

* * * *

When they eventually arrived home Archie and Bernie found to their relief that all was well on the island, although Bernie soon heard from Ailsa that she was having difficulty managing the school now that it was operating in two different buildings. She had obviously just had a difficult few days, something Bernie knew only too well could happen from time to time at the school.

So Ailsa wondered whether, now that she was at home, Bernie would be willing to help out occasionally by supervising the younger children, who were still being taught in the original building, enabling Ailsa to take charge of the older students, some of whom were now fairly boisterous teenagers. She was aware that Bernie would now have additional calls on her time but, if it were possible for her to help out occasionally at the school, she would find that really helpful.

This presented a dilemma for Bernie. She was very fond of Ailsa, but she didn't want to raise expectations regarding her own availability. Nevertheless, she still felt she owed her sister a deep debt of gratitude for so readily agreeing to take over her Eilean Shona responsibilities and make it possible for her to pursue a new career in Glasgow. And she had always enjoyed being involved with the school. She just needed to be careful not to make too many commitments, especially as she had agreed to accompany her husband on as many of his estate activities as she could and he would also no doubt be required to attend the House of Lords on a regular basis from now on. She would need to work things out carefully over time, she and Archie concluded when they discussed the situation.

They invited Ailsa to come up to the Big House one evening while the others were still away and by the time they had finished eating, Bernie noticed how much happier her sister seemed to be. Neither Bernie nor Archie wanted to disappoint Ailsa as she and Bernie had always done their best to support one another over the years, and anyway, they all attached the utmost importance to maintaining the quality of the teaching and the happy atmosphere that the school had always enjoyed.

* * * *

Meanwhile Archie had returned to some very welcome mail. First, he had received a letter offering congratulations from Sir James Anstruther on his formal ennoblement and seeking His Lordship's consent to attend luncheons in the office with clients and other significant Edinburgh businessmen from time to time. He envisaged that these would be held, say, three times a year on dates to be agreed well in advance.

Several of these contacts had expressed a wish to meet the newly elevated Lord MacDonell. Sir James added that his partners had agreed to offer an increase in Archie's share of profits if he were willing to make this commitment – he was conscious that hitherto they had perhaps not adequately remunerated His Lordship for the use of his eminent name and reputation.

Secondly, Archie had received a letter from Lord Angus Kilwhinnie, the convenor of the Scottish Tory peers (of whom there were nine now, following his own recent ennoblement), giving him the dates which he should reserve for the next Parliamentary year. There were to be five such meetings, all to take place in Edinburgh and to be held approximately once every seven or eight weeks, with an interval of three months during the summer recess. In addition, Kilwhinnie anticipated that his attendance would be required occasionally in the House of Lords but these occasions were rare at present as he, as their convenor, held proxies for all nine Scottish Tories. This followed a deal made with the Whigs to save time and travelling expenses for Scottish peers on both sides of the House.

With his own commitments in London now likely to be much less time-consuming than he had previously expected, Archie wondered whether he was making a misjudgement in investing the proceeds of his Edinburgh property in the purchase of the house in Chancery Lane. The developer had again delayed the sales of the Chancery Lane properties so there was an opportunity for him to withdraw his interest. It certainly appeared that the bulk of his time was now likely to be spent on the island, which would no doubt please the islanders as well as his mother, who had recently read further public criticism of absentee landlords all over the country.

But Bernie persuaded him that the purchase of a house in a fashionable part of London had to be a good investment – no doubt in the years to come there would be times when Archie found himself attending the Lords rather more often and she would wish to accompany him to London. It was up to him, of course, for as a married woman she had no right to own property herself. But she felt sure that with their respective obligations they would be glad to have a place of their own in the capital. They would live to regret it if they withdrew from the Chancery Lane purchase.

* * * *

In the autumn of 1836, after the various formalities required by the British Museum had been completed, the Seal of Promise collection finally returned to Eilean Shona in immaculate condition. They had now re-named it 'The Forty-five Rebellion Exhibition' and an appropriate plaque had been provided, to be affixed to the glass case in which it was to be kept. The two staff who had travelled with it were able to install it in the Big House library, which Lady Elspeth suggested, and Archie and Bernie readily agreed, was the most appropriate location as well as the least disruptive to the Laird and his Lady's likely commitments and requirements. As soon as they had completed its installation, the Museum staff asked if it would be possible to contact the elderly priest, Father Thomas, who had been so helpful when they met him on their previous visit.

As usual, Father Tom was delighted to be invited to assist and within twenty-four hours he was on the doorstep, more than happy to meet again with the British Museum researchers. He was particularly pleased to see the exhibits now displayed so professionally. He looked straight at the box and immediately commented that it was just like the old bible boxes in which he remembered spare bibles were kept at both the seminaries where he had studied in his youth, including that at Samalaman.

After some thought, Father Tom suggested that the Seal must have travelled to Scotland with Prince Charles who on his arrival in Moidart, in August 1745, would no doubt have chosen to deposit it for safe keeping with local Jacobite supporters rather than risk losing it on his march south. He probably left the glove with them at the same time, as his typical Stuart mark of gratitude. However the scroll, which had not been signed until 24th October 1745 – when the French king would have first become aware that the Jacobite uprising was gathering momentum – must have been brought to Moidart later that year before being entrusted to the same local supporters.

These, Tom suggested, were probably a small group of monks who were known to have worshipped at the old chapel at that time, long before it became a seminary. Together, these items would have been of huge value to them if and when Prince Charlie succeeded in seizing the throne but a potential death warrant if the uprising failed. It appeared that they must have kept these items in the bible box, both for their safety but also for ease of disposal in case searches began to be made in the area. Cumberland's forces were constantly on the lookout for reasons to arrest known Jacobite sympathisers.

Father Tom thought it very likely that, as news from the Jacobites became progressively worse, the monks would have decided to hide the box outside the chapel, somewhere they could locate and retrieve it if they wished but where searches would be much less likely to uncover it. The failure to include the glove inside the box, if that was indeed what had happened, might suggest they had hidden the box in haste. As devout Catholics they would certainly have feared that possession of these items would have been seen as proof of their active support for the Jacobite cause.

In conclusion, Father Thomas emphasised that the burial and preservation of their box would have given them the option of producing them if and when it became wise to do so, for example if the Prince had reached London and seized power. As it happened, they had evidently remained hidden underground for over seventy years, presumably without anyone becoming aware of them until Lady MacDonell had, as a child, fallen on top of them in the presence of her future husband.

* * * *

"Well, there you are," said Wilson, the archaeologist who was heading up this project for the British Museum. "That does seem to me to be a very plausible explanation. In fact, I find it extremely difficult to imagine any other such explanation. I suggest we should all be most grateful to Father McNaughton. Meanwhile we will keep our files open and we would very much like to maintain close contact with yourselves, Your Lordship, and Your Ladyships, and with you, Father, by mail if you are happy with that. We will always welcome any further thoughts you may have at any time, indeed any plausible alternative explanations that may occur to any of you. And, of course, if any of your island inhabitants wish to see the exhibits, we would encourage you, My Lord, to permit that – indeed if you held an open morning, say once a month at a time convenient to you and Lady MacDonell, and your mother of course, that would of course meet the Crown's stipulation. And you never know what helpful suggestions or comments such visitors might make. Finally, I would like to suggest that for the foreseeable future we pay you occasional follow-up visits ourselves, perhaps annually for the time being, and maybe with other members of our research team from time to time, so that we may continue to monitor and explore the significance of this extraordinary find."

* * * *

Bernie was excited by the idea of having the Seal of Promise hoard displayed so splendidly in the library. The family, it seemed, rarely used that room and although they had a fine collection of books of all kinds – history, drama, even some of the novels by Jane Austen and Sir Walter Scott – those who read them tended to take them to their bedroom or some other place, and then return them to the library when they had finished with them.

Having the exhibition on display would bring this room to life. Bernie was keen to instil as much life and activity to the Big House as she could and this was a prime example of how that could be achieved. She would be happy to host an 'open house' morning each month to satisfy the Crown's requirement for public viewing.

Archie was happy too. He had been relieved to learn that he would not now be expected to spend too much time away from home, at least for the foreseeable future. He could cope with the five Scottish Tory meetings a year in Edinburgh and three lunches at Anstruthers, also in Edinburgh of course. He might try and persuade Anstruthers to hold these before or after his Scottish Tory meetings, to save a few journeys. As far as London was concerned, he promised Bernie that he would go ahead with the Chancery Lane purchase, with an eye to the longer term, but also so they would soon have a place of their own in the capital.

However, he hoped they would still be spending most of their time at home on the island, for he wished to perform his role as Laird in the way his father had always endeavoured to do. His father had lived his life for the sake of his family and his island and estate, and for all the people who made it the happy, friendly and resourceful community it was. Bernie nodded and added that this was why they had all loved and respected him so much.

But Archie was still keen to lay the whole mystery of the Seal of Promise to rest. He had listened to the experts from the British Museum, and to the Duke of Wellington's concerns, and most recently he had listened with great respect to his former school teacher, Father Tom. Yet he still didn't feel that the mystery of the Great Seal's reappearance, after apparently being thrown into the River Thames; or the purpose of the French king's letter; nor indeed the dropping of an old Stuart glove near to the box, had been fully addressed. Apart from all being supportive of the Stuart cause, what was their connection with one another? Some time, he and Bernie should explore the area around that isolated stone in more detail, perhaps with spades and a team of volunteers from the island.

"Spades? Us digging under the ground? Not me, not just yet, please," said Bernie. She had been waiting to break some important news to her husband.

"Not for a while yet, unless you wish to do it without me. You see we're going to have a wee bairn, darling. I hope that won't be a political embarrassment for you now, if I'm soon seen to have a bump!"

"Oh my beautiful, wonderful Bernie," he said. "I've had some good news over these past few months but this is the best news I've ever had. Sorry, the best news WE'VE ever had. Shall we go and tell my mother? She should be the first to hear. And your mother and father too, of course."

"Och! We'd better tak' some Scotch when we gang an' tell ma pa," she said.

So the search for further clues to the mystery of the Seal of Promise was put on hold while they waited for the wee bairn. "We can return to the Seal some other time, my love," said Archie.

"Aye, my darling," said Bernie, "some other time." And they went in search of Lady Elspeth.

The End